One size fits all
and other holiday myths

Mary Louise —

Hope _all_ of your
holidays are very
happy ones!

Sam Venable
1991

D1114619

One size fits all
and other holiday myths

A walk through the four seasons
with Sam Venable

Cartoons by Martin Gehring

The Knoxville News-Sentinel

In memory of Big Sam, a right jolly ol' elf

Contents

Mistletoe and MasterCard: it must be winter   **151**

Foreword

Once was all right. Twice was stretching it! But thrice?

That's asking a little much of someone. Just how many good things can be said about Sam Venable?

Actually, plenty.

I had the privilege in 1985 to write the introduction to Sam's first News-Sentinel book, "A Handful of Thumbs and Two Left Feet" — a collection of his best outdoor stories. At that time, Sam had switched from outdoors editor to The News-Sentinel's general columnist.

"Two or Three Degrees Off Plumb," which followed in 1988, is a collection of Sam's columns and his unique look at life. This, naturally, required a second introduction to be written.

Now, just as a swarm of locusts can be expected to appear like clockwork, here is the third of Sam's books, "One Size Fits All and Other Holiday Myths," a collection of seasonal yarns from various festive events including Groundhog Day, April Fool's Day, Income Tax Deadline Day, the Fourth of July, Labor Day, Thanksgiving and Christmas. He even throws in a few you've probably never heard of.

That's because Sam looks at the world differently than we do, and for that we should be thankful. Sam has a special writing style whether it be humor, pathos or sarcasm. It can bring a chuckle or a tear, but most of all a nod of agreement with a silent, "You tell 'em, Bubba!"

Before Sam basks in too much glory from this segment in a trilogy of introductions, the credit for this book must be shared with two others, Susan Alexander and Martin Gehring.

Susan, The News-Sentinel's public service director, compiled the columns for this book — just as she did for Sam's other books. Martin does the cartoons that illustrate Sam's columns. His works illustrate this book. Martin also did the cover design.

Obviously, I'm a Sam Venable fan. We assume you are, too, or else you would not have plunked down cold cash for "One Size Fits All." We hope you enjoy it.

Harry Moskos, Editor
The Knoxville News-Sentinel
August 27, 1991

Author's preface

My life has always revolved around seasons.

When I was a lad, each year had four distinct seasons: Christmas season, Birthday season, Out-of-School season and In-School season. Unfortunately, these four were not divided equally. Christmas, Birthday and Out-of-School season lasted only about 15 minutes apiece, while In-School season droned on for 136 years.

But then I discovered the ability to anticipate, and the seasons took on new meaning.

Christmas season began to stretch from late November till well into the new year. Birthday season (mine's in May) hatched as soon as the first spring blossoms appeared and could be milked until the fish were biting and pond water was warm enough for swimming. Out-of-School season, one of the most joyful celebrations of life since humans began walking upright, came on the heels of Birthday season and could be enjoyed until Labor Day season.

In-School season, on the other hand, continued for 136 years.

As I grew older and entered high school, my seasons abruptly changed. There was Football Practice season (January 1 of each year through, oh, roughly, December 31); Football Playing season (approximately 12.5 seconds every Friday night from September through November); Hunting season (Saturday mornings and afternoons during Football Playing season); Fishing season (Saturday mornings and afternoons when there wasn't any Hunting season) and Dating season (Saturday nights during Football Practice, Football Playing, Hunting and Fishing seasons).

In-School season still existed, of course. And it still lasted 136 years.

After college — I discovered many unique and exciting seasons in four years at the University of Tennessee, but since my momma and my kids might see this book, you'll have to figure them out for yourself — I bounced around on a couple of newspapers before winding up at The News-Sentinel as outdoors editor.

That's when the seasons exploded. I needed a calculator to keep track of them: Dove season, Duck season, Deer season, Jigging season, Rabbit season, Quail season, Grouse season, Crappie season, Turkey season, Trout season, Spinnerbait season, Topwater season, Fly and Rind At Night season. It was only because I was such a dedicated hunter and fisher . . . er, I mean outdoor journalist, that I was able to cram 28 months of activity into each 12-month period. Since I was pursuing these activities on News-Sentinel time and News-Sentinel money, I felt a personal and professional obligation to devote a full two weeks per year toward writing articles about them.

But by 1985, the big cheeses around this joint finally figured me out. They made me come into the office regularly (Necktie season) and attempt to act dignified (Impossibility season). It was like In-School season all over again.

Then one day, I was flipping through a calendar and it dawned on me how many honest-to-gosh seasons there actually are. Wow! I could write about these times of the year; that way, I could pretend to have a real job!

Thus far, the plan seems to be working.

That's how this book came to be. Susan Alexander, The News-Sentinel's public service director and books division editor nonpareil, suggested we incorporate columns from the four seasons of the year and mother-henned the operation from A to Z. Editorial assistants Dee Dee Booher and Chrystal White helped translate newspaper clippings to computereze, editor Harry Moskos was bribed (cheaply) into writing a flowery introduction, eagle-eyed copy editor David DeWitt caught the errors (sue him, not me, if you find mistakes), Jack Kirkland shot the back cover photo and the talented pen of my little buddy Martin Gehring did all the illustrations. For their help, I am deeply grateful.

Me? I sat around and spilled coffee and made socially offensive noises and offered unheeded suggestions and generally enjoyed every moment of Get In the Way season.

Hate to run, but Leave Office Early season has just started, and I don't want to miss a moment of the celebration.

Venob
August 16, 1991

Chapter One

IN SPRING THE WORLD WAKES UP — AND GROANS

I know what you're saying —

"Venob is SOOOOO ignorant. He starts the spring chapter on Groundhog Day. What a goober. Doesn't he know Groundhog Day is in early February, and the first official day of spring doesn't roll around until late March?"

Of course I know. But, as I tell editors at least five times a week, people who adhere to rules have absolutely no sense of adventure.

Groundhog Day is when we begin to have thoughts of jonquils and robins and tender green grass, right? It's the first time of year when we say to ourselves, "Hmmmmm. Maybe winter won't last forever, after all. Maybe it'll be possible to go to the mailbox without a goose down jacket and insulated boots."

That's why I decided to start spring on February 2.

Of course, you never know when to take spring seriously in East Tennessee. We could have a couple of 70-degree days in February, followed by a 12-inch blizzard in April.

Our weather never adheres to rules, either.

High on the 'hog

February 2, 1986

Rise and shine, Boss Hog. This is your one day of glory. Then you can go back to sleep and we'll forget we knew you until this time next year.

Americans delight with mixing fact and fiction on holidays, and never is there a better illustration than Groundhog Day.

According to legend (isn't it neat how things like this can be attributed to The Great Legend and then no one will argue?), the groundhog will emerge from its den today. If it sees its shadow, it will run back inside, guaranteeing six more weeks of winter. But if skies are cloudy and the animal isn't frightened, spring is on the way. Right?

Hog wash. Give me TV's pretty boy meteorologists any day, even if I must wade through hurricanes in Houston and blizzards in Bangor before I find out if it's going to rain tomorrow in Knoxville.

Groundhog Day is also when the people on Punxsutawney, Pa., gather to wake their four-footed hero, Punxsutawney Phil. Phil — could be Phyllis, for all we know — will be paraded around by men wearing black tuxedoes and top hats. Flashbulbs will pop, and Phil's predictions will be broadcast worldwide. Then both Punxsutawney and Phil/Phyllis will be forgotten for another 364 days.

I really shouldn't get steamed up about this. There's nothing wrong with civic festivities or tampering with biological fact. Certainly not if The Great Legend is to survive.

But the fact of the matter is that unless it has been an unseasonably warm winter, you couldn't rouse a hibernating groundhog this time of year with a 2-by-4 and a pitchfork. That's especially true in the animal's northern ranges.

So just what is this beast in whose paws the meteorological fate of America rests for the next six weeks?

Sadly, no one seems to know very much. In an age of environmental awareness, of detailed study into the intricacies of flora and fauna, groundhogs are little more than ecological lepers. Few researchers have spent so much as a day with them.

Groundhogs certainly have not aided the process. It seems they have done everything under their furry hides to alienate themselves from mankind. Except on February 2, of course.

What gets the groundhog into trouble most often is its fondness

for veggies, particularly the lush growth found in pastures and gardens. Ah, but he's not a strict vegetarian. Ed Warr, a biologist for the Tennessee Wildlife Resources Agency, said he has caught groundhogs in live traps set for raccoons and baited with, of all things, sardines.

In addition, hundreds of car owners — including News-Sentinel columnist Harold Julian — have learned over the years that groundhogs have an insatiable appetite for electrical wiring and rubber hoses.

Before he acquired Ralph The Groundhog-Killing Dog, Harold was plagued with these pests every summer.

If they're not munching green beans or wiring, the blooming things are burrowing under fields, creating a network of tunnels that can collapse and damage farm equipment. So says University of Tennessee wildlife management professor Dr. Mike Pelton.

On the other hand, groundhogs don't always stay in the ground. They have been seen sunning atop fence posts, feeding in apple trees, even climbing as high as 40 feet in a sycamore.

But none of this rhetoric should be construed as an indictment against the species. All animals, gnats to elephants, have a unique niche in the life of this planet. Pelton says what limited study has been done on groundhogs indicates their abandoned burrows provide shelter for a wide variety of other animals, including foxes and possums.

And if you're willing to dabble in things bizarre, you might discover groundhogs make acceptable pets. Dr. Bromfield Ridley, biology professor at Tennessee Tech, tells of a farmer who owned one:

"She could come and go as she pleased. She had run of the house. She'd even climb up on the sofa and let you scratch her belly."

But there was one major drawback. "That same ol' groundhog," says Ridley, "would bite the fool out of you."

If she was mine, she'd bite me once. After that — shadow or no shadow, six weeks of spring or six weeks of winter — I'd be eating groundhog stew.

The card shark

February 11, 1990

If you're having a tough time picking the perfect card for your Valentine, talk to Frank Kelly. When it comes to sentimental selections, he always finds the last word.

Then he buys it.

Trust your Uncle Venob on this matter: Kelly knows cards. After more than 1,000 purchases, he's a storekeeper's best friend. Look for him in a Hallmark shop, the corner drug store, newsstands, the greeting card section of Kroger's — any place he might discover the newest verse.

Thursdays are what got him into this binge nearly 12 years ago.

"We got married on a Thursday," says Nancy Kelly. "June 15, 1978. The next Thursday, Frank gave me a card. Then he got another one the following week. He's never missed a Thursday since."

Once you start the card-buying habit, it's extremely difficult to shake.

"I get them for any and all occasions," Nancy said with a laugh. "New Year's Day, April Fool's Day, Valentine's Day, Groundhog Day, St. Patrick's Day.

"Sometimes they're comical; sometimes they're very sentimental.

"During the Christmas season, cards start showing up on Dec. 1. They keep coming, non-stop, until Christmas Day. I've saved every last one of them — boxes of them, in fact.

"It doesn't even have to be a special day. A card will just appear. Frank is a very thoughtful person. Something will happen during the week and he'll find a card to match it.

"It's the same thing when he looks for a gift for me or anybody else. He never shops just to have a present. It's always something special for that particular person."

Kelly rarely mails cards to his wife. That's too easy. Instead, he hides them. Everywhere.

"I never know myself where the next one will be," said Kelly, head of the water and wastewater department at KUB.

"Nancy and I fish a lot, so sometimes the card shows up inside her tackle box. Or under the boat seat.

"Sometimes it's under her pillow. If I'm going to be gone for a few days, I hide one somewhere in the house. Then I call the kids and tell 'em where it is and they deliver it for me."

We are talking a marital game of cat and mouse of epic proportions.

"Frank goes to work early," said Nancy. "He's usually at his desk by 5:30. When I get to my office (Merit Construction Co.), a card might be taped to my door.

"His best trick was getting one delivered in the middle of the Caribbean. I was on a seven-day cruise with my mother. When we got up that Thursday morning, somebody had slipped a card under the door. It read, 'With all my love, Frank,' just like all the others."

How did he do it?

Kelly just smiles. Magicians never give away their secrets.

Except, perhaps, the secret to a happy marriage.

Helpless and hopeless romantics

February 12, 1989

I hate to be a holiday spoilsport. But before you get too wrapped up with the Valentine spirit, please be advised that we are living in a most unromantic section of the United States.

How unromantic? That's the rub. The people who are supposed to know about such things couldn't tell me. All they said was Knoxville is not among the 10 most lovey-dovey cities in the country.

It's worse. They claimed we don't even rank in the top 75.

In fact, if the findings by a California champagne company are correct, Knoxville is the celibacy capital of the free world. I'm surprised City Council hasn't banned kissing outright.

The Department of Romance, Weddings and Entertaining — I did not make that up — for Korbel Cellars is responsible for this study. The people there inspected records for the nation's 75 largest metropolitan areas and graded each one on its inherent romance. They figured heavily on the marriage and divorce rate per capita, plus sales of flowers, wine and diamonds.

"Since Americans' most romantic activities include being wined and dined, a walk on the beach, watching a sunset and watching a romantic movie, Korbel's study also factored in the number of good restaurants and theaters per capita, miles of coastline or shoreline and number of sunny days," said company spokeswoman Joyce Jillson.

Armed with such information, Korbel came to the conclusion that San Francisco is the most romantic city in the land.

I could not agree more. From what I have heard and read about San Francisco, everyone is in love. Bruce loves Bill, Fred loves Ralph, and Alice thinks Beth is the hottest stud in the neighborhood.

Others in the top 10, in descending order, were Honolulu, Los Angeles, West Palm Beach, New York City, Miami, Rochester (New York), San Diego, Boston and Grand Rapids (Mich.).

Honolulu and West Palm Beach certainly qualify in my book. I can even imagine San Diego and Boston.

But Los Angeles and Miami? Good grief! If it's romantic to gag on smog or dodge flying slugs from an Uzi, I've got a lot to learn about love.

Oh, and how do cutsey couples get their jollies in Grand Rapids? Sit around and talk about new cars?

Only two Tennessee cities made the list. They were so far down, we might as well write ourselves off as the Barney Fifes of love and be done with it.

Memphis, on the basis of its healthy marriage rate, snuck in at 57th. Nashville, which leads the state in nuptials and sales of diamonds and flowers per capita, ended up a meager 24th.

Nashville's low ranking really surprises me. After reading about the horse racing and bingo bribes over there, I was under the impression everyone in Music City was in bed with someone else.

But ugly ol' Knoxville was nowhere to be seen. Zip. Nada.

"I can't even find your city on the list," said Debbie Bronstein, who works for the champagne company's public relations firm.

Well, I never. Surely we rate somewhere in the also-rans of romance, don't we? Just because we East Tennesseans are bad about marrying our first cousins at age 14, that means we don't know nothin' about love?

This whole episode has me hopping mad. I just hope I'm over it soon. Don't want to spoil the atmosphere when I treat Mary Ann to our annual Valentine's Day shindig on the town.

We'll start out with dinner at the Krystal, then share a six-pack of Weidemanns, and wrap up the evening with a long, loving stroll down the sporting goods aisle at Kmart.

Hey, do I know how to woo a gal or what?

St. Patrick's Day

Green? Gag!

March 17, 1989

Green is a marvelous color. It is soothing to the eye as well as the soul. I'm glad whoever invented the color spectrum saw fit to squeeze green in there between blue and yellow.

That being said, however, let me issue a St. Patrick's Day warning: By sunset this evening, we will have been assaulted by so much green, everyone in town will be — if you'll pardon the expression — green around the gills.

Green neckties. Green shirts. Green blouses. Green dresses. Green coats. Green hats. Green gloves. Everywhere, green.

Even the O'Malleys, O'Sullivans and McConnells, a group of people given to raucous frolic on this day, will ultimately suffer. They will drink green beer, and it packs a frightful punch, particularly when it is quaffed from noon until midnight.

What I'm trying to say is that there is good green and bad green. If St. Patrick had spent more time driving out the bad kind of green instead of worrying about those stupid snakes, the world would be a better place.

Consider green veggies and green fruits. Most of them are good. Spinach, okra, celery, asparagus, broccoli and limes, for instance.

Without spinach, Bluto would have stomped Popeye's guts into the dirt decades ago. Without okra, the South would've had one less claim of natural superiority over the North. Without celery, asparagus and broccoli, adulthood would barely be worth the trouble. And without limes, no one would ever have experienced the joys of key lime pie or gin and tonic.

But there is a dark side to green fruits and veggies. A sinister, ruthless, cowardly chapter. An evil mutation that has haunted humanity since the dawn of creation.

Do the words "brussels sprouts" ring a bell?

Think about a big pile of brussels sprouts on your plate. They look like mushy green midget brains. They stink worse than gym socks that have hidden in the back of your locker for an entire semester. Summer semester. Even then, I'd rather eat the socks.

Then there is the kiwi fruit, a slimy green algal growth that godless restaurants have recently begun sneaking onto the salad bar.

Think about this for a minute. The kiwi is a long-billed, flightless bird from New Zealand. There is also a brand of shoe polish called Kiwi. Surely a raw kiwi bird or a can of Kiwi shoe polish has a finer flavor than a slice of green kiwi fruit. There are no tiny black seeds in shoe polish, either.

Want more evidence of good and bad green? Think about television.

Mister Greenjeans was the good variety. He was Captain Kangaroo's buddy. He had a calm, gentle voice. He taught children all about plants and animals.

Lorne Greene, on the other hand, is best remembered as Ben Cartwright, the rich old coot who ran the Ponderosa. All he ever did was dispatch his sons, Adam, Hoss and Little Joe, to do his fighting. Did you ever notice how Pa always managed to ride up just as the last punch was being thrown?

Later in life, Lorne Greene played second fiddle to golden retrievers and dalmations in dog food commercials. Served him right.

And then there was Mean Joe Green. He vacillated between good and bad.

During a football game, he could have taken on the entire Cartwright clan, including Hop Sing, and never bruised a finger. But off the field, Mean Joe was a pussycat. When he tossed his dirty jersey to that little boy in the Coke commercial, I almost burst into tears.

On the other hand, I bet that awful jersey stunk worse than a whole room full of brussels sprouts.

Losing o' the green

March 17, 1991

There is no better time than St. Patrick's Day to discuss matters of green. Specifically, the green you'll be handing over to Uncle Sam before April 15.

My tax return is finished. If you saw me in the flesh right now, you could tell for yourself. My neck is no longer ridged with blue veins, my fists are not clenched, I do not foam at the mouth, and my kinky gray hairs have sprung back into shape after being stretched like banjo strings during 1,040 fits of rage.

Actually, I shouldn't complain. Nobody should. That's because the average American spends very little time preparing a tax form. If you don't believe me, turn to Page 4 of your 1990 tax information guide and look at the chart.

According to the Internal Revenue Service's bean counters, it only takes 3 hours and 8 minutes to keep all the records necessary to fill out Form 1040. That's less time than we spend taking out the garbage over the course of one year.

I'm not sure how the bean patrol came up with that figure. For all I know, teams of accountants were assigned to every Whipstichet, Hinkleding and Glagmire family in America, and they spent months following members around their respective houses, timing them as they stubbed checks and stuffed drug store and charity receipts into the sock drawer. Whatever. If the feds say 3 hours and 8 minutes, so be it.

Next is the average time required to learn the law or consult a tax form. Two hours, 33 minutes. We're not talking about CPAs, comptrollers, actuaries and others who invest years in higher education so they can make sense out of tax laws. Rather, this is Joe and Jane Sixpack, whose grasp of economics is limited to How Much Foldin'

Money We'uns Got In Our Jeans.

Preparing the form? That's the toughie. According to the IRS, the typical American, parked at the card table with pencil and calculator, will spend three hours and 17 minutes actually filling out the papers.

And then there's the task of copying, assembling and mailing the form to the IRS. Chalk up 35 more minutes.

Punch all those figures into your pocket calculator — *clickety, clickety, click* — and you see that your standard, red-blooded American gives Uncle Sam a mere 9 hours and 33 minutes of time preparing his/her income tax. Considering the liberties and freedoms afforded by our republic, this is a very small investment.

Ah, but then there's the dollar side of the equation. According to a Washington organization called The Tax Foundation, your standard, red-blooded American will work until May 5 before he/she satisfies his/her tax burden for the year.

Which means you could have started figuring your taxes after breakfast on New Year's Day and finished in plenty of time to watch Tennessee whip Virginia in the Sugar Bowl. But then to pay the stupid $%*&!¢ bill, you gotta work until long after the Orange and White spring game is history.

Time is money? Not hardly.

First days of spring

If it can go wrong, it will

April 6, 1990

Spring is officially here. The Dogwood Arts Festival is officially under way. Trees are officially in leaf. Flowers are officially in bloom. And come 3:30 this afternoon, school will be officially out for Easter week.

But if you think we can sit back and take it easy for the next 4 1/2 months, what an official goober you are.

How come?

FAPPOSAS, that's how come. Famous And Prophetic Phrases Of Spring And Summer.

FAPPOSAS ruin everything. From the first pale bud in April till the leaves begin to change color in September, FAPPOSAS butt into the lives of humans all across the country.

It doesn't matter what you plan — picnics, vacations, family outings, hiking, fishing, skiing, boating. You name the activity, and FAPPOSAS will kick it squarely in the teeth. I guarantee it.

Still not convinced? Then utter one or more of these FAPPOSAS and see what happens:

"There's no need packing a rain suit. The forecast shows clear weather for at least 48 hours."

"I don't care what the map says. I've been on this trail a dozen times. And I *know* we can cut across that ridge and save ourselves a good two or three miles."

"Don't worry about bringing any food. We'll catch lunch and supper from the lake."

"You haven't water-skied in 18 years? Big deal. It's like riding a bike. Nobody ever forgets."

"What's a little lightning? Was Ben Franklin scared?"

"Granny Smith never refrigerated her potato salad, and she lived to be 92."

"Thank goodness I had the car checked before we left home. Now we don't have to worry about anything going on the fritz."

"Of course I can get those hooks out of your arm. They had an article about it in last month's Field & Stream."

"These boots won't leak. Says so right here on the label."

"I used to cook this stuff when I was a Boy Scout. You'll love it."

"Yes, I brought the film. It's somewhere in my backpack."

"Boy, that old abandoned wasp nest would sure look good in our den!"

"Haven't seen a rattlesnake around these parts in — oh, I'd say at least 15 years."

"Sunscreen? Naaaa. I never burn."

"No more driving all over creation looking for a motel these

days, honey. I called their 800 number, and they guaranteed us a reservation for tomorrow."

"The rangers don't mean it when they tell you not to feed the bears. It's one of those things the government makes them say."

"No need carrying extra gas for the boat. One tank is more than enough to get us back up the river."

"The best part about this place is we're never bothered by mosquitoes."

"Trust me. Bass will fight each other to grab this lure."

"Relax, Mister Worrywart; I distinctly remember putting the plug in the boat."

"Disregard the growl. Wild animals are a lot more scared of you than you are of them."

"Let's see, now. . . .What's the ol' poison ivy jingle? 'Leaves of three, let it be,' or 'Leaves of three, and you're home free'?"

"Wet wood's no problem. If you want a quick campfire, nothing works like a shot of lantern fuel. Here, stand back and let me show you how it's done."

Eggstra! Eggstra!

March 24, 1991

If you feel smitten to communicate with me in the next few days, please use the mail, telegram, fax, carrier pigeon or personal courier.

For that matter, you can even belt out an old-fashioned East Tennessee hog squall.

But do not use the telephone. There's only one line to my desk, and I want to keep it clear.

When news of my latest scientific experiment gets out, I know the Nobel committee — or, at the very least, an envoy from the International Academy of Smart People — will try to call, and I don't want them to get flusterated with a busy signal and wind up bestowing their high-dollar prizes on someone else.

I have just solved The Great Vernal Equinox Egg Balancing Mystery. Please hold your applause until this column is finished.

According to centuries-old legend, eggs will stand upright during the vernal (spring) equinox — which, for 1991, occurred at 10:02 p.m. last Wednesday.

I don't know how this legend started, but I occasionally see stories about it and hear about it from newspaper readers — complete with photographs of eggs standing at perfect attention on the tops of bars, kitchen counters, tables and desks.

Last Wednesday night, I tried for myself.

(In all honesty, this was the *second* time I dabbled in egg-standing experiments. During the fall equinox last September, I made a brief attempt at balancing two or three eggs at home. All of them immediately toppled over, creating the makings for an omelet and dispelling the legend in one fell swoop. But then someone told me autumn didn't count; it only works in spring. So I've waited all this time to try again. We high-level scientific researchers are a patient breed.)

I went to the refrigerator around 9:45 p.m. and withdrew all 13 eggs the Venobs had in inventory. So as not to upset the delicate balance within our 'frige, I also withdrew a 12-ounce can of malt beverage from the other side of the tray.

The first few eggs I tried to balance fell over, just like the ones from last September. So I put them aside and reached for more.

And that, dear friends, is when it happened.

Starting at 9:55, the eggs no longer fell. One by one, they stayed put when gently placed on their larger end. By the time the digital microwave clock flashed 10:02, seven of the 13 were sitting up like miniature bowling pins.

I am not lying. Cross my heart and hope to die; stick a needle in my eye. I was so astounded by this shocking phenomenon, I nearly drained the 12-ounce can in one pull.

My wife and children will vouch for my story, even though they were less than enthusiastic about this monumental scientific feat. Consider daughter Megan's comment to her mother:

"Was Dad this much of a geek when you all were dating?"

Barbs from ingrate teenagers aside, I opted for the Ever-Important Acid Test to prove the theory. I dotted the stand-up eggs with a pen and put 'em back in the refrigerator with the non-standers.

At 7 the next morning, long after the 1991 equinox was history, I retrieved all the eggs and tried the experiment one more time. That's when I made the amazing dicovery which will surely lead to a prize from the world's scientific community.

(A drum roll, please). THE VERY SAME EGGS THAT STOOD UP AT THE WITCHING HOUR OF THE EQUINOX ALSO STOOD UP THE NEXT MORNING!

In other words, equinox, schmequinox. The time of day or year has nothing whatsoever to do with it. Some eggs are just flatter on the end than others.

Or, as they say down at the poultry plant, all oviducts do not create equal.

Signs do not lie

February 24, 1987

I am typing these words a full five days before they are due to appear in print.

Working so far in advance on a weather-related topic is risky, even during the monotonous dog days of summer. But at this time of year, it's downright treacherous. At the snap of a finger, we can go from 55 degrees and sunshine to -10 and 6 inches of snow.

In this instance, however, timeliness matters not a twit.

You can take the news I am about to lay upon you and carry it to the bank and never worry about the check bouncing. I don't care if you are enjoying your first sunbath of the season when you see this column or whether you are shoveling snow and ice off the driveway.

All I want to say is that spring is *juuuust* around the corner.

Trust me. I know it for a fact. Within the last couple of days, I have seen and heard the signs. Signs do not lie.

First, I have already seen jonquils in bloom. Nearly 10 days ago, in fact. Mind you, these were outdoor garden-variety jonquils. Not something nurtured in a greenhouse.

When jonquils start unfolding their yellow hats, you can begin to rearrange garden tools in the basement. Yes, they sometimes tamper with the truth; many's the jonquil that has dropped its petals onto snow. But they're not nearly so bad about false starts as, say, the crocus.

Second, I have heard thunder. Real, ol' timey, just-like-an-April-shower thunder.

This occurred one morning last week when the heavens couldn't decide whether to hurl rain or snow upon us. I suppose there was a fierce disturbance going on up yonder, with cold fronts striking warm fronts or whatever. In any event, it evoked two nice rumbles that were music to my ears.

Some types of thunder are not friendly. If you are caught in an August thunderstorm and lightning is crashing all around and your ears are about to burst from the racket and you are so scared you can't swallow, it is difficult to harbor pleasant thoughts about thunder.

Aaah, but when thunder rolls in the distance — especially on a cloudy spring afternoon when the hillsides are painted in various pastels — it produces a soothing effect you'll never find in a bottle of pills.

Finally, I know spring is nigh because a little bird told me.

It was a dumpy, brown bird with an outrageously long bill and short, stubby wings that whistle when it flies off the ground. If you haven't guessed by now, I speak of the woodcock.

Woodcocks are migratory birds. About the only time you will find them in East Tennessee is for a brief period during the fall and spring migration. They are moving northward as we speak, for I have already heard their courting songs — I use the term loosely — on my evening walks past an overgrown field near the house.

In addition to their outlandish looks, woodcocks have a weird way of saying sweet nothings. When a male is trying to attract a young thang, he sits in the leaves and yells, "veeeeeent!" to her.

(Sorry, but "veeeeeent!" is as close as I know how to reproduce. It's one of those sounds you simply cannot duplicate with letters. The closest noise I can relate it to is the drone of a jarfly in midsummer. But once you hear it, you'll never forget.)

After singing, he leaps into the air and flies a high, circular pattern, all the while emitting a warbling whistle.

This sort of jive talk may not turn your crank, but it works wonders for female woodcocks. Countless generations have been criss-crossing the North American continent for thousands of years.

So there you have it: iron-clad evidence that spring is nigh. Let us hear no more groaning about winter, no matter what dire reports weather forecasters may concoct in the coming weeks.

If this keeps up, I may run outside and mow the brown grass and wild onions in my yard, just for the sheer joy of it.

What, me angry?

April 5, 1987

The dove perched on the back of a patio chair outside my kitchen window appeared to understand the situation — and disagree with it — as much as I did.

Meaning he was utterly miserable.

There he (maybe it was a she; who knows except other doves?) sat, mumped up, feathers fluffed like a duster, a first-class foul fowl. He kept turning his gray head from side to side. He looked up. He looked down. He went side-to-side again. I nearly got dizzy just watching.

Or maybe it was the whirlwind of snowflakes that made my mind blur. Millions and millions of flakes, they were. Enough to pile up 12 inches on the deck before the day was through.

Finally the dove fluttered to the windowsill and began pecking at a pile of sunflower seeds. If ever there was an angry bird, this was it. I swear I saw him scowl. His attitude seemed to match mine as I shoveled another bite of cold cereal down the hatch, longing with every chew for a cup of hot coffee.

The power was off. The house was cold. The last of my winter firewood — dry and begging to be burned — was stacked beneath four pickup loads of freshly split green wood. I was not a happy person.

In fact, I was brewing a blue-ribbon mad.

Here it was Friday, the first full week of traditional turkey and trout seasons. I could have been out in the mountains, watching the world burst into glory once again. But no; I have to sit inside a cold, dark house. And brood.

"Just think," a sickeningly cheerful voice announced inside my head, "if you were camping, you'd probably be eating cold cereal and enjoying every bite. Besides, it's really not *that* chilly in here."

"But I'm *not* out camping, you idiot!" snapped a hateful voice, to the thunderous applause of other angry emotions. "And I'll thank you to keep those cute, upbeat opinions to yourself!"

Thus, the internal battle raged.

I know this never is a problem with you emotionally stable people in Readership Land, but I take it personally when the weather is unseasonable. I know the weather gods have it in for me and me alone. They always cooperate for other people. But they've never liked me.

Spring is supposed to be green and warm. Summer hot and humid. Fall crisp and splashed with color. Winter cold and snowy. Period. East is east, west is west, and don't —*bah-humbug!* —go switching the channels.

But while I was basking in the warmth of self-pity, I decided to venture out. A birch tree in my side yard was bent precariously under the weight of wet snow. It and others needed a good cleaning. So with all the "pshaw-be-dang-habengratchits" could muster, I pulled on boots and heavy clothes and stepped from the basement.

That's when "it" happened, much to the chagrin of my marvelous hateful emotions: Spring was in full progress, just like the blizzard never occurred.

Robins, red-winged blackbirds, cardinals and song sparrows were in full throat. I knocked snow off heavily flowered dogwood, redbud and forsythia limbs, and a rainbow of colors burst through. Four-foot-tall loblolly pines — beaten down and huddled like sleeping fawns — sprang erect when I tapped them with a broom. It was incredible.

In fact, I was so awestruck by the eerie scene, I dashed back inside, loaded a camera and captured closeups in color. "I may be an old man before an opportunity like this returns," I thought to myself.

That's when "it" happened again.

Like a lightning bolt, the thought struck me that I wasn't angry at the world anymore.

Aaarrrgh! How could this be? Where had I failed? What if — *gasp!* — word gets back to my wife and kids?

Dang. I just hate it when my mad is whistling at full steam and something comes along to cheer me up.

A fool and his games

March 31, 1987

I'm giving you this information a full day in advance, which is plenty of warning. If you don't take advantage of it — and your friends do and you wind up looking like a jackass — don't blame me.

At the stroke of midnight and continuing for the next 24 hours, people all over the land will be trying to trick each other. It is the rite of spring known as April Fool's Day.

The custom sprouted roots in France during the mid-1500s.

According to "The American Book of Days" by Jane Hatch, this was when Charles IX adopted the reformed calendar. Prior to that time, the new year celebration began March 21 and ended April 1.

When the start of the year switched to January, some old clodhoppers clung to the traditional date. They came to be known as "April fools." It wasn't long before the habit of pulling pranks arose, spreading first to England, then to the rest of the world.

In France, I am told, the victim is called an "April Fish." In Scotland, he or she is known as an "April Gowk." Weird, perhaps; then again, you gotta wonder about a country where muscular men prance around in skirts. But that's neither here nor there.

Some of the pranks played in America this year will be harmless. Downright nerdy, if you ask me. Like telling your Uncle Floyd his shoe is untied, then gleefully shouting, "April Fool!" when the jerk glances at his feet.

Some will be a bit more testy — like slipping a loaded cigarette into a friend's pack. But this is still ho-hum material.

The April Fool's pranks I like to see have punch. They have spice. They have life. (Or at least 8 to 10 years, with time off for good behavior.)

Consider these possibilities for mirth, merriment and mayhem:

• Sneak out tonight and attach a burglar alarm to your neighbor's new car. Soon as it sounds off, call the cops and tell 'em to get there pronto.

• Replace your office mate's pipe tobacco with coffee grounds. (Be prepared for this to backfire, though. He might prefer the change.)

• Send some TV preacher a check for $3 million. But don't sign it.

• Submerge a plastic shark in your neighbor's swimming pool. Scatter shoes, a shirt and a pair of pants around the side. Then toss two packs of red dye into the water, scream and hoof it.

• Family frolic: Squirt Nair into Dad's hair restoration tonic, shake talcum powder into Mom's blow dryer, squeeze shaving cream into Junior's toothpaste tube and stir Hershey's sauce into Sis's makeup. Ha-ha-ha, ain't it neat to belong to such a fun-loving family?

• Bribe the public address operator at work to announce the

office smarty-pants' name during coffee break and say the blow-up doll he ordered has arrived.

   • Send your boss's name and address to the PTL Club and include this message: "I want Heritage USA to be the beneficiary of my $100,000 life insurance policy. Would a representative please call as soon as possible?"

   There. That oughta keep you occupied for the better part of April Fool's Day. Go ahead and have a ball with your friends, family and fellow workers.

   Just don't try anything on me, 'cause I'll be out of town. Yeah, that's it; and there's sickness in my neighborhood, so don't start anything around my house.

   Besides, I don't use hair restoration lotion and I don't have a pool or a new car or any of that stuff, so none of those tricks will work on me. And no matter what anybody says, I didn't order that blow-up doll.

   Really, I didn't.

And we lived to tell about it, too

April 1, 1986

   There's an awful problem about an April Fool's Day story. No matter how obvious the joke is, a few knuckleheads will believe it.

   Sometimes, they cannot swallow fast enough. I'm talking about hook, line, sinker, rod, reel, boat, motor and trailer. In one gulp.

   On April 1, 1974, The Knoxville News-Sentinel carried a bold-face sports story about how the University of Tennessee had recruited an 8-foot basketball player from Africa. His name was Ghroheuover Glhoehck — pronounced, the article said, "Grover Glick."

   The piece was fraught with giveaways. Among them:

   Glick's coach was Arlis W. Davison. (At the time, UT had an assistant coach named A.W. Davis.)

   Glick had been reared in the home of a British nobleman, Lord Seward Alberteen. (Another UT assistant was Stu Aberdeen.)

   The man who had alerted UT to Glick's talents worked for the land-holding company of Manging, Haywood and Woolruff, Ltd. (UT Athletic Department officials were Gus Manning, Haywood Harris and

Bob Woodruff.)

The "Ethiopian Broadcasting Co.'s" top commentator, Jan Word (for Voice of the Vols John Ward) was to broadcast Glick's debut as a Vol.

A sportswriter from the "Addis Ababa Sand-Times" also figured heavily in the story. His name was Harvin East. (The News-Sentinel's UT writer in those days was Marvin West.)

And if that wasn't enough, the final paragraph of the story read as follows: "So there you have it, Big Orange fans, an 8-footer for the Vols. Mark down the date of this historic signing — April Fool's Day, 1974."

Surely no one believed it, eh?

"They flooded us with calls and letters, hundreds of them," said sportswriter Ted Riggs, mastermind behind the trick. "You know how UT fans are.

"People thought I was the greatest sportswriter in America to get such a scoop. When they learned it was a hoax, they turned on me. Women would call in and say vulgar, mean things.

"The next year, I suggested another April Fool's Day story," Riggs continued. "I proposed to write that UT was building the largest athletic complex in history. It was to include a dorm for athletes, an indoor golf course and a basketball arena seating 58,000 — to be shared with a professional team that was coming to town.

"I got a flat rejection from the editor. He said it was too believable."

The News-Sentinel even has the distinction of scooping itself on an April Fool's Day story. That occurred March 30, 1979, when Mark McNeely was our Nashville correspondent.

"It was late one week, and I had a Sunday column to write," McNeely recalled. "I noticed that Sunday happened to be April 1, so I worked up a big April Fool's Day piece." It, too, was laced with obvious fiction. In virtually every paragraph, McNeely had politicians reversing themselves on important pieces of legislation. The biggie surrounded state Rep. Tommy Burnett of Jamestown, who had been a staunch opponent of funding for the Tennessee Amphitheater at the 1982 World's Fair.

The spoof not only had Burnett reversing his stand, but at the same time, he was to accept a seat on the board of directors of (fair bigwig) Jake Butcher's United American Bank.

Guess what happened. Yup, someone in our newsroom glanced at the story as it moved across the wire and failed to notice the "April Fool" caveat at the top. The paragraph about Burnett was plucked from the column and used, as is, as a separate news bulletin on Page 1. It was one of those "stop-the-presses-we've-got-a-bombshell" things. With the deepest shade of red face, the newspaper apologized the following day.

For weeks, every editor in the joint was in a foul mood over that one. All us peons thought it was hilarious.

We still do, and that's no foolin'.

Taxes and other hassles

Giving till it (yeee-ouch!) hurts

April 14, 1991

For millions of procrastinating Americans, and you know who you are, this is the worst weekend of the year.

Instead of sipping a leisurely third cup of coffee as you shuffle through the Sunday morning newspaper, you've been working at the breakfast table since 5:30. You have emptied your filing cabinet, and now the floor is ankle-deep in receipts, carbon copies, federal forms and other official documents. You've pigged all the AA batteries from the supermarket so your calculator and pencil sharpener won't quit when the going gets tough. And you've laid in an emergency supply of junk food, not to mention aspirin and antacids.

Welcome to the PITT — Panic Income Tax Time.

Sure, you've had since January 1 to prepare your Form 1040. But noooooo. You weren't going to give the government one red cent any sooner than necessary. You were holding out until April 15.

So as you and jillions of other last-minute filers stand in line at the Post Office, transferring your hard-earned treasures to Uncle Sam's quivering, outstretched hands, I have a few figures you might want to bounce around.

How does $4.5 million sound for starters? That's how much of your money Congress has appropriated to Huntington, W. Va., so the Keith-Albee Theater can have four screens.

This project is one of dozens of costly capers funded by the good men and women you've sent to federal office. I found it listed in the "1991 Congressional Pig Book Summary" published by a Washington group called Council For Citizens Against Government Waste.

The council says it is working to eliminate Congress' insatiable appetite for expensive, wasteful (which is redundant) porkbarrel programs. It's a worthy goal, for sure, one that consumer groups, taxpayer unions, environmental coalitions and gobs of others have sought for years.

Regrettably, these well-intentioned people rarely achieve success. Porkbarreling is as much a part of political life as campaign speeches and testimonial dinners. Politicians know it. Bureaucrats know it. Civic officials know it. The press knows it. It's a never-ending, ever-escalating game of spending where the blame inevitably falls some-where else.

A Tennessee congressman can, and will, scream about an Arizona highway project that is costly, environmentally disastrous and benefi-cial to only a handful of drivers. In Arizona, however, the politicians, bureaucrats, civic officials and press will hail the project as a penny-pinching savior of the citizens.

Two months later, the same Tennessee lawmaker will introduce legislation authorizing an equally costly, destructive and useless highway project here. The folks out West will scream, "Porkbarrel!" Ironically, the Tennessee politicians-bureaucrats-officials-press will disagree. They'll praise it as the best use of asphalt in the history of public works.

Once you understand the system, it makes perfect sense.

And it is why, according to the citizens' council's latest list, Congress has approved such juicy projects as $850,000 for a bicycle path in Macomb County, Mich; a $10 million executive training center in Avondale, Md.; $1.3 million in "job retention" for farm laborers at a

privately owned sugar mill in Hawaii; $350,000 to restore the House
of Representatives' beauty salon; and $25,000 to study the location of
a new House staff gymnasium.

Admit it. Doesn't this news make standing in line at the Post
Office a lot more fun?

One size fits all and other holiday myths

March 27, 1988

Your mama warned you about listening to other people's lies,
didn't she? She tried to tell you there are some things in this world that
simply are not true, no matter how glorious and realistic someone may
make them out to be.

But you had to learn for yourself, didn't you? You had to throw
your mama's wisdom aside and plunge in over your head — and then
scream for the life buoy, right?

Well, don't worry. Everybody has to make these mistakes. Even
your mama did. It's part of the maturation process.

Falling for a lie like "the check is in the mail" or "I'm from the
government and I'm here to help you" isn't that much of a crime on
first offense. If, however, you continue to be taken in by common lies,
perhaps you should talk to a trained counselor. Either that, or talk to
me about the prime Florida swamp property I have for sale. Cheap.

This time of year — with spring just waiting to explode, with new
fashions in every store window, with the air adrip in thoughts of
summer holidays — we are smitten by two of the worst lies ever
visited upon humankind.

They are vicious. They are mean. They need to be outlawed by
Congress. These are the two lies of:

One size fits all.

I defy you to look at a mail order catalog and not find this statement on any number of garments. It doesn't matter if the catalog is
advertising shoes or hats, gloves or shirts. Somewhere in the glitter,
you will see those four false words.

"One size fits all" does not mean the particular article of clothing
will magically expand or contract to cover each individual body. Not
on your life. What it REALLY means is, "We only make this thing in

one size, and if you happen to be of that dimension, which is along the lines of an Australian pygmy, it will fit perfectly."

It is fun and relaxing to stretch out under the broiling sun at the beach.

This lie is repeated at least 26,482,849 times every spring. Sometimes more often than that. It has become the stereotypic mental image of the words "vacation" and "beach holiday."

Certainly, visiting the ocean is an exciting experience. It is marvelous fun to play in the water and build sand castles and collect sea shells and walk along the beach as the surf gurgles between your toes.

But to just lie there like a rack of ribs on a grill, staring at the sun? Aaaargh! I have a suspicion this is what hell is truly like.

The advertising people would have us believe that people reclined so comfortably on the beach do not have a care in the world, that they exist in an eternal state of nirvana.

Baloney.

The truth is that sweat is pouring off their bodies like Niagara Falls; they will suffer first-degree burns in less than 10 minutes; and when they do attempt to get up and stagger to the motel room, they will carry 2 1/2 cubic yards of sand with them — most of it hidden deep within nooks and crannies that have never seen the light of day, let alone served as a repository for sand.

I have at my desk this very moment a travel brochure photograph. It shows a man leaning against the base of a palm tree beside the beach. He is supposed to be asleep.

On first glance, he did appear serene. Then when I looked closer, I realized what an excruciating position his body had to be in, all bent up around that gnarled, twisted tree trunk.

It dawned on me that this poor man was either (1) a circus contortionist on vacation, (2) one of those weirdos who loves pain or (3) dead.

And I'll bet if you peeked at the label inside his swim trunks, it would say, "One size fits all."

Why not go back to sundials?

April 7, 1991

Before this weekend is over, I will do my part to help our sovereign republic spring forward into Daylight Saving Time for yet another year.

I will pull the stem on my wristwatch, rotate the winder do-hickey with thumb and index finger to advance the minute hand one complete revolution, and then push the stem back into place. The process will be finished inside of 10 seconds.

Other people will experience a greater degree of difficulty.

Contorting their hands into pretzels and punching buttons with three or four fingertips, they will attempt to reset their digital clocks and watches. This exercise in frustration will leave them with vein-ridged necks, an exciting new vocabulary of vulgar terms and rooms full of timepieces blinking "12:00" in bright red characters.

I have never liked digital clocks and watches, I will never like them, and that is the end of that. If this attitude puts me in the category of gray-headed geezers who thought everything was better when Ike lived in the White House, so be it.

Perhaps my first experience with the infernal beasts is what soured me.

In the late 1970s, when I was writing a book about a hunting club in southwest Louisiana, the guy I was working for gave me a digital wristwatch at Christmas.

I was not the only recipient. The fellow must have purchased a truckload of them, because everyone — kennel cleaners to duck pickers to biologists to cooks, plus wives and children thereof — unwrapped a digital watch that year.

As digitals go today, these were not especially whiz-bang fancy. They kept time and date and had an alarm, but they had no built-in calculator, time-zone indicator, phone number catalog or any of the high-tech functions available in the 1990s.

Nonetheless, nobody had the foggiest notion how to set the stupid things.

Directions? Of course we had directions. But they were printed on several pages, in itty-bitty type, and the few of us who took time to read quickly discovered it would be easier to carry a sundial in a backpack.

The buttons were minuscule. If you tried to push one with the tip of your finger, you wound up hitting two or three. So instead of setting the time, you activated the alarm or accidentally changed the date.

It was a zoo. At any given moment on Little Pecan Island, 25 watches would show 25 different times and dates. Once, we tried to synchronize our alarms, and the resulting high-pitched "beeps" that cranked up over a 45-minute period sounded like a convention of drunken tree frogs.

So I did what any thinking person would do. I carefully nestled my watch back into the original box, put it in the closet and gave it to someone else the following Christmas. So help me Hannah, another Little Pecan employee — apparently not realizing I had been part of the original watch crew — gave me his that same year.

This watch-giving fury continued for a good three or four Christmases — much like the traditional receive-and-give cycle for a fruitcake — until the island was finally purged of the beeping demons, and we all happily went back to our old, familiar, wind-up timepieces.

It is impossible to keep my distance from all digitized readouts. Like any other typical American family, the Venobs own a microwave, VCR, radios and automobiles equipped with digital clocks. Getting them to agree on hour and minute in the early stages of DST will be a chore for my wife and chillen.

I will set my wristwatch and the grandfather clock, thank you.

Other than that, I refuse to participate.

Sorry to be so stubborn. But sometimes, a man simply has to make his stand.

Forget the fad; it's our future

April 22, 1990

Just to be different from everyone else, I think I'll chop down a tree today. Or clean my paintbrushes in the creek. Maybe scatter a week's worth of garbage along some lovely country lane and laugh as foam cups and plastic wrappers go skittering off with the breeze.

Tee-hee. Just teasing. Honest.

I merely wanted to see if you were paying attention to the fact that this is the 20th anniversary of Earth Day. Surely you've heard. It's been in all the papers.

Perhaps we do need to laugh occasionally about the sad plight of our fragile planet. If for no other reason than to keep from crying.

Despite the problems, too much breast-beating tends to make us forget Earth's simple, blessed joys that are there for the asking: The beauty of a sunrise. The aroma of a meadow after a June squall. The chorus of Canada geese on the wing. The crunch of fresh-fallen leaves on a crisp October afternoon.

But as refreshing as they may be to the soul, laughter and pleasant thoughts won't solve the crisis we have brought upon ourselves.

Neither will parades, posters, banners, petitions, catchy slogans, media specials, political speeches and other trendy trappings of this environmental celebration.

The posters and banners will be gone tomorrow — banished, ironically enough, to landfills and incinerators. Catchy slogans will fade from the tongue. The press will find a new cause. So will politicians. And the basic problems of environmental degradation will still go begging.

No, not until the hearts of people change — change permanently — will the Good Ship Earth be assured of smooth sailing on friendly waters.

It doesn't matter if you are the CEO of a chemical company, a homemaker in the suburbs, a small-town farmer or a sales clerk. If you're willing to compromise your ecological birthright for profit or convenience, you'll never be part of the solution, no matter how proudly you profess to be "an environmentalist."

Sometimes, I grow so pessimistic it's scary. It doesn't take many Alaskan oil spills or polluted Pigeon Rivers to convince me the sands in Earth's hourglass have all but trickled away.

Then I'll climb to the top of a mountain — as I did in the Cumberlands a few days ago — and pig out on the sight of a jillion-billion trees putting on their summer clothes, and I get to thinking that maybe Doomsday is little more than a bad dream brought on by too much pizza.

Can we live in closer harmony with nature? Of course we can. As long as we don't backslide.

Americans proved it on a small scale during the 1970s when we honed in on energy conservation.

Our vehicles got better mileage. We turned out unnecessary lights. We insulated. We recycled. We carpooled.

But then the crisis passed momentarily, and we slipped back into gluttonous ways. If you don't believe it, compare an automobile ad today with one from 1979.

I know a guy who suffers a serious heart condition. A smoker. When the docs finally carved his chest apart, he threw away his cigarettes and cursed the day he took the first puff.

Then a funny thing happened.

The incisions healed. The pains went away. His ticker began to behave properly. His life expectancy took a quantum leap. And the last time we talked, he was lighting one off another.

Maybe he figured what the heck; tomorrow's going to come soon enough, so I might as well enjoy today. And perhaps that's the attitude too many of us have taken about the environment.

If so, there's a serious flaw in the reasoning.

It's not only *our* tomorrow that's coming. It's our children's and grandchildren's, too.

Shhhh! The leaves have ears

April 29, 1990

Assuming Ed Wagner's theory is correct, trees all across America should be wagging their tongues right now.

Wagner, a physicist, runs his own research laboratory in Grants Pass, Ore. He has dedicated the last two decades to proving the notion that trees communicate with each other. Especially when their trunks are being assaulted with a chainsaw.

Wagner has done some high-tech listening. When a tree is cut, it sends out what he calls "W-waves."

These are silent screams to you and me but supposedly quite detectable on Wagner's devices. What's more, trees near the victim join in with a chorus of protests.

In a recent news report from the lab, Wagner admitted his work has met with considerable skepticism. "For some people, it's so contrary to what they think that they won't bother to read the evidence," he commented. "But it's just a matter of time."

Far be it from me to say this guy is wrong. For all I know, the forests of America have been clamoring all week. Now that Earth Day 1990 is history, trees surely have a million stories to tell each other.

All it takes is a trained ear to eavesdrop. As per:

"Orville Oak! Is that you? You ol' son-of-an-acorn, where you been keeping yourself the last 50 years?"

"I've been right behind you all along, Mike Maple. Not that you'd ever turn around and say howdy. Lord knows I've been hollering till my cambium is nearly cracked."

"Sorry, Orville. My hearing's nearly gone. And at my age, it's getting tougher to glance back over the ol' branches. Besides, I've been keeping an eye on Dolly Dogwood down in the hollow since '68. Or maybe '78. Time gets away from me anymore."

"Yeah, I know. Seems like only yesterday we were sprouts. But it's high time you started acting your age, you old coot. You're making an absolute fool out of yourself, waving your limbs, turning your leaves and dropping those stupid little helicopters all over creation. You think she'd ever be interested in the likes of you? Hah!"

"You never know, Orville. One of these decades, she's going to notice. I'm sure of it. Anyway, it's good to see you survived Earth Day. How'd it go for you?"

"Not bad. The Clumsy Climbers Hiking Club didn't do me any favors when they came through Saturday morning. The knobby soles on those boots — YEE-OUCH! It'll take me a good four years to work the kinks out of my roots. But it wasn't as bad as the time Euell Gibbons chowed down on my bark."

"At least those guys' hearts are in the right place. Besides, I get a kick out of their funny little hats. What a riot. Do all people dress like that?"

"Naaa. Some are even crazier. Ever see a deer hunter in a blaze orange jumpsuit? Wheee-doggies! Brighter than the sun on an August afternoon."

"Hate to change the subject, Orville, but did you hear about the Pine family?"

"The Pines? No! What?"

"Loggers. Got the whole lot of 'em. Peter and Peggy, plus the youngins, Paul and Princess, as well as Uncle Purvis and Aunt Patty. Whacked 'em off at ground level."

"That's what all the screaming was about last month on Ledford's Ridge?"

"You got it. They say it was awful. Herman Hemlock told me. He heard it from Laura Locust, who got it firsthand from Floyd Fir. Floyd was afraid they'd get him, too. But he made like a fence post, and they never noticed."

"Lucky for him."

"Indeed. It was so quick on the Pines, though, most of 'em went without a fight. All except Purvis. He twisted on the stump just as he was goin' over and tried to hit one of the loggers."

"Nail 'im?"

"Nope. Close, but no cigar. Scared the wits outta the guy, but he got away with a few scratches. Guess ol' Purvis wasn't as quick as he used to be."

"I reckon not. In his prime, he could fling a limb 75 yards uphill. I used to love the way he tormented squirrels with pine cones. Gosh, this is terrible. I'm sure gonna miss the Pines. Reckon whatever became of 'em?"

"That's the saddest part of all."

"Huh?"

"They got turned into Earth Day posters."

How to stay on schedule

March 22, 1990

The 1990 dogwood trees and the 1990 Dogwood Arts Festival have a serious communication problem. As usual.

Despite a recent cool snap, Knoxville's trees are on the verge of full flower. As we speak, many are laden with pale mini-blooms. At the mere suggestion of sunshine, they shall burst into glory. Trouble is, the festival doesn't start for two more weeks.

Great, just great. By then, the trees will be well past their peak. And by the time the festival closes at the end of April, "spring" will be a word mentioned only in Ancient History 111.

Some years, this situation is reversed. The festival cranks up and everybody is walking around in their warm weather finery, eager to gaze upon beautiful white and pink blossoms. And what do the stupid trees do? They sit there, nekkid as skinny-dippers, just like it was New Year's Day.

I used to take personal offense at this miscarriage of botanical justice. I always wanted to grab an out-of-synch dogwood and shake it into its senses.

"You (bleeping) ingrate! The people of this city have gone to a lot of trouble to throw a celebration in your honor! But do you appreciate their efforts? Nooooooo! You bloom (fill in blank: ahead of schedule/behind schedule)! There you stand (blossoms on the ground/blossoms still in buds), and we end up looking like a bunch of goobers who wouldn't know a dogwood tree from a quart of chocolate milk!"

But I don't feel this way anymore.

I have learned to control my temper, for one thing. For another thing, I have learned that police fail to appreciate the humor when they see a grown man shaking dogwood trees and cursing their barren branches.

But the main reason I don't feel this way anymore is because I just got off the phone with a woman at the old church in San Juan Capistrano, Calif. And brother, have I seen the light.

According to the famous legend, swallows always return to Capistrano on March 19. This has been going on since 1776, when Father Junipero Serra founded the Catholic mission and noticed birds funneling into the eaves on March 19.

Most church custodians would have attacked the invading birds with a broom and sent the chirping, pooping vermin elsewhere. But the guys at the mission enjoyed them, and over the years this annual custom has evolved into a huge civic celebration. This year, for example, some 5,000-7,000 people were on hand to witness the first arrivals. But I digress.

"It ain't fair," I said to myself. "Our dogwood trees, which stay in one place all their lives, are too stupid to bloom on schedule. But their birds, which migrate plumb to Argentina, manage to return to California precisely on March 19. How come?"

I called the mission to find out. And in so doing, I discovered The Secret To Split-Second Biological Events That Are Worth Tons of Money To The Local Community (patent 3245797).

"Occasionally, a few birds do arrive early," said mission spokeswoman April Robinson. "Like any type of migratory animal, swallows send out scouts. The main flock starts arriving March 19 and continues to build up in the following weeks."

Translation: The swallows come back to Capistrano when they damn well feel like it.

If birds show up ahead of time, they are pronounced "scouts." If they wait until, oh, let's say, April 2, they are the "remainder of the flock." But when a few of them happen to twitter to the roost on March 19, it's yipee-hoorah-praise-the-Lawd; those sweet little darlings have done it again.

Now that I understand this biological secret, I am happy to

change my once-pessimistic report of this year's dogwood crop. Instead, here is the exciting news of the 1990 Dogwood Arts Festival, straight from the Mission de la San Juan Venob:

"The unusually large buildup of scout dogwoods indicates the remainder of the trees are going to explode into gorgeous flower on opening day of the festival — right on schedule!"

Sexy seeds and other garden lies

March 16, 1989

If members of Knoxville's Adult Oriented Establishment Board really want to crack down on pornography, they oughta start with seed catalogs.

Just look at the shameless smut I discovered the other day while browsing through the latest brochure from Burpee:

"Pickalot Hybrid Cucumber — The first all-female . . .well-shaped, dark-green fruits."

"Sweet 'N Tender Hybrid Corn — Its ears are more tender . . . well-filled right up to the tip."

"Stella Sweet Cherry — This is a rarity . . . self-fruitful, needs no other variety for self-pollination."

"Burpee's Ambrosia Hybrid — Luscious melons with unique flavor . . . extremely thick, firm flesh is delicious right down to the rind."

I wanted to read on, but I was sweating profusely as it was. Besides, I heard footsteps coming and didn't want the kids to catch me looking at such trash.

The reason I picked up the catalog in the first place is because spring is nigh. Time to start having thoughts of warm weather, sunny days, a green lawn, a lush garden.

Of course, the thought stage is as far as I go. It is easier for me to pick beans off the shelf at the grocery store than pull them off the vine in the garden. You don't have to bend over, for one thing. And it's air-conditioned.

My wife, a woman who never met a plant she didn't like, disagrees completely. She enjoys growing her own. This year, she's even started all her garden plants — tomatoes, peppers, okra, the works —

from scratch. Our den looks like Luther Burbank's office. Little green squiggly things sprouting by the multiplied hundreds.

Nonetheless, I do enjoy leafing through her seed catalogs. The pictures are fun to look at, although you and I both know they are the products of trick photography.

The tomatoes are never blemished, the pumpkins are perfect spheres, the corn has nary a tassle out of place, and the apples aren't bruised. This is as fake as fishing-catalog photos of anglers catching huge bass and clothing-catalog photos of middle-aged men with flat stomachs. Lies. All lies.

It's also interesting to see what gardeners will buy when their green thumb itch breaks out.

Did you know people actually sell dandelion seeds? It's right there on page 130 of the spring Burpee book. A pack of 1,500 seeds for 95 cents. Once they take root, you can flip over to page 197 and order a dandelion weeder. It costs $4.95.

How SAM views veggies

Finally, there is the eternal marvel of how advertising geniusii can pour out thousands of words to describe everyday fruits, flowers and veggies.

Take carrots.

I always figured if you've seen one carrot, you've seen 'em all. Not according to Burpee. On page 122, there are 617 words devoted to 10 varieties of carrots. I counted them.

To distinguish one from another, copy writers used such terms as "flavorful deep orange roots with high Vitamin A content" . . . "fine-grained, tender, rich-flavored" . . . "1 1/2-inch across shoulder, tapering to blunt end" . . . "cylindrical with small core and smooth skin."

That's funny. They all looked like carrots to me.

In fact, the only thing on the entire page that made sense was a chart. There was a length index alongside. It proved, scientifically and conclusively, that some carrots are short and stubby and some are long and skinny.

I always wondered why that was.

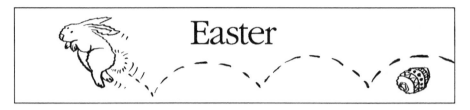

Easter

Scents of the season

March 30, 1986

The smell of spring is upon us, and I don't mean flowers.

Thanksgiving smells like roast turkey and cranberry sauce. Christmas smells like cedar and balsam. The Fourth of July smells like watermelon and charred meat — animal or human, depending on what touches the grill first. But Easter always smells like vinegar.

If you have to ask why, go make an appointment with a shrink. Quick. You surely had a deprived childhood, and it's important to vent these frustrations before things get any worse.

Vinegar is an integral part of Easter because that's what mamas everywhere use when they mix dye for Easter eggs. Don't ask me why. I'm sure some high-flung chemical reaction must occur before those little colored pellets dissolve and impart their hues to the shells of eggs.

Never question this phenomenon. Just accept it as one of the many secrets of life that must be taken on faith. Sorta like how you can open the refrigerator door and there's always milk inside.

When you think about it, Easter egg dyeing is not that exciting. In fact, it's rather gross — especially if your eggs happened to crack during the boiling process and the dye leaks inside and streaks the white part. I'd rather eat a roach than a three-day-old, room temperature, green and yellow, streaked, hardboiled egg that has been hidden six times behind a fencepost near places where cows have paused to meditate.

I think the real reason kids love to dye Easter eggs is because it's such a limited activity. You get to do it only once a year. If parents had any sense, they'd use the same logic in other areas of child-rearing. Like trying to get kiddies to eat yucky food.

"Mommy, how much longer until Brussels Sprouts Day?"

"Oh, it's a full week, honey. Try not to think about it, and it'll come sooner."

"But, Mommy! Can't I have just a little taste right now? Pleeeeeze?"

"No, dear. You'll have to wait. It wouldn't be fair to your brothers and sisters to cheat, would it? When Brussels Sprouts Day finally comes, you can eat all you want."

"Oh, goody! I'm not going to eat any candy for a whole week, just so I'll have more room for a fourth helping!"

But the real reason I have mixed feelings about Easter eggs is because mine never turned out the way they looked on the dye package.

Sure, your basic one-color egg wasn't a chore. All you had to do was seat an egg in the bent-wire holder and dunk it into a cup of dye and let it sit while you read two pages of Sunday funnies. The longer you read (and it bathed), the deeper the color. Big deal.

What I always wanted was one of those gorgeous, rainbow striped eggs, the sort of thing Karl Faberge would have created for a Russian czar.

First, I would take a clear wax pencil and inscribe the outside of the shell with intricate designs.

Then, using the bent wire holder, I would dunk it in various positions in different dyes. That was to create the rainbow effect.

But it never worked for me. The hateful egg always emerged looking like a bruise.

Every time she saw my bruise-colored eggs, my sister would make fun of me. But I could always get the last laugh.

I would just remind her of the time she was a little girl and thought the colored pellets were candy and ate a handful of them and scared mama half to death because she thought her baby had been poisoned.

No harm done, of course. The stuff was only food coloring. A day later, nature took its course, and the entire episode had a happy ending.

Quite a colorful one, too.

Endless cycles of renewal

March 26, 1989

I was sitting at the edge of the forest, drinking in the splendor of an early spring morning, when the pleasant scent hit my nostrils.

It came from dirt. Fresh dirt. The damp, warm, heady — well, earthy — smell of a new year's beginning.

This particular aroma happened to be wafting from a recently scraped roadbed. It was a road the landowner was cutting through the woods to link two fire service roads from adjacent hollows.

But little matter about the source. It could just as easily have been a freshly plowed cornfield, a just-turned garden, or even a spade-sized wedge pried from the back yard as an eager lad filled his tin can with angleworms.

No, what really mattered was the very scent of the dirt itself. It let me know that spring, at last, was officially here.

We may have another cold snap or two. Indeed, April snow is no stranger to these hills. But once you get a snootful of newly exposed dirt, you can bet Old Man Winter is glancing nervously around the room, searching for a door or a window to make his hasty escape.

Maybe it's just my nose, but dirt has a different smell in spring. It is stronger. Bolder. More compelling. Bracing. "Alive," you might even say.

How far removed it is from the musty odor of fall and winter, when millions of leaves are piled, one upon another, to mildew and rot until they return to the earth whence they came.

Make no mistake; the aroma of a freshly littered forest floor in October — especially when enhanced by an all-night rain — is perfume to the nostrils. But this springtime sensation of loam and humus and clay — well, it's just different, that's all. It's like the aromatic difference between chicken that is frying in your grandmother's black iron skillet and a blob of breaded thighs bubbling in deep fat at the Colonel's. You can either sense it or you cannot. And if not, you have my deepest sympathy.

I am not a student of soils. Not a technical one, anyway. Even though there are probably dozens of different soil types in Knox County alone, I am content to lump them collectively as "dirt."

Let scientists debate the fine points between Fullerton and Dewey, Bland and Nolichucky, Cumberland and Bolton and others of the red-yellow Podzolic group. Let them inspect samples of Lindside, Congaree, Staser, Chewacla and other alluvial soils and think learned thoughts about where each type might be found in and around our town. As long as I am familiar with red clay and "yallar mud" and river bottom silt and that grainy, abundantly rich, black gold from steep, north-facing hollows, however the minds of science wish to classify them is OK by me.

Strange, you might be saying to yourself, that something so lowly and seemingly inconsequential as dirt would be the subject of an Easter morning essay.

Quite the contrary. Dirt is the very essence of our being. Born of the old, the dead and the decayed, it brings forth the promise of life anew every year.

It is fresh. It is vibrant. Indeed, it is very much alive.

And just sitting here at the edge of the woods, looking at a strip of new dirt and swooning on its perfume, gives me blessed assurance that the cycle will continue as long as life itself exists on this planet.

An Easter to remember

April 7, 1985

It was dull, drab clothing, issued by Uncle Sam. Not the sort of stuff you'd normally wear to church on Easter Sunday.

But that didn't bother Howard Ownby. He couldn't have been happier in a silk suit. After nearly a month in squalor, Ownby had finally enjoyed the luxury of a shower and a shave. The shirt on his back was clean.

Best of all, he was free.

Ownby doesn't recall much about that Easter service on April 1, 1945. It was held in the open, next to a field hospital. He couldn't remember what religious denomination the minister represented.

"All I know," he says, "is that I sure was happy to be there."

You better believe it. Only three days earlier, Ownby had been liberated from a prisoner of war camp near Hattenrod, Germany.

Today marks the 40th Easter that Howard Ownby has celebrated his freedom. If the folks at Meridian Baptist happen to hear him singing louder than usual, perhaps they will understand.

"We had an assault across the Rhine River near Dusseldorf," said Ownby, 66. "We captured several Germans. But then we got surrounded. On orders from the company commander, we destroyed our weapons and surrendered."

Ownby and some 25 other GIs were taken to Stalag 12-A for interrogation. All they gave was name, rank and serial number.

"When we wouldn't tell anything else, they marched us into a courtyard and made us stand at attention. It was German attention, with your arms stiff at your side and your fingers pointed straight down.

"They brought me back in twice, after an hour each time, and questioned me more. The third time, I had to stand there for six hours. It was pretty cold, peppering some snow, and we didn't have coats. But we still didn't tell 'em anything."

The men were housed in cramped, cold quarters, two to a tiny bunk. They were given little food. Then they were packed like cattle into boxcars for the journey to Hattenrod.

"We didn't get off that train for seven days," he said. "They gave us a little food and water, but that's all. Some days, the train wouldn't move. We either stayed inside a tunnel or at a siding. It was very unsanitary."

The outfit was freed on Thursday, March 29, 1945. When the men celebrated Easter the following Sunday, they knew what "new life" was all about.

Ownby, retired vice president of Tri-State Roofing Co., is commander of the Smoky Mountain chapter of the American Ex-Prisoners of War Inc. He is one of more than 100 East Tennesseans who gather monthly to remember the not-so-good old days.

They, in turn, are among some 80,000 American POWs still living. Next week, the annual observation of National POW-MIA Day will recognize the sacrifices they made.

Members of the local group are compiling their experiences. They intend to give the volume to McClung Museum. If you want to be spellbound, run your finger down the membership roster. Anywhere it stops, you'll find a story.

There's Robert A. "Bob" Asquith, a former Knoxville resident who now runs the Etowah Health Care Center. Asquith was a POW in Germany from October 1944 until three weeks after Easter the following April. He weighed nearly 150 pounds when captured, 106 upon release.

When Asquith and his buddies reported after liberation, they noticed tears in their company commander's eyes.

"I couldn't understand this until I looked at my buddies and realized how decrepit we were," he said. "We had arrived on May 8, which was V-E Day. It was also my birthday, my 21st. What a present!"

Or perhaps you'd be interested in hearing from Roscoe C. "Piggy" Word Jr. He was captured by the Japanese in May 1942 and forced to do dock labor for two years. Then he was sent to the coal mines. Word wasn't freed until the Japanese surrendered.

"I guess I remember the spiritual aspects of Easter services more than anything else," says the 74-year-old retired senior vice president and attorney for Home Federal of Tennessee. "Not long after I was taken prisoner, I received a small Bible. I managed to keep it with me the entire time. It was very meaningful. I memorized a lot of Scripture."

Word talked of Easter Sunday in 1942, not long before his capture. The service was held on a beach at Corregidor. Japanese bombers overhead cut the sermon short.

Word also discovered human nature during his confinement: "When men are starving, all they talk about is food. When their bellies are full, all they talk about is women. And there's a strange connection between fear and religion. Whenever we were in danger of being killed, there was perfect attendance at services. When things slacked off, so did the crowd."

Despite the happiness of this holiday, Word says Easter is a particularly sad time for him.

"It's the same at Christmas, too. I had so many friends who didn't come back. I especially remember them."

So do thousands of others who suffered, struggled and survived.

'Happy' Mother's Day?

May 12, 1991

This is for all the mothers around the world who cook and clean and feed and wash and dry and mend and scrub and teach and comfort and counsel and guide.

Especially:

• The mothers who cook over an open fire in the squalor of a refugee camp.

• The mothers who clean their babies in stagnant pools, praying the unknown killer in the fetid water will spare them its misery for just another day.

• The mothers who feed scavenged scraps to their toddlers even as their own mouths cry out for nourishment.

• The mothers who wash their children's ragged clothing in a creek beside their mountain shack.

• The mothers who dry the tears of 2-year-olds and 22-year-olds with the same soothing, gentle words.

• The mothers who mend a son's heart, broken by love gone sour, while their own is being crushed by divorce.

• The mothers who scrub the shiny floors of someone else's house.

• The mothers who teach by flawless example that love can conquer bitterness and hate.

• The mothers who comfort victims of tornadoes, hurricanes, floods and fires while their own homes lie in shambles.

• The mothers who counsel daughters after their attackers have walked out of the courtroom on a technicality.

• The mothers who guide their children through treacherous mountain passes, deserts, swamps, battlefields, ghettoes and suburbs, plodding steadily on with nothing to sustain them save the faint hope of finding safety from fear and oppression.

For thousands of years, the mothers have borne these duties. And more. It starts when new life is wrenched from their bellies and does not cease until old life inside them goes back to the earth.

The mothers have cleared the land and tilled the fields and tended the stock and managed the stores and settled the accounts and run the companies and made the laws and kept the peace.

Believing in the cause but fearful for the sons of mothers everywhere, they have sent generations of children into war. And cried the anguished tears only mothers know when their gallant warriors came home in a box.

The mothers have done all of this since the dawn of creation. They will do it until the end of the ages.

And to think at one time they were called the weaker sex.

It wasn't my fault, honest

May 14, 1989

I never see a rose bush without thinking of my mother.

This is especially true if it's a large rose in full flower — you know, one of those fragrant, vegetative octopi slowly engulfing a wooden trellis.

When I was a boy, a rose bush like that grew in the Wilsons' yard, just down the road from our house.

The Wilsons lived next door to, and down the hill from, the Scruggses. The Scruggses' was where neighborhood lads converged daily for the Great Sports Contests of the 1950s. Gravity being what it is, our errant footballs, baseballs, softballs and basketballs always wound up at the Wilsons'.

If the stupid football hadn't rolled into the Wilsons' yard one particular day, none of this would've happened. I bet one of my stupid brothers, Ricky or Ronny, was to blame. They probably missed a pass or dropped a kick. Or maybe it was Jimmy Scruggs or Freddy Kautz. It had to have been one of them, because I never made mistakes.

Anyhow, the football roly-polied down the hill. It slowed in the dip that separated the Scruggses' yard from the Wilsons' yard. Then it came to a stop alongside the rosebush.

After chastising the other guys for their unbelievably sloppy handling, I raced downhill for the retrieve.

That's when it happened. Again, I stress it wasn't my fault.

Ricky or Ronny or Jimmy or Freddy or one of those other stupid boys probably yelled at me to kick the stupid ball back up the stupid hill. Was I to blame because the rose bush was in the way?

The ball barely cleared my shoe before the branches snaked out and caught it. Or tried to catch it, as the case may have been.

I don't know the foot-pounds of energy generated by a freshly kicked football, but it sure as heck is greater than the tensile strength of a rose bush. The stem snapped just above the ground, slick as spit.

My reaction was like that of any responsible 12-year-old. I ran home.

But my conscience began gnawing at my innards. My conscience must have been particularly hungry that day, for it gnawed and gnashed and chomped and chewed till I was a mere shell of my former self.

So I went to Mother and told all.

She listened patiently, although I noticed how she failed to comprehend the stupidity of Ricky, Ronny, Jimmy and Freddy. At times, mothers can be amazingly thickheaded themselves.

"Go back to Mrs. Wilson and tell her what you did," she said. "You know that's what you should have done in the first place."

Quietly, and in excruciating emotional pain, I knocked on the door. If you try to apologize but nobody answers, it still means the slate is wiped clean, right?

The doorknob turned.

Mrs. Wilson, bless her soul, was most understanding. She said not to worry, that the rose bush would probably grow back. Then she added the zinger I didn't want to hear.

"Thank you for being honest enough to tell me about it. Some boys would have just run off."

I'm telling you this story because last Tuesday evening there was a bumpity-crunch next to my own house. Mary Ann went to the front door to investigate. There stood young Justin. He lives up the street.

"I'm sorry, Mrs. Venable," he said. "I ran into your bush."

Mary Ann assured Justin it was OK and thanked him for telling her. Then she walked back into the kitchen and related the incident to me.

"You mean that hateful ol' pyracantha?" I laughed. "I detest that bush. Holler at Justin to come back and try again. I'll even get the hedge clippers so he can do the job right."

Mary Ann was not amused.

But at that very moment, a full 30 years after I'd gone through all that conscience-gnawing and palm-sweating, a sobering thought occurred to me.

Do you suppose Mr. Wilson hated Mrs. Wilson's rose bush the same way I hate our pyracantha?

From the mouths (buurp!) of babes

May 17, 1988

Get out your Di-Gel, folks. Also a few rolls of Tums and a gallon of Pepto-Bismol. Jeannie Doriot's annual recipe book is hot off the press, and already my stomach is tied in knots.

Doriot is a kindergarten teacher at Giffin Elementary School. Every year she helps her 5- and 6-year-old students make a unique

Mother's Day gift. She asks them to describe the best dish their mamas prepare. After recording this information straight out of the mouths of the babes, she compiles it in booklet form.

The results are hilarious — even if they would send Betty Crocker packing for a nunnery. For example, check out this formula for pound cake, courtesy of Matthew Dunlap.

"First, I believe you put the sugar in a pan. One pound of sugar because it's a pound cake. Boil it for an hour. Then you put butter on it — one pound, too. Then you turn it over so it can get brown on the other side. Then you take it out and put some syrup on it. Cut it up and it's ready."

It wasn't until I read the 1988 cookbook that I realized the lost art of alchemy has been rediscovered in kitchens near Giffin. Consider chocolate chip cookies from Matt Gerken and apple sauce from Mindy Floyd.

"Get some raisins — five," instructed Matt. "Then put some powder — cooking powder — in a bowl. And you stir it up. Put it in the oven for 15 minutes. While they cool off, the raisins turn into chocolate chips and you have chocolate chip cookies."

For apple sauce, Mindy said, "You get a quart of apple cider. And then you pour it into something, kind of like a milk carton. And put it in the freezer for about nine hours. Then it freezes for a little while and turns into apple sauce."

Phillip Norris, who must be somewhat of a numbers freak, also came up with a unique recipe for chocolate chip cookies:

"You need seven cartons of milk, three cups of salt, two eggs and some more milk after all that — seven more. Get five chocolate chips. Stir it a long time for a little bit and it'll get real fluffy. Get a pan and get one of those mixer spoons and put the cookies on the pan. Put seven cookies on. Put them in the oven and let them bake for an hour. Take them out when it dings. Let them cool and put them in a bowl for your children to eat."

Need a quick cake? Robbie Cochran can fill the bill: "Get a cracker. Put icing on the cracker."

Grant McMahan is my candidate for the Chamber of Commerce's Visit-All-The-Stores Award, although he may not be able to accept if he eats too many of these hamburgers:

"We have to get some meat at Kroger's — one package. Then get some bread or some buns, probably at White Store. Take the package off the meat and just put it on a bun of a hamburger. Then, put it in the oven. My mom leaves them in about 20 seconds or something — no, not that much. But that's probably plenty. Then you take it out. If you have any ketchup you can put it on there. Or mayonnaise."

Aljerome Grimes, on the other hand, is a devotee of longer cooking, as witness this formula for broccoli: "It comes in this bag. Let it cook for 11 hours. Take it out and put cheese on it and let it melt while it's in the pan. When you're through you eat it."

To top off the meal, I suggest Keyawna Bingham's strawberry cake: "You're supposed to put garlic in it — just one drop. Mix it up and then you're supposed to put something else in it. You should put a little more garlic in it, too. Then you should put it in the oven for about five minutes. Then my mama will check it to make sure it don't get burned."

Yum, yum. Is dinner ready yet?

Chapter Two

THOSE HUMID, HAZY, CRAZY DAYS OF SUMMER

KIDS, DON'T TRY THIS AT HOME!

I'm going to be honest. Summer is not my favorite time of year.

Oh, I love summer holidays, all right. And summer food. And summer vacation.

I do not, however, love summer's heat and humidity. When most people daydream about summer, they conjure up pleasant thoughts of baseball games and cookouts. I worry about survival in a sea of sweat.

You've probably seen that TV commercial where a fully clothed guy falls backward into a swimming pool and the background voice says, "Aaaaaah!" That's the way I feel about summer. We oughta be able to leap into a pool and cool off at the drop of a hat.

I even tried it once. It was hotter than a depot stove and I jumped —shirt, shoes, the works —into this guy's swimming pool. It was unbelievably relaxing. And everyone standing around marveled at what a fun-loving person I was.

When I realized my billfold was still in my pocket, they marveled at how fast a fat boy could swim.

Does summer really exist?

Getting ahead of ourselves

June 21, 1990

About the time you eat lunch today, summer will officially arrive.

If this auspicious moment occurs and you have not selected your fall wardrobe, purchased Christmas presents, addressed and stamped greeting cards, checked the anti-freeze level, split firewood, waxed your skis and settled on New Year's resolutions, you are a shiftless laggard who will surely be late for your own funeral.

Rushing the seasons is a rite cherished by Americans. We nibble Halloween candy on Labor Day, order Valentine's roses the day after Christmas and stock up on Fourth of July fireworks before Memorial Day crowds wipe out the supply.

But when it comes to summer, our leap-frogging addiction hops into overdrive.

The older I get, the more I feel sorry for June, July and August. Nobody pays attention to them anymore. They might as well be ripped off the calendar. At least then, their embarrassment would be over.

I was introduced to this seasonal inequity many years ago. Innocent babe that I was, I attempted to purchase a swimming suit during the month of August.

Never mind that the thermometer was too hot to touch without welder's gloves. Never mind that the first day of school was still locked safely inside The Great Beyond. Never mind that lakes, streams and pools in East Tennessee would be swimmable for the better part of two months. Never mind anything sensible like that.

I searched stores throughout downtown Knoxville — which should tell you how long ago we are talking about — without success. I might as well have been looking for a blacksmith's apron.

"Swimming suits?" clerks would ask in disbelief. "Lord have

mercy! We haven't carried them since February. But now that you're here, how about a pair of wool mittens?"

Innocent babe that I still am, I tried to buy a summer-weight business suit a few weeks ago. Surely, I thought, the selection would still be good in early June.

Hoo-hah.

In all honesty, several stores still had a summer suit or three left on their racks. A fair selection of colors and fabrics, too. And if I was Andre the Giant or a munchkin from Oz, I would have made a purchase. As it was, I had to settle for more mittens.

One clerk — I swear this is true — tried calling his store's catalog department. Sorry, they told him; summer suits are gone for the season.

So it came as no surprise when I got home the other day and found an eight-page flier from L.L. Bean in the mail.

"June Special Values," the cover said.

A closeout on hiking shorts and T-shirts, mayhaps? Surely you jest. This was a pitch for overcoats, sweaters, insulated jackets, corduroy jeans and flannel shirts.

"Quantities Limited — Order Early," it read. "Prices effective through July 27."

I was tempted to call the 800 number and make my selection. But then I thought naaaaah. When it's 90 degrees and the humid haze clings like a wet sheet, the last thing I'm going to do is buy a wool Eskimo parka with fleece lining, handwarmer pockets and a fur collar.

I'll wait till October. The swimwear and sandal selections oughta be great by then.

'Janarchaugember' and 'Februober'

July 7, 1989

Everytime I withdraw the mound of letters, papers, notes, clippings, magazine articles, sandwich wrappers and other printed garbage from my office mailbox, I find the same message.

"Juncolm," it reads in garbled Venobese.

I jotted this missive to myself approximately six weeks ago. It was to remind me to write a cutsey, seasonal, moody, think piece about the month of June.

You know the kind of essay I mean — a treatise about dew-sparkled mornings, warm afternoons, cool evenings. No school. The laughter of children around the swimming pool. The aroma of cookouts, honeysuckle, fresh-cut watermelon. That sort of stuff.

I've been meaning to get around to it. Honest. But June became history — Lord be praised — and we've already sliced a sizeable wedge out of July. And my June column remains unwritten.

Normally, I'd blame it on procrastination. Around June 2nd or 3rd, I would have had great intentions to write nice things about this tender summer season. That would have kept me going until, oh, say, the 10th or 12th. Then by around the 18th or 19th, I would have panicked and knocked out my June column, and that would have been the end of that.

But this year, we never had a June to write nice things about.

I kept waiting for the opportunity. The opportunity rusted.

I held out for just the right moment. The moment mildewed.

I was hoping for inspiration. All I got was perspiration.

I knew real June would arrive someday, allowing me to gush forth with golden prose in tribute to its wonder and glory. Instead, my sinuses clogged up and I growled at little children and puppies.

I'm starting to think we didn't experience June after all. Somehow, someone must have slipped in a new month on us. And if that is the case, it oughta be called "Janarchaugember."

In the short space of 30 days, we endured weather conditions more suited to other times of the year. The 1989 version of June was as dreary and cold as a typical January; stormy and damp as a typical

March; hot and muggy as a typical August; cool and gray as a typical November. And I am deliriously happy to see it in my rearview mirror.

But now that June is out of harm's reach, what has taken its place?

"Februober," that's what.

The calendar might say July, but be not deceived. This month is starting out as boring as February and drizzly as late October. And it shows little sign of improvement.

A couple of my Louisiana friends came to visit over the Fourth of July weekend. We spent the better part of one entire evening fishing for striped bass on Norris Lake. We shivered in long pants and jackets and rain slickers and tried to feel our way from Here to Yon through pea soup fog. The punishment we endure in the name of recreation.

It is bad enough to shiver in long pants, a jacket and a rain slicker in the "summer" month of July. But when you don't catch a fish, don't even get a smell, it is an interstate crisis not readily forgotten. My Cajun friends were quick to remind me we ALWAYS catch fish in Louisiana.

The whole mess is reminiscent of a cold, rainy week in the summer of 1984, when I trolled for salmon off the coast of Alaska. It was the most miserable summer weather I have ever seen. The only time I wasn't clad in longjohns and rain gear was when I was wrapped — teeth clattering — in bed.

Big deal. Alaska can be forgiven for such climatic miscalculations. Tennessee, the garden spot of the South, cannot.

Still, I shall not despair. This atypical weather cannot last forever. Sometime between now and the official start of autumn, I am quite confident we will experience two or three consecutive days — who knows? maybe four — of summer. Real summer.

But you never know. This could be the first year I build a snowman on Labor Day and go skinny-dipping on Christmas Eve.

 School's out!

Guidance, divine or otherwise

May 28, 1989

I'm saying a little prayer that Alan Langenfeld — a young man who landed in a stew of his own making — doesn't get the heat turned up too high.

Alan recently finished high school in Onawa, Iowa. Graduation ceremonies were held last week. As occasionally happens to graduating seniors, Alan fell into trouble with the law the night he received his diploma.

Alan's crime? He defied a federal judge's order by leading the audience in prayer.

Seems that a few days earlier, U.S. District Judge Donald O'Brien had rejected a minister's request to offer a prayer at graduation. The judge cited constitutional restrictions on religious practices at a public facility.

When the preacher was turned down, class member Langenfeld did the honors. He asked the 1,000 in attendance to recite the Lord's Prayer.

Alan's actions have upset Cryss Farley, executive director of the Iowa Civil Liberties Union. "It certainly is a very serious thing," she said, "when a ruling of the federal court is ignored."

Indeed it is serious. In principle, at least. If we are going to have a legal system of any substance in this country, procedure must be followed. And as a disciple of the constitutional separation between church and state, I concur with Judge O'Brien's decision.

At the same time, I daresay there is no group of people in greater need of prayer than high school seniors who have just earned their freedom.

As I see it, Alan's error was in saying the Lord's Prayer, the standard of Christian faiths. There are religious beliefs other than Christianity in this country, and there are people with no profession of religious faith whatsoever. So perhaps Alan would have been better off saying something with more universal application.

Maybe the very act of calling his exercise a "prayer" was offensive. If so, then the moment could have been termed "meditation." Or "thought." The name really doesn't matter.

But what does matter is this: There are times when human beings, those with religious convictions and those without, simply need to stop and reflect on what has taken place in their lives. Graduation is one of those times.

If I had been in Alan Langenfeld's shoes that night, I would have asked the seniors to think about the four-year journey they had completed. It's just short of miraculous, actually. Four years ago, they were children. Today, they are adults.

Then I would've asked them to think about what they will do with the rest of their lives. Seek immediate employment? Continue their education? Travel? Join the military? Get married? Raise a family? And I would've cautioned them if they hadn't given some measure of serious consideration to those options, they're already falling behind in the race.

Next, I would have asked them to think about their friends. And their precious memories. And I would have warned them to savor these last few moments together. Because once they leave the room, the ties that have bound them through the years will slowly, sometimes painfully, begin to erode.

Finally, I would have asked them to think about their parents.

It might not always be obvious, given the oft-tumultuous relationship between parents and offspring, but the men and women who brought these young people into the world are unbelievably proud of them.

Proud of them, yes. And happy for them. And excited for them as they begin carving a niche of their own. But scared as hell for them, too.

And that's why it's OK — court order or no court order — for parents to pray that someone, or something, will always keep watch.

Economics 111

May 3, 1991

In a few short weeks, students at the University of Tennessee will get the most shocking education of their college careers. They will attempt to earn a little summer money by selling their textbooks.

Those of you who attended college know what I'm talking about. For those who did not participate, here's how the process works:

I. Professor Blastfume, who specializes in Civil War history, writes a textbook. It joins 3,697 other college-level textbooks about the Civil War.

II. The college history department selects Professor Blastfume's book as required reading for all students enrolled in Civil War classes.

III. When school begins, students march to the bookstore and plunk down $49.95 apiece for Professor Blastfume's new tome.

IV. At the end of the semester, students return their books to the store because they have been promised HUGE CASH PAYMENTS! for used texts.

V. The HUGE CASH PAYMENT! turns out to be $4.17.

VI. At the beginning of the next semester, once-used copies of Professor Blastfume's book — still required by the history department — sell for $42.95.

VII. The semester ends, but no HUGE CASH PAYMENTS! are made. That is because Professor Blastfume's Civil War textbook is obsolete. Aaaah, but his colleague, Professor Sumpwater, has authored the 3,699th Civil War book.

VIII. Next semester, Professor Sumpwater's book, mandatory for history students, hits the market at $54.95.

This cycle has been a proud college tradition since Og and Ug graduated from Flintstone U. in 534 B.C. It's a proven fact the first cave wall message scientists ever deciphered read, "Those $&%* jerks! I paid 40 clam shells for my books at the start of the semester, and they only gave me three now!"

Of course, many professors advise their students not to sell their textbooks at all.

"You should start your own professional library," they say.

"These books will be very important sources of information in your chosen career. You will discover they are far more valuable than the pittance you get from the bookstore."

Translation: "Once you are well-established in your career, you will look extra cool if the shelves behind your desk are lined with rows of dust-covered books that haven't been cracked since

1978. Besides, Professor Sumpwater and I are collaborating on a new Civil War textbook, which will be required reading for next semester's courses."

Face facts, students. You'll never beat the system. Go ahead and take the store's HUGE CASH PAYMENT! and buy yourself a hot dog and get ready to fork over your summer wages for new books when fall semester begins.

Of course, if the English department makes Sam Venable's books required reading, you ought to buy a new set and think seriously about starting your own professional library.

Madness in the meat department

July 2, 1991

I recently shopped for Fourth of July cookout supplies and made the stupid mistake of not realizing I needed a Ph.D. in food technology.

Things started going wrong as soon as I entered the condiment aisle. I wanted mustard.

You remember mustard, don't you? It is a tart, yellow substance applied to hot dogs. At least it used to be.

These days, you have to search diligently to find plain, basic, slather-it-on-till-it-runs-off-the-dog mustard. First, you gotta dig through the spicy mustard, brown mustard, spicy-brown mustard, hot mustard, sweet mustard, hot and sweet mustard — I was starting to detect a distinct pattern by this time — Dijon mustard, Parisian mustard, honey mustard and honey-and-bourbon mustard.

Honey-and-bourbon mustard? Gag.

I like honey and I like bourbon and I like mustard. But I want them served the way God intended them to be served: individually. Some things are not meant to be combined. Once, in the bar at the Lake Charles airport, I watched a man mix Scotch with sweet milk and was relieved beyond description when I learned we weren't on the same flight. Anybody who'd swallow a purgative like that surely had a bomb in his luggage — if not in his stomach.

Mustard proved to be only the start of my troubles. I went to the bread department and attempted to pick up some plain, white, enriched-flour, hydrogenated-shortening, clog-your-arteries-and-make-you-fat buns.

They don't live here anymore, either, thanks to whole wheat, oat bran, garlic, sourdough and low sodium.

But then I advanced to the meat department and started wondering if July the Fourth was worth the effort after all. I asked the guy

behind the counter where the hot dogs were.

"What kind you want?" he said.

"Whadaya mean, 'what kind?' I'm not buying a car, pal. I want hot dogs. Plain, all-American hot dogs."

He gave me one of those hoo-boy looks.

"I mean what ingredients? Beef?"

"Is there any other kind?"

"Of course. We carry turkey hot dogs, chicken hot dogs and pork hot dogs, too."

"Well, I, er . . . Just give me the beef ones and I'll be on my way."

"Not so fast," he replied. "You want jumbo or regular size? Or were you interested in mini-wienies to serve in a sauce?"

"Look, Waldo. All I want is . . ."

"Cheese-filled or plain?"

"Cheese-filled? You mean they pack hot dogs with cheese these days?"

The man gave me another hoo-boy look.

"Yes," he said. "American or Swiss?"

Sweat began beading on my forehead.

"Hello? Hello? Is anybody in there? Baseball, hot dogs, apple pie, Chevrolet; does any of this register with you?"

The guy didn't blink. "Eight to a pack or 10? Zip-bag or shrink-wrap? Regular or light? For the grill or the microwave?"

"Forget the hot dogs," I said. "Just give me some chicken breasts."

"Will that be skinless, boneless, marinated, barbecue, lemon-pepper or Italian-style?"

I wonder if the Krystal will be open on the Fourth.

Nectar of the Southern gods

May 19, 1991

I hate to have to bring this up, but here is the blun t, awful truth:

People should acquire certain manners naturally, either in the womb or shortly upon arrival to the new world; and, alas, some have not gotten the message.

We have in our midst a breed of social hooligans.

Ruffians.

Rogues.

Unwarshed heathens.

Call this trash what you wish; they all have one thing in common: They don't know nuthin' about iced tea.

The summer season is here, and that means iced tea consumption throughout the South is about to increase.

It also means, unfortunately, the amber slop passed off as iced tea will begin to flow as well.

In order to discuss what true, lay-your-ears-back-and-pour-it-down iced tea is about, let us start by spelling out what it ain't.

It ain't instant, for one thing.

Instant iced tea is a culinary abomination that should be dumped into lead-lined concrete vaults, sealed, then buried like toxic waste. The people who invented instant iced tea are communists or aliens from another planet or both. In any event, they seek to disrupt life as we know it.

Real iced tea is brewed. With boiling water, teapots, and real iced tea bags.

Another thing iced tea ain't is warm.

Read the name of this beverage again. Does the word ICED mean anything? As in cold, perhaps?

Apparently it doesn't at some of the eateries I have visited in this and other towns. Pouring freshly brewed tea into a glass and annointing it with two slivers of shaved ice does not qualify.

Instead, we are looking for magnum ice cubes. Clear ones. The kind you make in metal trays with levers on top. And lots of 'em.

Glass. That's another ain't to consider with real iced tea.

It ain't served in a shot glass or a juice glass or a foam coffee cup. It is served in a wide-mouthed jar, Mason brand if at all possible, or any other glass container capable of holding a minimum of 16 ounces. Twice that volume is preferable.

Something else Southern tea ain't is plain.

Plain coffee is fine. In fact, the Good Lawd hisself drinks his coffee black. But when it comes to iced tea, the Big Guy and all the heavenly hosts want it loaded with sugar and lemon.

Although it is written — Ezekiel, I think; maybe Haggai — that only pure cane sugar be administered to iced tea, it has become an accepted practice to do the deed artificially. We may all answer for this transgression on Judgment Day; but for now, those little blue and pink envelopes have official blessing.

However, accept no substitute when it comes to lemon. I mean it.

This recipe calls for real lemons — those sour, yellow fruits that grow on trees. "Reconstituted" lemon juice (reconstituted from what — dead polecats?) ranks second only to instant tea in Southern social disgraces. We are talking the eye-stinging, pulpy, real McCoy.

And I don't mean one of those paper-thin slices that cheapskate restaurant-cafeteria owners try to camouflage as lemons. Iced tea lemons should come in big chunks. When you squeeze them, juice should flow liberally into the tea, not simply moisten your fingertips.

Let's review: Brewed. Lots of ice. Large glass container. Much sugar. Real lemon in big chunks. Got it?

Then go and sin no more

The best melons are free

August 17, 1990

Every time Bill Vaughan takes a bite of watermelon he reaches the same conclusion.

"They don't taste near as good as they did in the old days."

Vaughan's critique has nothing whatsoever to do with pesticides, fertilizers, soil analysis or supermarket temperatures. It has, on the other hand, everything to do with the fact that his fruits are now acquired in a legal manner.

Bill Vaughan is a good friend of mine. He is a successful businessman. He is also a respected member of the econolegislative community, which is a very polite way of saying he is a Capitol Hill lobbyist.

But Bill is first and foremost a watermelon thief, and even though legal considerations on his transgressions have long since expired, I have persuaded him to bare his soul to society.

Besides, as Bill so astutely points out, "in 1955, watermelon stealin' wasn't stealin'. It was mischief. If the only thing kids did today was steal a few watermelons, there wouldn't be no trouble in this country."

Although he now wears pin-striped suits and ensconces himself in a high-rise building far above the

clouds over Knoxville, Vaughan immigrated from Jellico, quite likely barefoot in bib overalls. I am convinced he sneaked into our town when border guards weren't watching, but the statute of limitations has surely lapsed on that crime, too. We're stuck with him.

It was while he resided in Jellico that Vaughan perfected his larcenous skills. Like this:

"Son, there wasn't no interstate in those days. The main road in and out of Jellico was Highway 25W. And it wasn't crowded.

"Every summer when the watermelon trucks would come through from Florida, we had easy pickin's. They had to climb Peabody Mountain, which is between LaFollette and Jellico.

"It's steep out there. Real steep. The ol' boys drivin' those trucks would have to gear 'em down and barely creep up the mountain. We'd wait till dark and catch one comin' through and get all the watermelons we could eat or give away.

"All you had'ta do was pull a car up behind the truck. Get up real close where the driver couldn't see you in his side-view mirrors. Then somebody would jump out one side and climb on the truck and start pitching watermelons. Somebody else would jump out the other side and run beside the truck. The guy who was driving the car would go on and pass. He'd come back later and help us load everything up."

I interrupted long enough to ask Vaughan the names of his accomplices. He couldn't remember. Which makes me assume: (1) there is no statute of limitations for watermelon-stealing in Campbell County, (2) there is loyalty among watermelon thieves or (3) produce trucks from Florida still creep up Peabody Mountain. In any event:

"One night I climbed on the truck and was slingin' those melons fast and furious. I got so bogged down in my work, I forgot we'd made it to the top of the mountain. We started down the other side, and that ol' boy behind the wheel really put it in the wind. I mean he was haulin'.

"I figured if I didn't want to end up in Ohio or somewhere else, I'd better be gettin' off. So when he slowed down at a curve in Jellico, I jumped. Landed in Dr. Ausmus' yard. I got a little bruised and shaken, but it wasn't nuthin' bad."

Was the truck driver ever aware of what was taking place?

"I really don't know," laughed Vaughan, a human beanpole whose legs begin roughly two inches below his Adam's apple. "I put it in gear myself. There wasn't no way he was gonna catch me on foot."

Backyard Barbecue Lies

June 2, 1989

I can't believe it. Here we are, nearly three weeks ahead of the official start of summer — the first beads of sweat have hardly trickled, for Pete's sake — and already the lies have begun.

Backyard Barbecue Lies.

I was watching television the other night and witnessed this seasonal untruth. The next evening, on another channel, it happened again. Last night, on yet a different station, I saw it for the third time. There is no denying this monster's existence any longer.

You have probably seen one of these evil Backyard Barbecue Lies, too.

You're sitting in front of the tube, absorbed in a ball game or a documentary, and a barbecue commercial comes on. Experience warns you to ignore it. Your brain is screaming, "Change channels! It's a lie! Don't watch!"

Fool that you are, you watch anyway.

It doesn't matter what the product is. Could be charcoal. Or charcoal lighter fluid. Or charcoal that doesn't require lighter fluid. Or barbecue sauce. Or chicken, beef, pork, watermelons, aluminum foil, plastic bags, paper plates. Or any of the 234,782,593 other products traditionally associated with outdoor cooking.

The first part of a Backyard Barbecue Lie goes something like this: You meet Joe, the quintessential Guy-Next-Door. He is wearing a chef's hat and apron. He points to a perfect bed of white-hot charcoal. He is smiling.

Here is the truth: Unless they are auditioning for a barbecue commercial, real people do not wear those stupid chef's outfits. They wear worn-out blue jeans or a pair of coach's shorts, plus a sprung-neck T-shirt that says "Running Dog Tavern, Chockalooka, Mississippi" in faded print.

Real people have never seen a perfect bed of white-hot charcoal. They do all their cooking on a jagged mound of briquettes — some already reduced to ashes, others unsinged — that reek of Coleman fuel.

Yes, real people appear to be smiling. But be not fooled by appearances. This is an involuntary contortion from fumes billowing out of the pit. Hardened criminals, freshly extracted from the gas chamber, often display the same expression.

How To Cook AN ALL-AMERICAN HOT DOG!

1 PLACE ON GRILL.

2 BURN IT.

3 FEED TO DOG.

4 GET ANOTHER HOT DOG.

GEHRING

In the second part of a Backyard Barbecue Lie, the camera switches to Joe's neighbors — all 65 of them — who have gleefully gathered to partake in the banquet. In a feat unparalleled since the days of five loaves and two fishes, Joe is about to produce unlimited quantities of T-bones, chicken breasts and shrimp from a 14-inch grill.

Deftly, he positions the choice cuts upon the grate.

Gently, he slathers each piece with a thick, tantilizing sauce.

Graciously, he serves up this ambrosia amid rounds of applause from admiring friends.

Now for the truth: Real people cook hot dogs and hamburgers. Attempt to cook them, I should say.

Their hot dogs roll off the grate and plop onto the driveway. Those not chewed beyond recognition by the dog are repositioned above the flames, assuming no one is watching.

Real people's hamburgers stick to the grill, refusing to budge for spatula and fork alike. Then at the last second, they crumble like a dry biscuit and rain upon the ashes.

Real people's neighbors accept a backyard barbecue invitation for the free beer, not for the meal. They pig-out on potato chips, pretzels and cheese puffs, hoping to deaden their tastebuds against the inevitable assault of meat to come. Smart ones have even pre-programmed their beepers to signal an emergency summons to the office shortly before the main course is served.

Keep this in mind the next time you see a Backyard Barbecue Lie on TV. Or when the guy next door calls up and say, "Why don't you and the missus come over Saturday night? I'm throwing a big cookout, and I'd hate for you folks to miss out on my skills."

Being a father

June 16, 1985

It's strange, this business of fatherhood.

Twenty years ago, I could have told you everything you needed to know about it. Surely more than you wanted to know.

But armchair quarterbacking is easier than calling plays in the huddle. When you find yourself standing in a father's shoes, that vast storehouse of knowledge suddenly evaporates.

I should be well-versed on the subject. For 37 1/2 years, I've either had a father or been one. The only gap occurred between June 17, 1972, when my dad died, and Jan. 3, 1973, when my first child was born.

Despite this experience on both sides of the fence, the answers do not come readily. And the more I search for them, the less I am certain of what I've learned along the way.

I came into this world in 1947, just as the baby boom's first tremors were being felt. From a materialistic standpoint, my genera-tion — all 76 million of us — arrived at the greatest time in American history.

The Great Depression was little more than a distant, unpleasant memory. World War II was over, and the men who won it were back home with their young families. Technology was becoming an indus-try unto itself. High-paying jobs were opening. The future dripped of golden promise.

All across the United States, fathers were putting their children on their knees and telling them how good things were going to be.

"I want you to have it better than I did," they would say. Just like Big Sam was saying to me.

Those weren't idle words. They were spoken by men who had suffered hard times and endured danger and weren't about to permit the same tragedies to be visited upon the fruit of their loins.

They made good on their pledges, too.

They treated my generation to a better education than any before it. We comprise 57 percent of all living college graduates.

They gave us a standard of living unmatched anywhere in the world. Two incomes flow into 54 percent of our families.

But the one thing they did not give us was the mastery of this stage in life known as fatherhood. They could not give it to us because they did not have it themselves. Instead, they were having to learn it one step at a time, just as their fathers did. And their father's fathers.

They struggled. They made mistakes. They enjoyed heart-warming successes and heart-shattering failures. Just as we do today.

Which is not to imply that fatherhood is an onerous task. Quite the opposite. I say without hint of reservation that being a father has been, and continues to be, the highest point of my life. But for all of its joys, fatherhood brings with it so many concerns.

I worry about what the future holds for my kids. I worry just how long this opulence we are immersed in, this monetary squalor spawned by a generation intent on making things better than they had it, will continue to spiral dangerously upward.

I worry about drugs. About war. About whether my children will be happy in the careers and lifestyles they choose or fate chooses for them.

I worry about spending enough time with them. About making the right decisions. About whether I'm being a positive influence on their lives.

At least it is comforting to know I am not alone.

A few days ago, I renewed acquaintances with Tim Elledge, the newest member of our editorial staff. In the late '60s, Tim and I worked together at a newspaper in Chattanooga. I had not seen or heard from him since the day I left Hamilton County.

Tim rode into Chattanooga on the first anti-establishment wave. He was our token radical at the arch-conservative News-Free Press. One assistant city editor always accused him of being (gasp!) a hippie.

Tim wasn't fond of neckties. His hair was long by the white-sidewall standards of the day. He hung out around the college campus, prompting the editor to wonder aloud whether Tim covered demonstrations or started them.

In the ensuing years, Tim has led everything but a 9-to-5 life. He has worked for newspapers in Texas and Maine. He started a whitewater rafting service and led trips into Canada. He moved the company to Alaska and ran wild rivers there "until I got tired of living in a tent." He got back into writing via United Press International's bureau in San Francisco.

Then Tim and his wife had a child. And the next thing you know, he's back in sleepy East Tennessee.

"San Francisco is a great place to live if you're single or don't have children," he was telling me. "But I didn't want my little girl growing up with green hair and a safety pin in her nose."

Fathers everywhere should understand.

Father's Famous Foolish Fables

June 18, 1989

Fathers are full of advice. If you don't believe me, just ask.

They can dish out sage guidance on any topic. Money, education, careers, love, marriage, trendy fashions, business, religion — you name it. A father perched high upon his soapbox can orate, opine and pontificate until the very soles curl up beneath his wingtips.

Fortunately, no one pays attention, so there's little damage done.

Dear ol' Dad means well. He truly does. It's just that the brand of wisdom he dispenses has usually aged far beyond its time. He heard it sometime back, but he can't tell you where — or even what it means.

To him, it sounds good. It sounds intelligent. It sounds — well, it sounds fatherly.

To everyone else, especially his children, it sounds like something out of a script from "Leave It To Beaver." And if you take it too seriously, you'll grow up to be a creep like Eddie Haskell.

But be of good cheer, kiddies everywhere. As you shower Pappy this morning with gaudy neckties and pig-breath cologne, count your blessings. Dad will be so choked with emotion (not to mention his allergies), he probably won't issue any advice for a full day.

After that, brace yourself. You never know when to expect another dose of Father's Famous Foolish Fables. Such as:

Satisfaction in a job well done is the best reward.

Baloney. Satisfaction is 20 bucks. If the job's not done right, tell your old man to fix it the way he wants it.

Sticks and stones will break your bones, but words will never harm you.

Oh yeah? If words don't do any harm, how come Junior always gets his mouth washed out when he says them?

When the going gets tough, the tough get going.

Of course they do. They go right out the back door and leave their mess for somebody else.

Early to bed, early to rise, makes a man healthy, wealthy and wise.

It does nothing of the kind. He misses "The Tonight Show" and "Late Night with David Letterman" and then wakes up to the stupid bickering between Bryant Gumble and Willard Scott. That makes him grumpy all day.

Happiness is where you find it, but rarely where you seek it.

All depends on where you've been looking.

Neither a lender nor a borrower be.

Why not? It was great while it lasted for Jake and C.H. Butcher and all their friends.

Honesty is the best policy.

Possibly, but only after your lawyer has arranged a cushy plea-bargain agreement.

Build a better mousetrap, and the world will beat a path to your door.

Pa-leeeze! Stick with a marketing scheme like that, and it's

Bankruptcy City by noon tomorrow. If you expect recognition these days, get ready to shell out six figures for an ad agency contract.

A fool and his money are soon parted.

See, it's like this: You've got this nifty new mousetrap, and I've got media contacts from here to L.A. For a measley 100 G's, I'll be happy to put you in touch with the right people.

Beauty is only skin-deep.

Beauty-schmeuty. If her old man is loaded, she can look like a yak.

The only difference between a champ and a chump is "u."

It's the only difference between yak and yuk, too. But if "u" are whoopin' it up in Europe on Daddy-In-Law's money, who cares?

If you can't say something nice, don't say anything at all.

Or else become a newspaper columnist.

A lesson from Big Sam

June 19, 1988

If my dad were still alive, I would not buy him a necktie today.

Even if I did, I doubt he would wear it, for Big Sam and I did not share tastes in clothing. Certainly not in neckties. He was particularly fond of the clip-on variety.

No, if he was still around, what I would do is switch roles and give myself a Father's Day present at his expense. I would sign myself up for one of his classes.

My old man would not want me to do it, and he would protest mightily. Of this I am certain. That is why Sam Venable Jr. never took a course under Sam Venable Sr. at the University of Tennessee.

My father insisted that a college professor should not have one of his own children in class. It was a matter of principle to him, and with Big Sam principle meant everything. If there was a potential for conflict of interest, he wanted no part of it.

The fact that he adhered so rigidly to his values is one of the many reasons I remember my pappy so fondly on Father's Day.

Perhaps it was his upbringing that made him the way he was. Perhaps it was his years as an Army officer. Perhaps it was watching in disgust as less-principled people swayed like sea grass in the winds of public opinion. Whatever the reason, Big Sam knew there was right and there was wrong and ne'er the twain should meet. You never had to wonder where he stood on an issue. Any issue.

Twenty-five years ago, it was not important to me to sit in my dad's class. In fact, I was rather happy he felt the way he did about the matter. But now I judge things in a different light.

First of all, I'd simply like to see how he went about earning his living.

From the time I was old enough to comprehend such matters, I knew my father taught health, physical education and recreation at UT. I often accompanied him to The Hill and shot basketballs in Alumni Gym or hit golf balls or swam with my brothers in the downstairs pool while he went about his tasks.

I watched him grade tests at home and even went over a few of them with him. I became friends with many of his fellow professors and the graduate students who worked under his guidance.

But not once did I ever see him in action.

Children need to watch their dads on the job, and it is unfortunate when a father's work occurs in an environment inaccessible to them. The son of a surgeon cannot sit at his father's side and watch him perform his skills like, say, the son of an auto mechanic. That is a loss for all concerned.

The second reason I wish I could be there is because, quite frankly, I'd like to shoplift some of Big Sam's material.

My father was a very funny man with a marvelous gift for telling stories. Whatever sense of humor I may possess, I inherited from him.

He could find humor anywhere. Everywhere. And as much as he

loved to laugh at others, he loved to laugh at himself even more.

This trait was not spared on me or my brothers and sister. Big Sam could rule with an iron fist, but sometimes when we would pull a particularly offensive sin, he was reduced to, as he put it, "laughing to keep from crying."

I have talked to any number of former UT students who took classes under my father. Almost to the person, the first thing they tell me is how he started every class with a joke or anecdote. Only after everyone was in fine spirits, they say, would he turn to the text and begin his lecture. Not a bad way to start the day.

So if I could pick my gift on this Father's Day, I'd want nothing more than to sit in the classroom at the end of the hall in Alumni Gym, with my notebook in hand, and watch my old man do his thing.

And when the bell rang at the end of the hour and all the other students filed out, I think I would stick around long enough to tell Professor Venable how much I enjoyed hearing what he had to say.

And how proud I was of him.

And how much I loved him.

Damn. Why do we never think about the really important things in life until it's too late?

Giving them their wings

June 16, 1991

It wasn't that the father didn't understand the son's need to go. Quite the contrary. He understood completely. Twenty-five years earlier, almost to the day, the father had boarded an airplane of his own and headed west to work in the mountains.

He was going to real mountains. Mountains of spruce and fir. Wilderness mountains with churning rivers and deep gorges and broad, endless vistas. Not the rolling oak-hickory forests of Southern Appalachia where he had grown up.

Thus, the father was not surprised when the son announced his intentions to go west as soon as high school ended. The son wrote the necessary letters and filled out the forms, and before the father could say, "Be sure to change your underwear," the son was bound for

Yellowstone National Park until college kicked off in the fall.

Yes, the father understood all of this. He was happy for his son and proud of him.

But the father had never dealt with an empty nest before. And as he and the son walked toward the waiting plane, his happiness and pride were tempered with the truth that a major chapter in both their lives was coming to an end.

The boy handed his ticket to the agent and the father studied him closely, longing to preserve a mental image of their last moments together. He could not imagine where 18 1/2 years had gone.

Wasn't it only last week that he had driven — driven, nothing; "raced" is more like it — along a rainslick interstate toward the emergency room as the baby beside him wheezed through the first of what would become a series of asthma attacks?

Surely it was only last Christmas, wasn't it — not Christmas of 1974 — that the son had spent his holidays in a hospital room, tethered to tubes?

The father blinked his eyes and snapped back to reality.

This was no youngster he was watching. He was just as tall as his old man, but lean as a beanpole, taut as a bowstring. The duffle bag he checked was crammed with jeans and thick shirts and high-topped leather boots.

Then suddenly, the father did not see an adult anymore. He was looking at a toddler in baggy PJs and Bert and Ernie slippers.

The son broke the awkward silence the same way his father would do. With humor. Of the many bonds between them, perhaps none was stronger than their love of a good laugh.

"Don't walk away from your stuff in the airport, not even for a minute," the son mocked Fatherly Admonition 122-C. His mother's brown eyes danced with glee.

"Tip the people who carry your bags. . . . Watch out for those crazy druggies. . . . Don't hike alone in the back country."

The smiling son was on a roll now. He spat out Fatherly Admonitions like a mouthful of watermelon seeds:

"You know, buddy, those grizzly bears out west are a lot meaner than the black bears around here. . . . Be sure to take your pills and inhalers. . . . If you have an asthma attack, get hold of a ranger."

On and on the son mimicked as they walked. And then they stood at the gate.

The father hugged his son. "I love you, boy," he said. "You go out there and give 'em hell."

The son nodded and swung his backpack across one shoulder. He walked on and never looked back.

The father turned away and headed down the hall.

"Hey, Dad!"

The old man spun around. There stood the son, grinning, giving his trademark under-the-chin goodbye wave. It was one of those silly family traditions, something the boy's father and his uncles had started when they were kids and passed along to the next generation.

The father laughed and waved back. He walked to the window and watched the jet roll out.

He swallowed hard as the burning lump in his throat grew from a BB to a baseball. His eyes welled up as the 727 gained speed down the runway, hurtled into the brilliant eastern sky, banked north and turned due west. His gaze never faltered as the silver streak shrank into a dot.

He blinked once more and it disappeared.

The father swallowed again, but the lump refused to go away. Nor would it be gone two hours later when he sat down at his desk and began to type.

If anything, it had grown.

In the good ol' summertime

The extinction of sunburn

June 7, 1991

I know this makes me sound like a geezer who can't string 25 words together without including "times were a lot tougher when I was a kid," but you'll just have to forgive me.

Folks *do* have it better today. They don't sunburn anymore. At least they don't if they remember to put on sunscreen.

As far as I'm concerned, sunscreen is one of the miracles of modern living. When we send an airplane into outer space and bring it home with pinpoint accuracy, I am not impressed. When we design computers that do the work of 250 people in 1/250th the time, I yawn. But when we develop a potion that keeps people's hides from turning into epidermal lava, I want to flip backwards and shout hosannas.

With each passing summer, I am more impressed with sunscreen products. You can take your basic snow-white East Tennessee cave dweller and rub on some sunscreen, and then stake him down in the broiling rays and he will not so much as turn pink.

Times were not always this good. Back when I was a boy, people warmed up to the summer sun the old-fashioned way. They cooked.

It was a metamorphic process not unlike the life cycle of an insect. People would venture into the season's first brilliant beams, turn redder than a rooster's comb, suffer two or three days, then peel their outer shell and start over. This process would continue three, four, five, maybe six, times until a thick level of bronze carcinogens had built up on the head, neck, shoulders, arms and legs.

At that point, these people would be declared "healthy" and . . . what's that? Did I hear someone just say, "Why didn't Venob use suntan lotion back in the old days?"

Oooooh-ha-ha-ha-hee-hee-hoo-hoo! What a laugher!

Suntan lotion did as good a job of blocking the sun's rays as cellophane tape. It was little more than mayonnaise laced with dye and fragrance. Advertising claims notwithstanding, it had only one real function in the cooking process: basting.

When lily-skinned mountain people ventured to riverside or lakeside (after TVA), they lathered on thick layers of suntan lotion and settled back to listen to their skin sizzle. This pleasant sound continued throughout the day, only to be replaced that evening with a gentle, "Eeeeee-iiiiiiii!" as they tried to roll over in bed.

But the advent of real, honest-to-gosh sunscreen changed all that.

I have tried different brands and different strengths. They all work. You put it on and you don't burn. It's that simple. If the Defense

Department could develop an anti-nuclear-chemical-poison lotion along the same lines, we could stick out our tongues at our enemies and save jillions of dollars on rifles and tanks.

Sure, I'm just as sentimental as the next guy. Sometimes I do get nostalgic for the good old days, when third-degree sunburn was as much a part of summer fun as broken arms and food poisoning.

When those moods strike, all I gotta do to is toss a few handfuls of carpet tacks and broken glass into bed. Then I can hop into the sheets and spend the next eight hours in a miserable, toss-and-turn snooze down memory lane.

No, this isn't the exact sensation as sleeping on beet-red sunburn. Not quite as painful.

But what the heck. Progress does have its price.

Etiquette afloat

June 7, 1990

The first thing newcomers to East Tennessee notice, besides pickup trucks with gun racks, is the vast supply of water in this part of the state.

"Holy Toledo!" they exclaim. "I thought I was moving to the mountains. This place is covered with LAKES!"

(Technically, these immigrants don't exclaim, "Toledo!" They use a more colorful, one-syllable word — one that rolls off the tongue easier than the cumbersome name of some city in northern Ohio. In newspaper jargon, this word is pronounced "&%$*!" But I digress.)

These people are correct, however, in their assessment of our water resources: We've got lakes on top of lakes.

If you leave downtown Knoxville and drive in any direction, you will soon be up to your axles in water. Assuming, tee-hee, you were stupid enough to keep driving after waves began lapping upon your tires.

These are not natural lakes. God had every good intention of creating real, live, honest-to-gosh lakes around here when he was building the world, but he ran out of money somewhere south of Minneapolis and had to settle for rivers and streams in East Tennessee. As fate would have it, TVA found the money (pre-Starvin' Marvin era), ran off the farmers, dammed the rivers and —*voila!*—We Be Wet.

This condition spawned a ripe market for boats.

For the last 50-ish years, natives and newcomers alike have purchased enough cruisers, johnboats, sailboats, bassboats, house-boats, runabouts, dinghies, tubs, prams, junks and scows to challenge the Sixth Fleet. If you took all the vessels in East Tennessee and arranged them, bow to stern, the line would stretch from here to Memphis. If you don't believe me, stroll from deck to deck across Fort Loudoun Lake some Saturday during football season and see for yourself.

I bring up the subject of boats because Memorial Day is history, and The Official Boating Season has begun. Which means — YEEE-IIII! WATCH OUT, YOU DUMB-&%$*! — the chance of finding 12 square feet of unoccupied water is an outright impossibility except between the hours from 2 to 4 a.m. on stormy nights when there isn't a bass tournament.

Given these conditions and the inevitable influx of new skippers, I am happy to provide three pointers gleaned from my many years as an outdoors editor. Read and heed, my friend, and you will have lots of neat experiences to swap when The Official Boating Season ends on Labor Day. Assuming you are out of the hospital by then.

First, remember most launch ramps are constructed extra-wide. This is so you will have plenty of room to back your trailer safely into the water. Resist the urge to move to one side so someone else can launch at the same time. Boaters enjoy 45 minutes of socializing at the top of a double ramp while others launch one-by-one. This is known as nautical foreplay.

Second, boaters and fishermen are among the friendliest folks on earth. When you go roaring by a pair of anglers anchored in a quiet bay, be sure to wave and shout, "Yoo-hoo! Catching anything?" If they have any manners whatsoever, they will return a one-fingered salute signifying they got the message and are wishing you a nice day.

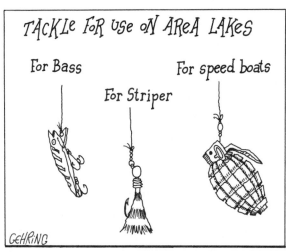

Third, lakes can be noisy places. What with the splashing of waves, the honking of geese, the quacking of ducks and the chirping of crickets, you can well imagine the potential damage to your ears. Do yourself and others within a 10-mile radius a favor by turning the volume knob of your boom box to Quadra-Max. Especially when a lively rap tune is being played.

By the way, are you starting to understand why we have gun racks in the back of our pickups?

Hurricane Sam

June 2, 1991

I'm putting everyone on fair warning: Treat me nice this summer or I'll sic my hurricane on you.

The World Meteorological Organization has just announced its official name list for the 1991 hurricane season, and "Sam" is included.

Don't expect me to strike anytime soon, though. I've gotta wait till Ana, Bob, Claudette, Danny, Erika, Fabian, Grace, Henri, Isabel,

Juan, Kate, Larry, Mindy, Nicholas, Odette, Peter and Rose are used up. So unless it rains 40 days and 40 nights, I'll never get the chance to strut my stuff.

Still, if you're going to have a hurricane named for you, it oughta be a good one. That's why I'm hoping Hurricane Sam will be a rip-snorting, shin-kicking, hog-squalling monster who keeps folks talking for years to come.

Not that I'd wish bad luck on my fellow human beings, for Pete's sake. If I have any control over my namesake hurricane, he'll stay offshore. None of this billion-dollar disaster business like Hugo delivered.

But that doesn't mean Hurricane Sam can't go on a wild streak out in the ocean. I can just hear the nation's meteorologists describe him as they pace in front of their maps:

"It'll be clear and sunny over the entire country for the next few days. But look here (pointing to black cloud symbol, lightning symbol, wind symbol, rain symbol, etc.) out in the Atlantic. Wow! That's Hurricane Sam, and boy, is he kicking up a fuss! The National Weather Service says he's the meanest hurricane since records have been kept. Fortunately, it looks like Sam's going to stay in the ocean, well out of harm's way. The mullet and marlin might not be very happy about the situation, but things look A-OK for us here on the mainland. And now for some temperatures in a city near you . . ."

Scientists give names to hurricanes to avoid confusion if several storms pop up at the same time. That could create a problem this year, however. If reporters on the 6 o'clock news announce, "Danny is angry and throwing a tantrum," we won't know whether they're talking about a hurricane or the vice president.

So for the sake of clarity, I recommend they skip Danny and jump down the list — even though people will surely keel over laughing at the thought of a big, bad storm named Fabian.

Speaking of names, how come they only apply to tropical storms and hurricanes? Why don't shingle-shaking thunderstorms, heat waves and blizzards here in the interior of the country get the same treatment?

It'd be a natural. You sit down with three good ol' boys on the front porch of a country store and within five minutes they'll be talking about the weather.

"It's hotter'n a depot stove," the first will offer.

"Shore is," says another. "Reminds me of the big heat wave in '81."

"Weren't '81," replies the third. "Hit was '77. Ah remember 'cause that was the year I ruint the gears on ma'tractor."

They'll start fussing and feuding, and the first thing you know somebody will have a bump on his head or several fragments of lead in his butt. But if these meteorological happenings were given names — especially localized names — conflict could be averted.

When a man says, "Hit ain't been this hot since Heatwave Cletus blowed through town," you can take it to the bank, partner.

Tacky tourists are my kind of people

July 5, 1988

GATLINBURG — You don't need $150 in your billfold to take in the finest sights this tourist city has to offer. All you have to do is spend 10 or 15 minutes on a sidewalk bench on a Friday night and let the sights stroll by.

Not just any bench will do, of course. For optimum cellulite gazing, it is best to position yourself at midtown, equi-distant between Duff's and Baskin-Robbins. That way, you can catch 'em going and coming.

There is another advantage to this location. It puts you within shouting distance of the Rebel Corner, Tennessee's headquarters for teddy bears, tom-toms, tomahawks, T-shirts and other Tacky Tourist Trinkets. We are talking prime ringside, folks.

Want to see the sights for yourself? Then put on your best polyester shorts, a faded tank top with the ketchup stains, sandals and over-the-calf socks.

Black. The socks have to be black. Unless you have green. Or red.

You'll need a snow cone in one hand and a notepad in the other. A handful of taffy and a funnel cake wouldn't hurt, either.

Ready? Then let's write down what we see and add a few thoughts of our own:

• Man wearing a plastic elephant nose and a hat that says, "Let It All Hang Out."

Looks like the type who would be comfortable at an office party, the Shrine convention, or Mardi Gras.

• Man and woman wearing his and her Camaro shirts.

How tender. The family that races together stays together. Mayhaps they have matching gas cans back home.

• Old man, bent of back and broad of belly, with T-shirt proclaiming, "Surf City."

Hope springs eternal, I guess. But who knows? There may be a Little Old Lady From Pasadena just around the corner.

• Two boys, probably high school vintage, in faded, tighter-than-skin blue jeans and alligator cowboy boots. No shirts. Heavy on bracelets and tattoos. Lots of blond punk hair.

If something like this ever shows up for a date with my daughter, I will send her to a nunnery. After I beat them with a hoe handle.

• Bronze, wavy-haired Muscle Daddy dripping with gold necklaces.

I wonder if they turn his neck and chest green when he sweats?

• Teenagers walking 10 steps to the rear of their parents.

I understand, kiddos. We were all there once. My own kids stay to the rear, too. Sometimes they go plumb across the street.

• Newlyweds.

At least I think they are newlyweds. They (1) have no children, 10 steps away or otherwise, (2) are holding hands, (3) carry bags from various shoppes (translation: lots of waiting and looking) and (4) are still speaking to each other.

• Preteen girl tottering on high-heeled shoes.

Mama probably told her to pack those nerdy old tennis shoes, but you know how dumb mamas can be. Oh, well; blisters acquired in the line of parental defiance don't hurt. In fact, they are badges of courage.

• Woman who could use a few meals of Lean Cuisine tugging at husband and shouting, "Oh, look! There's a fudge kitchen!"

What the heck, honey. Go for it. It's vacation. Eat, drink and be merry, for tomorrow you diet.

• Pot-bellied, middle-aged, gray-haired writer, replete in T-shirt, tennies, shorts and camo cap, sitting on sidewalk bench, watching the tourists and jotting down occasional notes.

Not that I would know anything about this, but I bet he's looking for an easy column.

The legend of Ol' No. 95

August 24, 1989

This has not been a good summer for bears. From the bears' point of view, I mean.

Hardly a day goes by without stories in the newspaper about how yet another bear has wandered out of the mountains and gotten its hide tattooed with bullets. I don't know whether this is an indication of an abundance of bears or a shortage of bear food. Maybe it's a combination. In any event, Smokey and his friends have really been taking it on the chin since the spring thaw.

The stupid things would be a lot better off if they stayed in the safety of the Great Smoky Mountains National Park or the Cherokee National Forest. But no. Bears, like humans, get tired of the same old diet. A few roots and berries can go a long way.

It happens so innocently. Just a little recreational garbage at first, maybe a leftover pizza or two. Next thing you know, they're hooked on Kentucky Fried Chicken and will do anything for a fix.

The latest event occurred last week near Pittman Center. A man claimed he was charged by a bear that had been hanging around a restaurant's garbage truck. He shot the bear, cut off its feet and gave away the carcass, all of which is a violation of state law.

But occasionally the bear wins, and Ol' No. 95 is a case in point.

John Stiles, who heads up The News-Sentinel's Blount County bureau, has written several stories about this critter. It has been tearing up campgrounds and picnic tables all around Elkmont.

Park officials did what they always do in situations like this: They shot the beast with a drugged dart, put a numbered tag in his ear and toted him deep into the woods.

But Ol' No. 95 didn't stay put. He invaded a home in Madisonville. The man and woman who lived there held him at bay — with a mop, of all things — until the bear police showed up with another knockout dart and hauled him to the forest once again.

Maybe it'll work this time. I hope so. If Ol' No. 95 comes to town again, he might get shot with the real thing. So before his taste for apple pie puts him in front of someone's rifle sights, I'd like to dedicate a song in his honor. To the tune of ''Thunder Road'' —

Let me tell the story. I can tell it all.
About the Smoky bear that ate folks' food and had a ball.
The campers set their tables. The bear'd let out a whine.
And then they'd run and scream while Number 95 would dine.
(Chorus): And there was corned beef! Rye bread! Junk food
everywhere!
It took two weeks of groceries just to satisfy this bear.
And there were Moon Pies! French fries! His belly nearly burst!
The hunters swore they'd get him, but the lawmen got him first.

In the midst of August, nineteen-eighty-nine,
The rangers ruled that 95 no longer was to dine.
They drugged him high as Woodstock, packed him to the sticks,
And told themselves they'd heard no more about his dev'lish
tricks.
(Chorus).
Still, the bear out-slicked 'em; took him just a week.
He crossed the ridge and came to town 'cause folks' food he did
seek.

Once more they drugged and moved him; hoped he wouldn't run.

'Cause if he did they knew the good ol' boys would have some fun.

(Chorus).
So if some day you're munching, on a leg of lamb.

Or carving up a steak, pork chop, meat loaf or loin of ham;
And 95 comes calling, scratching at your door,
Just grab a mop and fend him off — no need for .44!
(Final chorus).

The Fourth of July

Fun and frolic on the Fourth

July 4, 1986

Brace yourself. The Fourth of July is upon us once again, and that means we have to be "festive."

No matter who you are, no matter where you live, somebody will be telling you how to have fun today. The planning process has gone on for weeks. Nay, months.

Virtually every civic and business organization has laid out a schedule of activities to make your Fourth of July complete. All you have to do is find the 7,683 hours required to cram the schedule into one day.

Here in Knoxville alone, you can run in a 5,000-meter race or listen to music at the World's Fair Park or take in a crafts show or watch skydivers or view a fireworks display. And that doesn't even scratch the surface.

You say you want a less vigorous agenda? No sweat. Just sit in front of your television, 7 a.m. until noon, and mainline the telecasts from the Statue of Liberty.

Or if you really want to get away from it all (chuckle, chuckle), you can visit an area lake and ski, fish, swim, boat and picnic along with 150,000 of your closest and dearest friends.

This is well and good for people who make traditional holiday plans and enjoy traditional Fourth of July celebrations. But what about the thousands of Americans who have no traditions? What happens to these people when a holiday rolls around? Doesn't anyone ever think of them?

Not until now.

That's why I am proud to offer Venob's Offbeat Ways to Frolic on the Fourth, Preferably With a Fifth (patent pending):

• Call the TV stations and demand to know why the Detroit Lions-Green Bay Packers playoff game is not being televised.

• Buy 2,000 watermelons and coat them with brown paint. Then invite your neighbors over to help you eat the big pot of baked beans that just arrived from Chernobyl.

• Spray ground beef with Right Guard and then ask your picnic guests if they'd like to see the new way you've discovered to press hamburgers.

• Run along the shore at a popular swimming area, waving your arms and screaming at the top of your lungs, ''The piranhas are loose! The piranhas are loose!''

• Observe meatless Friday by substituting large dill pickles for hot dogs.

There. That oughta keep you busy for a few hours.

And now that my chores are finished for the day, I shall repair to the den for the Statue of Liberty specials on TV. Then it's on to the big family gathering for pig-out time.

God bless America, and pass the Pepto-Bismol.

Reflection amid the revelry

July 4, 1991

All across this country today, Americans will be celebrating. It's going to be a wild, exuberant, flag-waving, song-singing, cheerleading sensation, one we've grown quite familiar with the last 11 months.

Perhaps too familiar. To the best of my calculations, the celebrations have lasted longer than the Gulf War itself.

Not that we weren't overdue a dose of old-fashioned strutting. From the mid-'60s and on through the '70s, even into the early '80s, outward demonstrations like this were not high fashion. Every time I see a pricey Old Glory necktie or a red-white-and-blue sweater today, I have to chuckle. There was a time you couldn't have given them away.

But situations and circumstances change. It's been more than half a century since Americans united, philosophically and politically, to stop barbaric military aggression halfway around the world. Verily, we have earned the right to wave our banners and sing our songs.

Knoxville is getting in on its share of the action, as well. I doubt there is anyone living within the reach of newspapers, radio or television in this area who does not know there is a big parade today. It is called Hail the Heroes, and it'll be a grand sashay through downtown.

In one sense, I'm really looking forward to it. When the starting whistle blows, I'll join other employees from The News-Sentinel, as well as those from WBIR-TV and radio station WEZK, to help carry a 15-by-25-foot flag along the parade route. Bands will play. Military units will march. Confetti will fly. There will be tears and cheers from one end of town to the other.

But in the midst of all this gaiety, I suspect my mind will also be wrestling with the fact that over 200,000 human beings, many of them children, were killed in the war whose victory we celebrate so joyously. More are dying as we speak. Their homes and cities lie in ruin.

War is not a football game, not some fictitious scrimmage played for bragging rights. The players do not arise when time expires and walk to the showers together. They stay on the ground, twisted, contorted, limbless, rotting and fly-blown, like tens of millions of war victims before them.

So do we have a right to be happy today?

Yes, because we are happy the awful thing is over. And thankful, too, that so many of America's husbands, wives, sons, daughters, mothers, fathers, brothers and sisters returned safely.

But we should be sad, as well. Sad in the short range because the situation in the Middle East has not changed all that much. And sad in the long range because we know war will forever be a part of the human condition on this planet.

A peculiar situation, this. We humans can pass along an education to our children. We can give them our money. Our time. Our talents. Indeed, each generation on this orb has the unique ability to pass along to the next the first and finest fruits of the harvest.

But there is one thing we cannot pass on: our experience. Our parents did not give it to us, and we cannot give it to our children. Until members of each generation have seen war, firsthand and up close, they cannot understand the ultimate uselessness of it all.

Oh, we try. Our libraries swell with books on the horrors of war. We produce documentary films about war. We write plays and ballads of the gory spectacle. So did other generations, and how much did we learn from them?

A few days ago, I was proofreading the final pages of historian Stephen Ash's "Past Times." These are vignettes of Knoxville history that The News-Sentinel is publishing in book form for the city's Bicentennial. Ash's selection from Oct. 9, 1890, struck me as particularly poignant. In it, he describes a reunion of veterans of the Civil War battle of Fort Sanders.

"The Knoxville reunion," Ash writes, "like others in that era, helped reunite a nation still divided by memories of the war. As one Knoxvillian wrote, 'There was not a Northern man who was here who will not go back to his home . . . with a friendlier feeling towards the South. There is not a Southern man here who has not a more fraternal feeling for his Northern brother.'"

And I couldn't help thinking to myself, "Why in the name of common sense does it take a war to make these feelings come out?"

Vacation vexations

And the winner is . . .

July 5, 1987

Nearly every summer, I try to find people who have experienced an awful vacation. Sometimes, I want to hear the gory details. Sometimes, I want to see their crazy souvenirs. Sometimes, I ask for stupid postcards. And sometimes, like this year, I invite them to share their worst nightmares on the road.

More than two dozen applied for the 1987 honor, and for the first time in the history of Venob's Vacation Vexations Championships, you folks nearly grossed me out.

I thought I had suffered through some humdinger vacation miseries in my life. Silly me. Compared with your woes, I haven't even hit a bump in the road. This year's entries were spectacular. Anyone could have taken the title.

There was Barbara Harper's thunderstorming night of terror aboard a houseboat on Norris Lake.

And Mary Reymer's ride from Pennsylvania to Florida with a grandmother "who weighed over 200 pounds, wore tents for dresses, and combat boots for shoes."

And Debi McClure's stay at a rustic cabin where "there wasn't a mosquito within five miles. The spiders ate them."

Not to mention Chuck Watson's account of "Tropical Storm Bob, which grew up to be Hurricane Bob, but should have been named Thor, God of Thunder."

Still, a choice had to be made. And this year's winner is Sherry Sullivan of Alcoa.

Last August, Sullivan and her family flew to sunny California. They returned with an account that makes the Bataan Death March seem like a sunrise stroll on the beach. I'll let her tell you about it in just a minute.

Sullivan's prize is the coveted Venob Hot-Dang-Super-Dee-Dooper, Anti-Emergency and Attitude Adjustment Kit. It contains more than $100 worth of important items — duct tape to Preparation H to Pepto-Bismol to jumper cables to flashlight to beer — guaranteed to smooth the edges of any rough vacation.

Even though there is no prize for the also-rans, I simply must make a few special presentations.

Patrice Kerr wins the Wordsmith Award for aptly describing no-see-ums as "flying teeth."

Catherine Rogers was first in the Sauna Division for enduring three days in an unventilated house (100 degrees) with the air conditioner on the blink. "And then the repairman fixed it, and it promptly broke again."

Jack and Debbie Thacker, still wed after 13 years, get the True Love bouquet for suffering a blown engine, thieves, illness and a tornado on their honeymoon.

Patricia Walker receives the Free Divorce Award for sitting beside a disabled car while hubby, in another car, had ''registered at the motel, walked the beach and gone out for dinner.''

The International Award, European Division, belongs to Nancy England for being pitched off a train — "no food, no sleep, no visa, no money" — at the Hungarian border.

The International Award, Mexican Division, is for Connie Robin, who spent five luggage-less days in beautiful Acapulco. Her bags arrived just in time for the trip home.

Kathy and Simon Barefoot win the Not-So-Sweet-Home-Alabama Award for braving rain, dead cats, forgotten tickets, mud and the jalapeno pepper quicksteps to attend June Jam in Fort Payne, Ala.

And Lynn Linebarger gets the Alabama Award, Plastic Worm Division, for his report on missed turns, busted motor, sunken boat, broken tackle, electrical fire and snowstorms during a spring bass fishing trip to Lake Eufaula.

Now, do you know why I'm counting the hours until Labor Day?

Without further fanfare, let me turn the stage over to Sherry

Sulivan and let her, in her own words, give you the agonizing blow-by-blow.

Me? I'm going over to the travel agency — to cancel all my flights for the next 20 years.

Day One: My husband, his parents and our two young children depart Knoxville, headed for California. Our plan is to arrive in Los Angeles, drive up the coast and depart San Francisco; but flying standby, you just never know. We finally get the last six seats on a 727 headed not for L.A., but for San Francisco. All our reservations are blown. The entire trip must be accomplished in reverse. It is an omen.

Day Two: Awake early, we rent a car to play tourist. It's freezing. Our first purchase is six sweatsuits. We tour Fishermen's Wharf, and our 3-year-old daughter is dead weight in our arms due to jet lag. Alcatraz tickets are sold out for the day. The line for trolley rides is three blocks long. We retreat.

Day Three: After a traffic jam in Chinatown, we arrive at the Exploratory Museum in an all-out effort to please the kids. It is closed for maintenance. At least the bridge is open.

Buried in road maps, we bid farewell to San Francisco. Three hours and 1,000 curves later, car sickness sets in. Our son loses his first tooth and bleeds profusely. Our remaining goal for the day, Hearst Castle, is also closed.

Printed on my husband's San Francisco sweatshirt is the term, "Are we having fun yet?" It becomes our family's motto, our vacation creed, our battle cry. We will have a good time. Somewhere.

Day Four: Confined to the car, the kids are near revolt. We find a nice beach in Santa Barbara. While my husband and father-in-law are visiting a local winery, our daughter falls into the ocean. We fear pneumonia. Back in the car, we decide no more stops.

Day Five: We promise the children guaranteed fun with a tour of Universal Studios. They are highly skeptical. We arrive early. Everything is going well — except for the ever-increasing pain in my stomach.

In the next four hours, my family sees Jaws, King Kong, the first aid station and a Burbank hospital where I have been taken. Late that night, my inflamed appendix is removed.

Day Six: I awake and my husband asks, "Is this the fun part yet?" I have no sense of humor.

With our vacation abruptly halted, my children and in-laws return to Knoxville. I stare longingly across the street at the NBC studios. If my luck changes, perhaps I'll catch a glimpse of Johnny Carson. It doesn't.

Day Seven: Pleading for an early release, I am discharged with staples in my right side. It is too late to catch a flight east.

Day Eight: We arrive early at the airport, only to be bumped off the first flight. We finally catch an eastbound, but miss our Knoxville connection. Will it ever end?

Day Nine: Back in East Tennessee, and home never looked so good! Our souvenirs include hospital bills totaling $5,174.

Now that, dear hearts, is a vacation to remember! Or forget, as the case may be.

An angler's anguish

July 24, 1990

The next time I get ahead at the office, I am not going fishing. Repeat: Not going fishing. I'll do something more productive. Like rearranging my paper clips. Or cleaning my coffee cup. Anything but fishing.

The story you are about to read is true, so help me Izaak Walton; I swear it on a stack of plastic worms. Even with a fisherman's imagination, I couldn't make up something so outlandish.

It all started one day last week when I found myself two or three columns ahead of schedule. This is quite unusual. Most of the time I barely finish a piece before the presses roll.

I called Ray Hubbard, a longtime angling buddy who lives in Blount County, and arranged a float trip down Little River in "Murph," our mutually owned johnboat.

(Ray and I bought Murph years ago, back when I was writing an outdoor column for this newspaper. We named it after Murphy's Law. Lately, we're thinking of a new name for our ship. "Exxon Valdez" leads the list.)

Our threesome was rounded out by Lowell Branham, another former News-Sentinel outdoors editor who now works on our copy desk. Lowell knows his stuff about boats. Including Murph. That's why he brought his canoe.

We dropped a pickup car at Wildwood, then headed upstream to Davis Ford to begin the journey. At the ford — while the other lads were busying themselves with boat-launching duties — I tossed a small Rapala crankbait into the current and promptly caught a 1-pound smallmouth bass. We began floating, and hardly 100 yards downstream, I added another to the stringer. Surely this was the day angling history would be made.

Not a quarter-mile into the trip, we stopped at a gravel bar to wade and cast. From that moment on, here is what happened; cross my heart and hope to die:

1. Catch small bass on plug. Reach to pluck it from water. Bass shakes abruptly. Front treble hook sinks waaaay past barb into my right thumb. Say two simple words: "YEEEEOWWWW!" and "%$&*-it!"

2. Bass, still attached to other end of lure, continues to shake. Invent newer, even more colorful, words as thumb is internally hamburgerized.

3. Finally grasp bass with free hand. Lowell and Ray — each of whom is far-sighted, neither of whom has brought closeup glasses — begin slow, arm's length process of clipping hooks with dull wire cutters. I stand veeerry still and invent more words. Louder, too.

4. Finally separate fish and thumb from plug. Hook is buried too deep for first aid. Decide to get into Lowell's canoe, paddle upstream and go to hospital for removal.

5. Capsize Lowell's canoe en route to car. Word index at all-time high.

6. Track muddy, wet footprints into emergency room of Blount Memorial. Fill out forms. Endure jokes from staff. Doc numbs thumb with square-ended needle the size of railroad spike. Word City. Hook out. Back on river inside of two hours. Day still salvageable.

7. Start catching fish again. Put eight bass on stringer in short order. Cross particularly rocky shoal and hear particularly loud pop-

I JUST WISH I COULD BE IN THE BOAT WHEN He GRABS iT

GEHRiNG

ping noise from stringer. Lift stringer. Discover it has caught on rock and snapped like thread. Words Revisited.

8. Raise graphite spinning rod just as Ray makes sidearm cast. Hear pariculrly loud snapping noise at tip of spinning rod. Look up to see end of rod dangling like limp rope. Don't know whether to attempt new litany of words or fall to bottom of Murph and weep uncontrollably.

9. Finally reach Wildwood and pull out of river. Drive upstream for other cars. Amazed to discover they are not sitting on cinder blocks.

10. Drive home. Beat dog. Scream at children. Go to bed repeating six new words: Read my lips! No more fishing!

LeRoy's last ride

August 29, 1989

The next time you have an unpleasant traveling experince, resist the urge to scream, pull your hair and curse your rotten luck. Think about Ann Dutton instead. Then fall of your knees and thank your lucky stars.

Ann is a hairdresser. She lives in Lenoir City and works at a beauty shop in West Knoxville. Not long ago, she decided to make a three-day trip to California to visit her daughter, Dena.

Simple enough. Except that as events began to unfold, the journey evolved from a friendly visit into a tourist's nightmare.

Ann sent me a letter detailing the experience. "I'm sure you can put it in the right words," she wrote.

No way. After reading her thoughts — and wiping tears of laughter from my eyes — I knew you'd rather hear it straight from the source. So without further delay, here is "How I Spent My Weekend Vacation" from Ann Dutton:

1. Wednesday afternoon, I made reservations with Continental Airlines.

2. Wednesday night, LeRoy (my husband) informs me that he plans on going with me. I changed all plans and made reservations with United.

3. I called all of my Friday customers to come in on Thursday. I did two days' work in one.

4. Got in bed at 2:30 a.m. Up at 5.

5. At 6:30, I backed my car into husband's truck. Did over $1,000 damage in all.

6. LeRoy walked to the street to get the paper to read on the way. Somebody had beat up the mailbox.

7. LeRoy was very short with my mother on the way to the airport.

8. My daughter had made reservations for us to pick up a car when we got to Los Angeles so we could drive to Bakersfield. We could not rent the car at Avis because they informed us our cash money would not get it. We had to have a major credit card. LeRoy told them what they could do with the card.

9. I tried to get a credit check, but because the time difference, everything was closed in Lenoir City. No good.

10. I went over to Hertz. They take a Sears credit card. But their drop-off station was no closer to Bakersfield than where I was. Another dead end.

11. I got lost. Spent the next two hours riding a bus around the airport trying to find LeRoy.

12. Discovered I didn't have my daughter's correct phone number.

13. Finally found LeRoy. He took his ticket and half the money and tried to come home, but there wasn't a flight till Sunday night. He could have changed planes, but that could have cost $75. All he had was $62.

14. Tracked down my daughter through the company where she

works. She told us to take a shuttle bus to Bakersfield.

15. Found out that 12 ounces of baby oil had leaked and saturated my clothing and suitcase.

16. Went to a dance. LeRoy was a toad, very unfriendly with my daughter's boyfriend.

17. On the way to the airport there was a wreck on the freeway. My daughter got lost and she and LeRoy got into a fuss.

18. Layover in Chicago lasted 5 1/2 hours. Air conditioner was off and we about burned up. I went to get some food. They changed the gate number and I almost missed the plane.

19. My mother was not at the airport to pick us up when we returned. We walked to the end of the road so she would see us.

20. Got home and discovered ice maker was torn up and flooded the kitchen and basement. Floor cover was buckled, wood swollen.

21. I had left two black garbage bags full of cucumbers on the floor. The water had gotten to them. They were rotten. House smelled like a dead dog.

And that, my friends, is where Ann Dutton's grueling story came to a close.

I gave Ann a call. She said time has healed everything. In fact, she and LeRoy have actually resumed speaking.

Will she ever go back to California?

"Sure, honey!" she quipped. "But I'm not traveling with LeRoy anymore."

A hot time in the ol' town tonight!

February 5, 1991

If Panama City has lost its polyester luster; and if you've done Disney World so many times Mickey and Pluto greet you by name; and if the thought of one more candy apple on the streets of Gatlinburg makes your stomach churn, have I got a vacation for you.

Just call your travel agent now and book a visit to the Chernobyl nuclear plant in the Soviet Union.

I am not making this up. In last Sunday's "Komsomolskaya Pravda" newspaper, there was a story about how Ukranian travel officials are promoting vacation tours to the site of the world's nastiest nuclear no-no.

Five years ago this April, one of the four reactors at Chernobyl exploded, killing anywhere from 31 to 500 people — the Soviets can't seem to agree on insignificant details like dead bodies — and spreading nuclear contamination from There to God Knows Where.

But, as they say down at the ol' borscht bar, vat's a leetle vadiation? Ve all gotta go sometimk, eh Baldski?

This ain't no quickie tour, Bubba Joe. We're talking the redline special, complete with side trips to the city of Chernobyl, plus a radioactive waste dump at Kopachi, plus the concrete tomb built around the defunct reactor, plus the town of Slavutich where thousands of nuclear workers still reside. And you thought the height of vacation ecstasy was the mongo-killer waterslide at Ogle's.

According to an Associated Press dispatch about this exciting possibility, "trips for foreign and Soviet tourists will begin and end with Geiger counter tests to check the visitor's exposure to radiation. If treatment at a radiological medical center is needed, it will be provided AT NO EXTRA CHARGE."

Those are my capital letters, of course. The AP and other wire services refuse to show emotion when reporting straight news. But in the spirit of international relations, I felt obliged to call your attention to the fact that those astute Rooskie travel agents think of EVERY-THING when it comes to your comfort and safety.

I can only imagine what other precautions Helga, your lovely tour guide, might offer along the way:

"Ladies and gentlemen, I don't mean to alarm you, but please refrain from sticking arms and heads outside the bus window. This area is inhabited by massive colonies of 50-pound ants which seem to have evolved since 'the incident.' If we do encounter an army of these insects, feel free to deploy the AK-47 we packed inside each box lunch. And now, if you'll be so kind as to look out the left window, please observe our famous five-eyed dogs and six-legged cats . . ."

I don't expect hordes of tourists to take advantage of this stupendous offer. Especially Americans. We have become a nation of petrified pantywaists, scared of our own whispers. Just because our skin might rot, our bones turn to mush and our life expectancies dwindle to, oh, say, 3-5 months, we blanch at the thought of traveling to a certified

vacation hot spot. Such is the shame we bear for being wimps.

Still, on the outside chance the Russians make a go of this thing, perhaps there are other exciting ports of call for tourists with gusto in their guts.

Charleston, S.C., during the height of Hurricane Hugo would have been a dandy. And how about standing atop San Francisco's Bay Bridge when the killer earthquake hit? Tommy Tourist surely would've given up a day at the beach for that experience.

But when it comes to 100-proof excitement and adventure, I recommend a lengthy tour of downtown Baghdad. Especially when allied jets are showering this scenic city with 600 million-jillion megatons of bombs.

Sign up now, folks. Reserved seats are going fast.

This wondrous season

An ode to August

August 10, 1990

I was enjoying the intoxicating splendor of a cool August evening, expounding upon the glories of autumn and fairly tingling with anticipation, when Good Friend Of Yanqui Extraction attempted to burst my bubble.

"This," he sniffed, "is *not* autumn."

"Huh?"

"Autumn is wearing a red plaid wool shirt," GFOYE harrumphed. "It is eating a crisp apple that splashes all over your face when you take the first bite."

"Of course it is," I replied, "but autumn has a lot in common with Christmas, your birthday and a two-week vacation at the beach."

"Huh?"

"Half the fun is getting there."

Having never lived Up Yonder, I cannot speak with authority about the process of summer's surrender to autumn. For all I know it happens like a clap of thunder. Everybody is sitting around in short pants and ka-blooey, the leaves turn from green to red.

"Aye-yup," they say, "4:17, right on schedule."

If that's the way it works, what a pity.

Here in the privileged southland, we rehearse and revere this annual passage. We call it August.

Please understand that August is officially summer. It can be hotter than the very hinges of hell, more humid than a Brazilian rain forest. Anyone of Southern breeding knows better than to buy a snow shovel this time of year.

Aaah, but August prepares us for the good stuff. North winds in the afternoon and midnight "freezes" of 55 degrees have a greater impact on the body and soul than a dose of salts and a weeklong tent revival.

August is laid-back, no-hassle, easy-going.

It is a time to cease fretting about fancy summer parties where guests sit in deck chairs and melt into pools of perspiration.

It is a time to abandon diets with a clear conscience because bulky sweaters, perfect for waistline camouflage, are soon to be shaken from storage.

It is a time to think great thoughts of social/cultural life in the South: from football games and county fairs to hay rides and hunting seasons.

It is a time to feast — gluttonously, if at all possible — on home-grown tomatoes, homegrown corn, homegrown okra and homegrown cantalopes. The miserable wretches who settle for store-bought produce this time of year either have no garden or no gardening friends. Whatever the case, they are to be earnestly prayed over, for they are in dire need of salvation.

Critics of August, swine that they are, sometimes accuse this regal month of flirting. They claim it tempts us with fallish tempera-

tures and fallish football fantasies, then slaps us back into reality with record highs and distant kickoffs.

Baloney.

The critics — who are aliens, possibly illegal ones from Up Yonder — don't understand this is all part of the process. Seasonal courtship, as it were. August's duty is to put us in the mood.

There will be time for enjoying genuine autumn when genuine autumn arrives — assuming we can arrange a bit of pleasure along with school's-back-in-session rushing and let's-plan-the-holiday-menu panics. With luck, there will even be lots of time for GFOYE's plaid shirt and crisp apples.

But for now, give me the music of katydids and jarflies at sunset.

Give me the beauty of purple morning glories, adrip with dew, climbing up the trellis at dawn.

Give me my sleepy, trusty, end of summer friend.

Give me August.

Chapter Three

FAT BOYS DON'T SWEAT IN THE FALL

Fall is the fastest season of them all. If every horse I bet on moved this quickly, I'd be a millionaire by now and wouldn't have to write books for a living.

Depending on the weather and UT's football schedule, autumn in East Tennessee begins in late August or early September. (And if you have backslid into that Venob-doesn't-know-his-official-seasons nonsense, I invite you to re-read my instructions at the start of the chapter on spring.)

This is a splendid time. The air gets crisp. Leaves take on a golden glow. There's excitement in the air. Of course, this excitement sometimes turns sour after the Vols' opening kickoff, but I digress.

So what happens? Fall ends and winter begins, that's what. Whooosh! We raise a glass of fresh-squeezed apple cider to our lips and before we can swallow, the dadburned stuff is frozen solid.

That's why many East Tennesseans discourage the consumption of fresh-squeezed cider. Long ago, they learned that the aged stuff won't freeze.

A reward unto itself

September 1, 1985

It was years ago — back before petroleum prices went sky high, back when station attendants pumped your gas and washed your windshield and checked under the hood and gave you green stamps with your change.

My wife was sitting inside her car as it was being serviced. She happened to glance at a nearby pump and noticed a huge sale had been rung up. Something like $20 or $30, which shows you just how long ago I'm talking about.

"Goodness, gracious!" she exclaimed to the attendant. "That's an awful lot of gas."

"Naw, it ain't," he replied. "That ain't nuthin.' I've seen a lot more gas than that sold around here."

With that, he cocked his head to one side in deep thought. "Matter of fact," he finally said, "the most I ever pumped was . . ."

And for the next five minutes, he regaled Mary Ann on the intricacies of 75- and 100-gallon gasoline purchases and how it takes a skilled service station attendant to handle such a job. He paused just long enough to give her a chance to pay her bill. Then she split.

Mary Ann and I have laughed about that incident over the years. But even as I chuckle at the thought of being pinned to a gasoline pump during such an oration, some very basic truths ring clear:

Here was a person who really enjoyed his job.

A person who did it well.

A person who took great pride in the service he was giving his customers.

To him and millions of other workers around the country, we tip our hats this Labor Day weekend.

On the surface, nobody enjoys working. Complaining about how we earn a living is an all-American tradition. You need look no further than country music singer Johnny Paycheck, who enjoyed several fat paychecks a few years ago with a tune called "Take This Job and Shove It."

Folks would listen to the lyrics and sing along and chug-a-lug a few beers and holler, "Tell 'em all about it, Johnny! I'm with you, son! I ain't workin' here no more, either!"

Then the next morning, they would pick up their lunch pails and punch the time clock and never think twice about it.

Why?

Because hidden beneath the veneer of moans and complaints, most people take great pride in their jobs.

We have been led to believe the American work ethic has evaporated since World War II. We've been accused of becoming fat, eager to cut corners and live on the dole. We are told that labor unions protect lazy slobs, that zipperheads in high management earn outrageous salaries for twiddling their thumbs.

Unfortunately, you do not have to search diligently to substantiate portions of the theory. But I absolutely refuse to believe it across the board.

I still think most people try to give it their best, assess their own mistakes realistically, and don't mind puffing their chests in the wake of a job well done. And I still think that most people, when they do find themselves in a meaningless job, actively look for something better.

That goes whether they're swinging a hammer or drilling teeth or cutting grass or computing taxes or ironing clothes or designing buildings.

Or pumping gasoline and philosophizing on subjects like the great American dream.

Send it on down the line

September 4, 1988

Gene Voiles is seated at a long wooden table. He is sorting through hundreds of one-inch brass valves. Four different types of valves are mixed together in the pile in front of Gene. His assignment is to separate them into individual containers.

Methodically, he picks one up. He inspects it carefully. Then he places it into a coffee can with others of its kind. As it drops with a crisp "plink," he smiles contentedly.

One down, many more to go. He plucks another from the pile, and the process continues.

Gene will perform this job until the end of the work day. He will do it the next day. And the next. At the end of the week, he might receive all of $35 for his efforts.

Gene Voiles couldn't be happier.

Neither could Jackie Graham or Rowena Carberry, seated at another table nearby. They are working with costume jewelry.

If a piece is broken or tarnished, Jackie tosses it into the reject pile. If it's OK, she passes it to Rowena, who tucks it into a box and sends it on down the line.

Across the room, Kevin Wells is grinding the rough edges off a section of metal tubing. He passes it along to Tim Kennedy, who inserts it into a larger piece and glues the two sections together. Down the line it goes once more.

Throughout the building, there is no talk of occupational burnout.

No complaining about working conditions.

No glancing at wristwatches to see how many hours must pass before quitting time finally arrives.

Gene, Jackie, Rowena, Kevin and Tim are among 160 Knoxvillians who clock in daily at Sunshine Industries, 3000 N. Central St. They bring their lunch boxes, a willing spirit, and an IQ of 80 or below.

A generation ago, these people would not be working. In all likelihood, they would be hidden in a backroom of the family home or isolated behind the walls of an institution until their cruel life sentence was served.

But thanks to an enlightened society and the emergence of "sheltered workshops" around the country, they and thousands of other mentally handicapped adults can experience the personal fulfillment that comes with being employed.

People of average intelligence would say the tasks at Sunshine Industries are boring and repetitive. They would say the wages, regulated by Department of Labor guidelines for the handicapped, are quite low.

And they would be right.

But this is anything but a make-work project to keep the retarded off the streets. Sunshine Industries provides a job — a useful, productive job — for people once considered unemployable. What's more, it serves as a training ground for those gifted enough to find a niche in the outside world. Last year, the company placed 30 workers in regular employment, largely in the fast-food business.

Sunshine Industries is a private, non-profit organization, an offshoot of the Knox County Association for Retarded Citizens. It grossed $1.2 million from production contracts last year.

The association receives a portion of its income from grants, government agency fees, the United Way and other sources. But 65 percent of its budget is self-generated. That's more than double the average for sheltered workshops nationwide.

Yet we are talking about something more important than dollars and cents here, something essential to the human psyche. We are talking about the pride and sense of belonging that come with having a job.

And we are talking about how these values are reflected in job performance. In the last few years, workers at Sunshine Industries' metal shop have manufactured 53,844 sets of bookcases. Three have been returned because of faulty workmanship.

Three.

As the Labor Day weekend winds down and you start groaning with thoughts of Tuesday morning, you might want to keep that little statistic in mind.

TGIF!

September 9, 1988

I'm going to make today's sermon short and sweet. We've all got busy schedules ahead of us, and we need to get cracking. I just need a few minutes to correct a grievous employee-employer misunderstanding, especially since this is the very week we honor America's labor force.

I have just finished looking at a study of worker performance published by Runzheimer International, a management consulting firm in Rochester, Wis. This report cited findings from a survey of personnel managers from around the country.

According to these people, Tuesday is the only day of the week when employees earn their pay. About half the managers (53 percent) said Tuesday was the most productive day on the schedule. Wednesday ranked second (19 percent), followed by Thursday (9 percent) and Monday (6 percent).

Friday scored the lowest. Only 2 percent reported Friday was worth a flying flip as far as productivity is concerned.

(I could point out that 53 percent added to 19 percent, et al, does not equal 100 percent of the work week. But I won't. I'm sure it was merely an oversight. By management.)

As usual, the experts are wrong. Dead wrong. Friday is, by far, the most productive day on the weekly calendar, and I can prove it. Let's take today, Friday, September 9, 1988, as a prime example.

All around Knoxville, workers by the tens of thousands are toiling furiously today. Their sense of dedication brings a tear to my eye and a lump to my throat.

You see, the University of Tennessee opens its home football schedule against Duke tomorrow, and many tasks remain undone.

There is the business of tickets themselves. Workers who haven't already secured their seats must spend hours on the telephone trying to cut a deal with their friendly neighborhood scalper. Before that, they've got to deliberate over parlay sheets.

Next is the matter of a pre-game tailgate meal. These things don't "just happen," you know. They call for planning, execution, split-second timing.

A deli tray needs to be ordered. Will it be ham and roast beef or turkey and cheese? What kind of cheese? Light bread? Whole wheat?

Cokes and beer need to be iced down, cookies need to be picked up — chocolate chip or butter pecan? — and potato salad needs to be made.

These chores do not occur at the snap of a finger, chum. If the job is going to be done right, it's going to eat up another three or four hours from an already hectic day.

That doesn't even scratch the surface. If you intend to travel by boat to Neyland Stadium, you've got to worry about fuel, provisions, the possibility of mechanical failure, plus a place to dock once you arrive. And I dare not even mention the planning and effort that must take place today if your post-game party at dockside is going to be a success.

Enough of Vol thoughts for the moment. Strange as it may seem, there is something besides football on the sporting schedule this weekend. This is also the opening of the wood duck season.

There are blinds to be brushed, decoys to be gathered from the basement and painted, calls to tune, guns to clean, licenses to buy. Busy, busy, busy!

So let's hear no more of this nonsense about how Friday is not a productive day. Quite the contrary. I don't know how we'd survive without it.

In fact, there's *so* much work to be done today, I may have to call in sick.

Peepoppy and his pals

September 11, 1988

For all you Dee-Does and Jo-Joes who bake oatmeal cookies and tell bedtime stories, this one's for you. Today is Grandparents' Day all across America.

Maybe this holiday isn't as widely known as Mother's Day, Father's Day, Valentine's Day and Christmas, but it's official nonetheless. The celebration started in 1978 when President Jimmy Carter put his pen to a proclamation designating the first Sunday after Labor Day as the time to honor all those proud grandfolk whose mission it is to spoil their grandchildren rotten.

I have no firsthand knowledge in this department — and please, my own teenage children, spare dear ol' dad the thrills for a good while — but I imagine one of the joys of being a grandparent is that you can get away with indiscretions off-limits to mere parents.

When you are a parent, you are supposed to ride herd on your children and make sure they don't stray from the straight and narrow. Yet the instant you become a grandparent, you not only condone unruly behavior, you encourage it, fund it, shape it, and run interference between children and protesting parents. I don't know why this double standard exists, but it has since the beginning of time and will continue to do so until civilization ceases. Amen and amen.

Another bonus of grandparentdom is the cute nicknames you acquire.

Well, maybe "cute" isn't exactly accurate. "Embarrassing" is more like it. Or "stupid."

At least they would be among adults in an adult world. You don't see many grown-up men addressing each other with the likes of "Bippaw" and "Boppaw." But between grandchildren and grandparents, these tender titles are golden sources of pride.

I took a walk around downtown Knoxville the other day and asked people what they called their grandmothers and grandfathers.

A good many of them used the ol' East Tennessee reliable: "I always called them Mamaw and Papaw," said Melissa Jeffries of her grandparents, Addie and Howard Miller.

Sandy Abel also used a familiar handle — "Nanna." But get this: Her grandmother's real name was Grit Martens. "I called my other grandmother 'Lovie' because that was her name. Lovie McCurdy."

Then there was Barbara Margiotta whose grandmom answered to the name "Walls." Good reason. Her name was Zilpha Walls.

Grandfather Alva Salyer is "Papaw Hound Dog" to granddaughter Faith Salyer because he owns a bunch of treeing dogs.

Betsy McKenry used "Mu" for her granny, Glessie Harber. Why? "I have no idea at all," she replied. "That's what everyone called her."

"Boobie" is what Mary Booher calls her grandmother, Josephine Walters. But that's not as weird as what some other relatives call the dear lady — "Gogine." (They had trouble pronouncing "Josephine," get it?)

Nancy Floyd also stumbled over pronunciations as a child. That's why she referred to May Williamson as "Grandmaw Wimpy."

Rich Keil used "Popo" and "Momo" for grandparents Henry and Dorothy Keil. Not to be outdone, they called him "Ree-Ree."

Clayton Lloyd's grandmother, Nancy Lloyd, was still in her 30s when he was born, so he called her "Big Mommie." "I reckon she'd jack my jaw if I called her 'Grandmother,' " he laughed.

Carmen McDaniel didn't have a grandpappy; thus, she used "Daddaw" and "Bobbaw," respectively, for grandmothers Martha Coppock and Mary Buckner.

Grandmother Janice Smith is "Mom-Moms" for Michelle Johnson.

Will Brown and other relatives refer to grandfather David Brown as "Peepoppy."

Gary Hodge used "Big Paw" and "Little Paw" to differentiate between his great-grandfather and grandfather, Noe Hodge and Dean Hodge.

Grandmother Jane Hayes is "Megger" for Lindsay Hayes.

And Stella Reed's love for cookies was turned into an appropriate nickname by granddaughter Susannah Stringfield.

She calls her "Oreo."

Start of school

Ciphering made simple

August 21, 1990

It's time for school to start. And, as usual, the nation's education leaders are worried sick because our students can't keep pace with students from other countries in the study of mathematics.

All is not lost, however. Our kids can still knock out everybody else's eyes in football, cheerleading, band, shop, senior play and dancing. But in matters of 2 plus 2, they rarely come up with 5.

(Or is it 7? That question always stumps me.)

The National Research Council is particularly worried about America's pitiful performance in math. In a recent report, "A Challenge of Numbers: People in the Mathematical Sciences," the council notes:

• By 1995, the college-age population will drop by about 22 percent from its peak in 1981.

• College-age white men, now dominating the science and engineering work force, will shrink by 34 percent, posing a problem for women and minorities who lag seriously in these fields.

• The popularity of mathematics among collegians has dropped sharply. Nearly 50 percent of undergraduates who start as math majors ultimately turn to other subjects.

At first glance, one is tempted to shrug and say, "So? Who gives a royal rat's rump? The good ol' U.S. of A. has mathematicians runnin' out its ears. Just look at what the boys at NASA can do. They can take a high-powered telescope, twist a few knobs, plot a couple of charts, figure some numbers, blast the thing into space and get pictures of . . . hmmmmm, on second thought, maybe we do need to brush up in the add-subtract-multiply-divide department."

Precisely.

But how do math teachers go about reaching today's students? With those dumb apples and oranges problems from 1953?

Certainly not. They need to chuck those relics out the window and speak in the learned tongue of today. Like this:

1. Billy buys five tickets to a New Kids on the Block concert at the face price of $22.50 each. He keeps two — one for himself and one for Bobbi Jo Quigglewart, who is hotter than a depot stove and would do anything to see New Kids.

Billy scalps the other three tickets — one for $35 to Junior Romines, one for $87.50 to LeRoy Brushberry and one for $125 to Bruno Jawsmashski.

Please calculate the percentage of markup for each of the scalped tickets. In addition, determine Billy's profit — less the $5 he bribed Bobbi Jo's runt brother for not telling what he saw in the driveway, plus the $100 doctor bill he encountered after LeRoy and Bruno realized what a bargain Junior Romines got and stomped Billy's foot.

2. Billy's football team, faced with fourth and goal at the 8 late in the championship game, draws two consecutive 15-yard penalties. Billy, hobbled by a recent and unexplained foot injury, limps in to attempt what will be a 55-yard field goal. His best is 41 yards.

Miraculously, he makes it, and the team is voted No. 1 in polls throughout the country.

Please determine: (a) the percentage increase in distance between kicks; (b) the amount of time Bobbi Jo Quigglewart spends with Billy after the game; (c) Billy's average monthly income from a $2.7 million pro signing bonus — less 31.5 percent for his agent.

3. Billy fills his nose with $750-a-day cocaine and washes out of the pros after two seasons.

Please calculate: (a) the monthly cost of Billy's addiction; (b) the loss of potential income over a 15-year career, given a 27.4 percent annual pay raise; (c) the total bill for his divorce from the former Bobbi Jo Quigglewart, including legal fees, alimony and child support.

Trust me, teachers. Give your kids a dose of this math, and they'll all be Phi Beta Kappas.

Looking 'cool' — I mean 'bad'

September 7, 1989

My son has shaved the sides of his head, and my daughter has dyed a red streak in her blonde hair. If that's not a sure sign of a new year in high school, I'll eat the logarithmic tables.

When you have teenagers in the house, you come to expect these things. Some years it's crazy hair. Some years it's crazy clothes. Some years it's both. I have given up trying to keep track of what is cool and what isn't.

Oops. There I went and showed my age again. I said "cool." It's not cool to say "cool" anymore. The correct term in most circles is "bad." But "bad" doesn't sound good to me, so I'll stick with "cool." Even if it is uncool.

Kids do strange things to their hair and their clothes in order to make a statement. It's an independence thing.

One reason is to set themselves apart from their parents. This doesn't apply in my son's case because I am losing hair myself. If I continue to shed in the front of my head and Clay keeps shaving on the side of his, we'll soon meet at a point northeast of our ears and can pass as twins.

Another reason for this change in appearance is so teenagers can express their own individuality. They adopt a style that reflects their distinct, unique personality. Of course, 75,000 teenagers in the same town are reflecting their own distinct, unique personalities exactly the same way, but that's neither here nor there.

In this respect, I'm lucky to have grown up during the '50s and '60s, a period in American history when parent-child rebellion was refined and polished to a bright luster.

Make no mistake. There is nothing new about conflict between the generations. Ever since humans walked upright, children have found a way to confound and confuse their parents.

It is a well-known fact that when archaeologists deciphered the earliest paintings on the walls of ancient caves, the message read, "The trouble with kids is they've got it too soft. When I was their age, I had to walk 12 miles through the tar pits to kill a brontosarus for breakfast. Then I went to school and studied spear-throwing and tiger-skinning for hours at a time. These days, all children do is hang around the cave and expect to be waited on. I tell you, today's kids will be the ruination of us all."

This generational sparring match didn't change very much until we Baby Boomers hit the scene. Then it turned into combat. Pick a crisis, any crisis. No matter what the issue was, the homes of America resounded with the same parental verse:

"Tuck in that shirt and put on some shoes, young man! If my old drill sergeant ever saw the likes of you, you'd be on KP for a month."

"Wipe that lipstick off right now, young lady! We didn't have money to waste on makeup during the Depression, and we got along just fine."

"When I get back from work tonight, that hair had better be cut! I didn't fight my way all over Europe just so I could raise a family of apes."

"Turn that radio off! I don't know why you want to listen to that garbage. You can't even hear what he's saying. You want good music? Try Bing Crosby or the Andrews Sisters."

Fortunately, we laid-back parents of the '80s don't react as emotionally as our own mothers and fathers did. We are not bound by dogma and tradition. We recognize the importance of letting our children be themselves. We acknowledge their need for self-expression. We welcome their independence.

If my kids pierce their noses, I'll kill 'em.

This is war!

September 1, 1988

Never again will I laugh at frenzied shoppers.

You would have thought I learned my lesson years ago, back when gasoline was in short supply and motorists had to wait — often impatiently — for a few meager gallons. How soon we forget.

A few nights ago, I took my children to buy school supplies. This was after classes resumed and teachers had outlined the items their students would need for the coming year.

Big deal, I thought. A few packs of notebook paper, some pencils, maybe a folder or two. This will be over in 15 minutes, max.

Silly me.

It never registered in my pea brain that every other parent in Knoxville had the same idea.

When we wheeled into the parking lot at Target, I was momentarily addled. The scene reminded me of the Christmas season. Here it was, less than 30 minutes before closing time, and both the store and the lot were packed. I finally found a parking spot in the lower 40, girded my loins and led the kids into the fray.

It's hard to say how many hundreds of people were "visiting" (that's a nice way of putting it) Target that night. Whatever the figure, fully 98 percent of them had designs on school supplies. The entire department was a sea of arms and hands. Reaching, groping, grabbing, tugging arms and hands.

My pulse quickened. My palms began to sweat. I got that squishy feeling in my guts. It was the kind I used to get when the teacher would call on me in class and I hadn't read the assignment.

So for openers, I opted for something easy. Notebook paper.

I checked every aisle, every shelf, every cubbyhole. Nothing. In fact, all I found was a sales clerk who looked like she'd just stepped off a cover of Time magazine. An issue about Belfast or Beirut.

"Where's the notebook paper, please?" I asked.

She stared back. Like maybe I had asked for the Hope Diamond or a three-volume cassette of "Chopin Does Reggae." Finally, her lips parted.

"We don't have a single sheet of notebook paper," she said in a monotone. Then she staggered away.

It was time to take emergency steps. I huddled the kids around me.

"Grab whatever you can! Accounting paper works fine in a typewriter, Megan. Trust me.

"You, Clay! Never mind that the only notebooks have My Little Pony on them. This is war, boy! You gotta make do.

"Now, let's go out there and win one for the Gipper. Oh, and if I don't make it outta here, tell your mother I love her. Ready? Chaaaaarge!"

While the children darted on their own missions, I sprinted into the folder section. I discovered stock clerks had quit piling wares on the shelf. Instead, they'd simply wheeled everything out in shopping carts. So I elbowed my way toward a buggy, grabbed a fistful of folders, took a bearing on my compass and set out for spiral notebooks.

I fought my way around a corner and — eureka! — spied another

shopping cart. It was heavy laden with spiral notebooks. But just as I exorcised a few, a woman's voice behind me boomed, "Hey, that's my cart! Leave those alone!"

I apologized briefly and set a course for erasers. In war, there is no time for elaborate I'm sorrys.

Bruised and bloodied at the checkout counter, I told Megan we could cut posterboard into 8 1/2-by-11-inch sheets and tell the teacher it was the latest thing in typing paper. Starched. She allowed as how it was worth a try.

Clay, on the other hand, wasn't certain he could convince his English teacher that his red and green pens were actually black and that perhaps she should be checked for color blindness.

Soon as we got to the car, I glanced at the gas gauge. It was just below full. Nonetheless, I whipped into an all-night station and pumped in two dollars' worth.

Be prepared, I always say.

Meet me at the fair

Nausea as entertainment

September 13, 1990

The problem with newfound courage is you have to keep testing it. Far better to remain content in cowardice and be spared the misery.

I reached this conclusion the other afternoon after stumbling off a gut-wrenching ride at the Tennessee Valley Fair.

It was called the Paratrooper.

If you are into nausea as entertainment, you will be rolling on the floor right now and saying, "Hoo-haa! What a wienie Venob is. I know 4-year-old children who ride the Paratrooper whenever it comes to town. Why, even my old Aunt Maude — who turned 87 last week and has had three heart bypasses — is a Paratrooper fan. She loves to knit while it spins her around."

Fine. More power to you, the 4-year-olds and Aunt Maude. I'll keep my feet in the dirt.

I have not been a fan of carnival rides since the age of 7 or 8, when a mongo-killer roller coaster in Cincinnati nearly caused me to become moist. Until that time, the scariest rides I'd ever encountered were in the kiddie corner at Chilhowee Park. When you step straight from the mini merry-go-round onto a roller coaster with 90-degree drops, it makes a believer out of you.

It also makes you afraid.

Heights and I never have agreed in the first place. And I consider motion sickness one of the top three diseases plaguing mankind.

That's why I maintained a near-perfect vow of celibacy at the fair throughout teenagedom and adulthood. The only time I broke this pledge was in the mid-1960s, when the brown-eyed girl I was dating gently convinced me to ride the double Ferris wheel.

"Quit crying, yellow-belly!" she shouted. "You're embarrassing me!"

It was awful. The hateful thing spun around like a washing machine, and then they stopped it while we were AT THE VERY TIP TOP! To make matters worse, Brown Eyes was swinging the seat back and forth like a porch glider.

I opened my mouth for a split-second and tried to scream, but nothing came out. At that precise moment, however, the concept of a disposable diaper for adults did cross my mind; but since I swore off carnival rides shortly thereafter, the idea drifted from memory and someone from Kimberly-Clark beat me to it.

I avoided scary, bouncing rides for 25 years. Then last month, while in California for the Pigskin Classic, I joined several writers and spouses for an evening at Disneyland. Someone suggested we do the

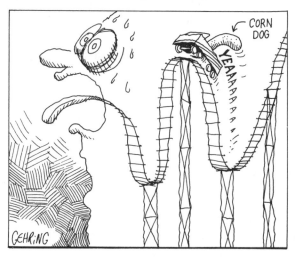

white-knuckle circuit. Matterhorn, Space Mountain, the works.

I screamed.

Mary Ann cut her brown eyes toward me. "Shut up, yellow-belly!"

We tried 'em all. And to my great surprise, it was fabulous. I laughed and hollered like Tommy Tourist From Tennessee and had a grand ol' time.

So when the fair opened in Knoxville, I couldn't wait to make the grand tour again. I grabbed daughter Megan — who had spent her carnival days riding with strangers because Daddy always stayed below — headed toward the Midway and climbed aboard the Paratrooper.

Beeeg mistake.

The thing spun at 14,500 rpms. It bounced like a kangaroo primed with Tabasco. It slung us sideways into a gluey, centrifugal mass of flesh.

Megan screamed with excitement. I, on the other hand, tried to remember the breathing techniques from Lamaze and dedicated the next five minutes to keeping a foot-long chili cheese dog from making a surprise revisit.

The torture finally ended and I staggered off like a drooling, grizzled-faced drunk.

"What do we ride next, Daddy?" Megan asked.

I didn't have to think twice.

"The car," I said. "The sooner, the better."

Battle in the barnyard

September 9, 1990

Pay attention, children. What Uncle Venob is about to say is very important.

The next time your science teacher starts jabbering about where milk comes from, don't believe a word. It's an outright lie.

I, on the other hand, will tell you the truth.

Milk comes from lots of places. It comes from supermarkets, convenience stores, restaurants and cafeterias. It comes from machines. It comes from trucks. It comes from glass bottles, plastic jugs and cardboard cartons.

It does not, however, come from cows.

I know this for a fact because I attempted to withdraw milk from a cow the other day, and all I got was a fine, white mist.

This feat was performed during opening ceremonies at the Tennessee Valley Fair. The folks in charge sponsored a cow-milking contest and invited a bunch of media types to participate.

Promoters do things like this for two reasons.

First, it gives the good ol' boys at the livestock pavilion their annual chance to make fun of city slickers. If there is anything more hilarious than watching a man in a starched shirt and necktie squat in manure-dotted hay alongside a cow with drool hanging off its nose, it's watching a woman in a fancy dress do the same thing.

Second, this is an excellent way to get cheap publicity for the fair.

If an executive from the fair walked into a newspaper office or a radio or TV station and said, "Hi, guys! How about giving me $5,000 worth of free advertising?" the news people would laugh out loud.

"Nice try, pal," they would say, "but we don't give away news hole and air time around here." Then they would walk him to the door.

But when he says, "We're sponsoring a milking contest. Would someone from your staff like to enter?" the news types snap their fingers and say, "Wow! What a terrific idea! Let's search through the newsroom and find the goofiest jerk we have. Someone who'll really screw things up. Let him get out there and make a fool out of himself and then write about it."

Which is why I found myself squatting beside this stupid drooling cow, squeezing her stupid ti . . . uh, whatever it's called, trying to shoot some stupid milk into a stupid Coke bottle — yes, a Coke bottle; isn't a pail supposed to be standard issue? — and dodging whenever the stupid cow tried to kick me.

And to think that all this time, I considered myself somewhat of an expert, harrumph, when it came to manipulating the mammaries.

They gave me my choice of five cows for this contest. Two Guernseys, two Holsteins and one Jersey. I ruled out the Jersey immediately. She was skinnier than a Q-tip and appeared to be in greater need of milk than I.

The Holsteins, on the other hand, were brutes. They looked like a team of black and white 747s. Never milk a cow, I always say, if it must be approached by step ladder.

So I settled on one of the Guernseys.

Bad choice. *Very* bad choice.

Maybe it didn't help our relations any when I walked up to the beast, slapped her on the flank, and said, "Give it all you got, honey, or the next stop for you is McDonald's." But for one reason or another, she produced not a drop.

Zilch.

Zip. Zero.

And please. Spare me your sermons about my milking technique. I'll have you know I spent a full afternoon of practice the day before at Breck Ellison's cattle emporium near Lenoir City. Quasi practice, anyway. Breck only had bulls in his barn. But big deal; some of his helpers extended their fingers and showed me what to do. So there.

I finally gave up on the Guernsey and switched to a 747. Too late. I got in one decent squeeze — producing enough milk to moisten a small postage stamp — before the judge, a man who looked like he could be cheaply bribed, called time.

When all the bottles were collected and their contents measured, WIMZ disc jockey "Diamond Jim" was declared the winner. I could swear I saw Jim pass the judge a $10 bill, but far be it from me to start an ugly rumor. Besides, all I had to offer was $7.54.

The day was not a total loss, though. I did receive a ribbon for my efforts. It was a black ribbon. For last place.

Even better, I was able to persuade the officials to change receptacles before next year's media milking contest. No more longnecked Coke bottles, thank heavens.

In my case, they said a thimble would be more than ample.

Those beautiful/hateful leaves

The best season

October 20, 1987

I think that I shall never see,
A poem as lovely as a tree . . .
A tree whose hungry mouth is prest
Against the earth's sweet flowing breast . . .
Poems are made by fools like me,
But only God can make a tree.

— Kilmer

I reckon I will never tar
Of seein' fall woods bright as far . . .
The red and gold and orange and yeller
Look mighty purty to this feller . . .
But boss, please don't think it's a trick,
If, during aut'mn, I call in sick.

— Venob

I don't know where the credit lies for the beautiful fall colors we are enjoying this year.

It could be the dry summer. Or maybe the early frost. Or possibly the fact that the Vols got off to such a fabulous start, ahem, on the 1987 football season. Whatever the reason, I make a motion we have a repeat every year.

Have you ever seen the woods so gorgeous? I'm sure there have been other bursts this bright, but I can't recall any in recent history.

The last time I remember such a splash was during the fall of 1968. The forests of East Tennessee absolutely glowed that year. The fact I was still serving a four-year sentence in college and was chained to the classroom and the library each day made the colors seem more vivid than ever.

(Dedicated student that I was, I made a concerted effort that quarter not to skip class more than three times a week. Unless it was absolutely necessary, of course. I have strived to maintain this record during the fall of '87. So if you happen to call my office and I'm not in, don't start asking questions.)

This year's beauty lies not so much in color pattern. Face it — fall is always attractive. But what sets this one apart from all others is the fierce intensity of hue.

The reds are nearly on fire. Sourwood, maple, dogwood and sumac look like they would burn your hand if you touched them. The purple of gum has taken on a velvet sheen. And the brilliant yellow of hickory makes me want to rip leaves off the limb and smoke 'em like tobacco.

The bitter side of all this splendor is knowing that wind and rain are about to bring the show to an end.

'Tis a chiseling effect at first. Just the tips of branches along the ridgelines begin to appear. Next, entire trees on the slopes stand bare. Then — boom! — the curtain falls. Almost overnight, the leaf thief streaks into the valleys. He starts ripping, hacking and slashing like a vandal. By morning, the once-painted hillsides are about as appealing as a billboard in the wake of a tornado.

Sometimes I wish it were possible to capture fall colors and serve them up on a drab winter day. Or even better, to enjoy a burst of October bliss during mid-August, when the humidity has a choke hold on the world and the thermometer is flirting with 100.

I don't mean preserving this beauty on film or videotape, either. My shelves at home are loaded with books containing pictures of fall foliage. Big deal. Looking at them in February is as useless as gazing at portraits of deceased friends and family members and trying to hear their laughter once again. If anything, it makes you miss them that much more.

Oh, well. Enough of matters melancholy. We can no more savor the delights of the autumn season in January any more than we can keep the warmth of the Christmas spirit alive after the wreath comes off the front door.

Perhaps that's the way it should be. Too much of a good thing, and we'd get downright spoiled.

So if you'll excuse me, I'm going back to the hills.

The worst season

November 18, 1990

Pipe-smoking and leaf-raking are two autumn activities Type-A people should avoid at all costs.

Trust your Uncle Venob on this matter. Pipe-smoking and leaf-raking both demand a great degree of patience, and we Type-A's haven't got the time to MESS AROUND WITH ANY STUPID &*%! PATIENCE, SO GET OUT OF THE WAY!

Oops. Please forgive me. I mentioned the P-word and nearly broke out in hives. I'll try not to do it again.

I smoked a pipe for three or four of the 10 or 12 years I spent as prisoner of war to tobacco. Tried to smoke it, that is. Ours was a relationship destined for failure from the beginning.

Dedicated pipe smokers are quiet, calm, collected Type-B's. They enjoy the foreplay of smoking — selecting a pipe that fits their particular mood, packing the bowl with a custom blend, applying a "cool" match, ad nauseam — much more than the hit of nicotine they get at the peak of arousal.

For a closet Type-A masquerading as a pipe-smoker, this is pure torture. We'd rather have our tobacco wham-bam-thank-you-ma'am style.

That's why we pack our pipes like soldiers loading a 105 howitzer.

It is why we torch the bowl to a red-hot coal.

It is why we suck on the stem with the force of two Texas tornadoes.

It is why we then throw everything — all the pipe tools, the pipe cleaners, the exotic blends, the imported briars — into the trash, GOOD %$& RIDDANCE, and run to the nearest convenience store for a pack of cheap-thrill Marlboros.

We have the same problem raking leaves.

If you believe the fiction of Norman Rockwell, leaf-raking is a contemplative exercise practiced in the crisp air of a color-splashed New England afternoon.

Hah! For a born-and-bred Type-A fat boy, nothing could be further from the truth.

We try. Honest we do. We step into the yard, rake in hand, and survey the blanket of golds, reds, oranges and yellows at our feet.

Aaaah, we say to ourselves. What a wonderful, calm way to spend a November morning.

Gently, we flit the rake along the edge of the sidewalk.

Methodically, we subject the tines to the exposed roots and gnarled base of the ancient maple tree.

Sensuously, we explore the flower bed.

It is sooooooo peaceful, soooooo refreshing . . . and then we come loose at the hinges. We run out of patien — AAARRRRGH! I AL-MOST SAID IT! —
and attack the job like a John Deere combine in 40 acres of soy-beans:

Rake-rake-rake-rake-rake-rake-rake!

Must-finish-this-job-for-Heaven's-sake!

Rake-jerk-slash-hack-jab-crash-boom!

If-I-work-real-fast-I'll-be-through-by-noon!

Oh, I suppose there is one saving grace for Type-A's. Raking gives us instant gratification in its purest form.

We drag the tines through a layer of leaves —*grrrrrruuuup!* — and expose a kelly-green swatch of grass.

Another *grrrrrruuuup!* and there are two swatches.

Again and again we *grrrrrruuuup!!* And the front lawn we last saw in September reappears in our wake.

But satisfaction is ever so fleeting. Ten minutes after the last *grrrrrruuuup!* the wind kicks up, and more leaves rain down from the sky. Our brilliant blanket goes undercover once more.

That is why you should never sneak up on a Type-A as he is furiously raking leaves on a windy day and make a stupid comment. Like, "Y'know, you're probably gonna have to do this job all over in a few weeks."

This is a particularly foolish thing to say if you are smoking a pipe.

 # Fall frustrations

How did we get here so quickly?

September 13, 1988

I happened to glance at the toe of one of my tennis shoes the other day. It was speckled with paint.

Millions of tiny speckles, it seemed. Blue. The color of a swimming pool.

My tennis shoes earned their speckles the same day several friends and I "painted" — you had to have seen us to understand what I mean — the walls and floor of our neighborhood pool. When you take a clumsy writer and team him up with engineers, salesmen and homemakers, and then stick paint brushes and rollers in their hands, you are flirting with pigmentatious disaster.

But somehow, we survived. Even more miraculously, the pool got painted.

All this occurred in late spring, back when summer still bristled with promises. Promises that would be broken. Again.

The longer I live, the more I am convinced that summer is nothing but a myth. We plan for summer and dream about summer and yearn for summer to get here.

And then — *poof!* — summer is gone and autumn's chill winds are blowing.

This doesn't happen to children. When you are young and full of faith in such things as Santa Claus, the Easter bunny and summer, the threshold of June is a gateway to infinity. You pass through those portals, confident that at least 3 million years will transpire before school starts, and you throw yourself headlong into the joys of an exciting vacation.

But something happens on the road to adulthood, something very cruel. Summer ceases to deliver the goods like it once did.

Instead of simply enjoying summer, we discover there are more important matters demanding our attention. Hundreds of them.

Or maybe the elements of summer — the stifling heat and killer humidity — are to blame. When you are a child, you are not aware that your skin is grimy and sticky. You go right ahead and play with your friends or ride your bike or hit a baseball and think nothing of it. I'm not so sure that central air conditioning, as much as I dearly love it, hasn't done more than its share to dispel the myth of summer for me.

Even worse is the bogus belief that summer is a relaxing time, a wondrous season of the year when the living is easy, the fish are jumping and the cotton is high. We have made summer everything but that.

We rush through summer like Long Island commuters. We shuffle our children to and from various camps. We take hurried vacations and spend the time fretting about jobs that wait for us when we return. We start a garden and then surrender it to the weeds, rationalizing that our time is too important to waste with a hoe. Besides, we tell ourselves, store prices fall in summer.

And before we know it, summer is gone once again, and we're standing there, wondering what hit us.

I drove by the neighborhood pool a few afternoons ago. The walls and floors were still blue, but the water had taken on a green tint. Since Labor Day is history, I strongly suspect the green tint will grow much darker in the weeks to come.

There were no beach towels or lawn chairs beside the pool. No laughing children engaged in water fights. No daredevils bouncing on the diving board. Nothing of the empty promises I made for having a grand ol' time at this place months ago, back when my shoes were earning their blue speckles.

What's so silly is that I told myself things would be different next year.

Shades of Robinson Crusoe

September 30, 1990

(Venob Verse: The embarrassing story you are about to read is true. My first inclination was not to write it. But I changed my mind after listening to humorist Roy Blount Jr. at the Friends of the Library's Book and Author Dinner the other night.

Blount, who told a tale of incredible stupidity involving a wrestling match between himself and a buck deer — you needed to be there — said writers are somewhat like business executives when it comes to blunders.

Business people get to write off their mistakes for tax purposes, Blount said. Writers, unfortunately, don't have that option. The only way we can write off a bad experience is simply to write about it. So here goes. . . .

And the first guy who calls me Captain Nemo gets it square in the nose, understand?)

None of this would have happened if the September heat wave had continued. As long as my home, my car and my office remained air-conditioned, I would have been perfectly content with those Key West mornings and Saudi Arabian afternoons East Tennessee was experiencing.

But no. The stupid weather had to change. A cold snap had to blow in and make me start thinking great thoughts of autumn.

I loaded my fly rod, a .22 rifle, some grub and an assortment of canned elixirs into my boat and snuck out of town before daylight. I headed for upper Norris Lake with the express purpose of wreaking great turmoil on local populations of spotted bass and gray squirrels.

This is a rite of autumn left over from my outdoor writing days. I am powerless against it. I go through this ritual six or seven times between late September and early November — or as often as I can steal away before some drooler at 208 W. Church Ave. gets wind and starts asking where the heck Venob is.

Norris Lake is deserted this time of year. No pleasure boaters, no waterskiers. Nobody but AWOL newspaper columnists. It's marvelous.

If I take a notion to fish, I fish. If I take a notion to climb a desolate hardwood hollow and hunt squirrels or poke around the lakeshore for arrowheads or stretch out in the grass and grab 4,327 winks, that's precisely what I do.

I do not, however, enjoy this experience so passionately that I beg to be marooned in it while my boat goes floating down the lake.

For that reason, I found myself sprinting out of the forest the other morning, racing across a barren rocky flat and baaaaarely grabbing the S.S. Venob before it drifted into the channel.

I had gone ashore to hunt briefly, you see, and thought I'd pulled the boat far enough out of the water. This was an incorrect assumption.

I had climbed only 75 or 100 yards before a puff of wind came up and tugged at the craft. If I hadn't heard the grating sound of aluminum against rocks and beaten a hasty retreat, it would have been Need Help City.

"All right, fool," I cursed myself at the next hunting location. "Don't just pull the boat ashore. Tie it. You've got a rope. Why not use it?"

So done. And sure enough, the S.S. Venob was securely lashed in place when I returned. I untied the rig, pushed off and prepared to step in.

What happened next remains a mystery.

Perhaps I tripped on a rock or a root. Perhaps I got tangled in the rope. Perhaps my boot caught on the trolling motor cable. Everything happened too fast. All I know is I lost my balance big-time and started to fall, one foot in the boat, one foot still in mid-air.

The human mind can perform brilliant feats of decision-making on occasions such as this. In the space of .0000000001-second, my brain sized up the situation and commanded me to spring back in the direction whence I came.

I obeyed immediately.

The leap was a thing of beauty. Despite an awkward start, it was executed with Olympic grace and strength. And to my great relief, I escaped with little more than damp boot bottoms.

Unfortunately, my brilliant, .00000000001-second brain failed to

remember that every action has an equal and opposite reaction. Which is why the S.S. Venob — minus its good captain — shot straight toward the middle of the lake.

I have never felt so alone, or so stupid, in my life. I was still clutching my rifle, and for a moment the thought of filling the

hateful, (bleeping) boat with holes flirted with my angry brain. Fortunately, sanity prevailed. There was nothing to do but say "pshaw-pshucks-pshoot" and start peeling clothes.

I didn't have to swim, thank heavens. Another puff of wind arose before I got buck nekkid. I had to walk down the bank a distance, but eventually the boat blew in and I was able to continue my Great Autumn Adventure without further incident.

I'll be back in a few days. It takes more than being stranded on an island to deter this kid.

But next time, Natty Bumpo here is packing a cellular phone.

Just call me 'Nub'

October 12, 1989

I was helping my Uncle Nelson install a bookcase several years ago.

It wasn't a particularly difficult job — certainly not for anyone with half a lick of sense about carpentry. All we had to do was measure the inside dimensions of a corner, make a few cuts and nail the whole works into place.

Trouble is, I don't have even a fourth of a lick of sense about carpentry. After several promising starts ended in miscalculation and bent nails, Nelson called a halt to the process.

"Stick out your hands just a minute," he said.

I dropped the hammer — barely missing his foot in the process — and presented my mitts. Nelson studied them intently. Finally he spoke.

"It's fortunate these hands know how to type, 'cause they sure aren't good for anything else."

I didn't have to be reminded. Ugly people know they're ugly. Fat people know they're fat. Geeks know they're geeks. And we of the non-skilled variety know we are klutzes.

Nonetheless, I will be reminded this week. Several times daily.

You see, the Fall Homecoming starts this morning at the Museum of Appalachia in Norris. By the time this popular folk festival closes Sunday night, my hands will be so ashamed of themselves they'll probably hide in the pockets of my jeans until it's time to drive home.

Whittling will be one of the reasons. My hands have never known the joy of picking up a chunk of wood and producing, say, a simple toy. As far as I'm concerned, the mission can be considered a rousing success if there is no blood.

But then I start walking the grounds at the Homecoming and run into dozens of people with whittlin' hands. People like Bill Henry.

Bill picks up a chunk of wood. Casually, he opens his pocketknife. Unlike my situation, there is no need for a tourniquet. With the same effort it takes me to make a cheese sandwich, he carves a replica of an ax stuck in a stump.

Then there is Rick Stewart, the cooper. He turns out cedar buckets and churns guaranteed not to leak water or cream — assuming you are silly enough to actually put his treasures to work.

At least Rick has a good excuse for owning talented hands. His grandfather, the late Alex Stewart, was a master cooper who made thousands of buckets and churns in the days before water was piped from the utility district and butter — honest-to-gosh, cholesterol-laden butter — was purchased in plastic tubs at Kroger.

Those guys are bad enough. But when I come to James Miracle, my hands want to detach themselves from my arms, scamper off in humiliation and wiggle deep into the confines of a leaf pile until the Homecoming is history. Not that I have an inferiority complex or anything.

James makes trays. Bread dough trays, I think he calls them.

Except when you first gaze upon them, they look amazingly like short poplar logs.

That's because they *are* short poplar logs.

But then James takes hatchet in hand and starts chipping off everything that doesn't look like a bread dough tray. And before you can say "How much wood could a woodchuck chuck," James is standing on a mountain of poplar chips, inspecting another masterpiece.

Once, I was tempted to show James I'm skilled with hatchets, too. As there was no kindling to be split, however, I elected to keep the secret to myself.

Besides, I had already given blood that month.

Maybe this year I'll play it smart. Maybe I'll sit at the writers' table all four days and not wander around the grounds to watch craftsmen at work.

Then again, maybe not. This show is too good to miss, despite the envy I must endure. So if you happen to visit the writers' area and see someone from Medic performing a transfusion, you'll know my stupid hands got the better of me and started tinkering with sharp, pointed objects once again.

Fall forward or backward?

October 25, 1988

Hoo-boy. Here we go with that time change business again.

At the stroke of 2 o'clock next Sunday morning, you're supposed to climb out of bed, stumble over the dog, trip on various electrical cords, kick the cat, bump your head, bang your shins, fall down the stairs, and turn all of your clocks and watches — including those fun-loving digital models — back one hour.

Or, if you are a spoilsport prudypants with no spirit of adventure, you can simply crank 'em back before you hit the hay and miss out on a swell time.

However you choose to perform the task, it makes up for the hour that was heisted from us last April. Once more, we will be safely back in the arms of Eastern Standard Time.

It's not that I have anything against Daylight Saving Time, per se. Indeed, the long-afternoon plan has its advantages in May, June, July, August and September.

But April is too early to start it, and October is too late to end it. The Good Lord had no intention of seeing the sun rise at 8 o'clock in the morning. We shouldn't either.

Nonetheless, this idea of toying with the clock to suit our fickle purposes bears further exploration. If an extra hour of daylight is so beneficial during the summer, why not save an extra day all year long?

That's why I am happy to announce Weekend Saving Time.

Presently, our system operates on a series of seven 24-hour days, right? That makes a weekly total of 168 hours.

Under my program of Weekend Saving Time, each week would still have 168 hours. But none of that mundane 24-hours-per-day stuff.

Mondays, Tuesdays, Wednesdays, Thursdays and Fridays would contain only 20 hours apiece. That's 100 hours.

Saturday and Sunday would have their usual 24 hours each, bringing us to 148.

And the extra 20 hours would be a free day!

(If Congress, as a measure of heartfelt gratitude, wants to name it Venobday, well — *blush, blush* — who am I to say no?)

Just think. Every weekend would be three days long. More time for sleeping, more time for recreation, more time for trips to the mountains, more time for anything but going to work.

Already, I can hear the nay-sayers telling me this plan isn't feasible. They say it won't apply to the millions of Americans who don't work a typical Monday-through-Friday week.

Big deal.

They can have, say, Wednesday-through-Sunday at 20 hours a clip. Then give them Monday and Tuesday at 24 hours each, throw in Venobday, and start their work week again on Wednesday. It's so easy, I'm surprised you have to be shown.

This revolutionary concept will be a veritable goldmine for the nation's business interests. Think what a blessing it's going to be for watchmakers, calendar publishers, schedule printers and others who deal in units of time. We are talking billions and billions of dollars. Good jobs at good wages.

Sure, it may cause a bit of confusion at first. Nothing truly innovative comes without a period of adjustment before things start to smooth out. Why, hasn't the switch to the metric system progressed just as slick as silk?

And if it does get out of hand, no sweat. We can always turn the whole program over to the fine folks in Congress.

Surely they can iron out the details of Weekend Saving Time as easily as they have simplified tax codes and balanced the federal budget.

Rushing the season

'Tis the season to make money

November 2, 1986

'Twas eight weeks before Christmas and all through the town,
The merchants were shouting and running around.

"Get moving, you lunkheads!"
They yelled to their men.
"We're about to let Christmas slip by us again!
Thank God Hal'ween candy is finally gone.
It's been on our shelves for the whole summer long.
Let's break out the trees and the tinsel and holly,
And all us wise businessmen sure will be jolly.
Throw out all those pumpkins and black cats and witches,
Then order a new bath of Yuletide sales pitches!
We want to hear cash boxes sing long and sweet,
So unwrap the reindeer and bolt on their feet!
Dust Santa's red nose and then clean out the sleigh;
It's time for big dollars the 'Merican way.
Don't fret that the calendar says it's still fall.
It's time to make money and that says it all!"
Thus, even before golden leaves fell away,
'Fore Election and Veterans and Thanksgiving Day,
'Fore frost nipped the land and the night air grew cold,
'Fore tales of the Pilgrims and Injuns were told;
The town by the river, so quaint and serene,
Leaped from summertime straight to the old manger scene.
But one of the merchants — quite new in the trade,
A young chap whose fortune had not yet been made —
Pondered aloud about rushing the season:
"Would someone please tell me just what is the reason?
I'm still wearing short sleeves! My front yard is green!
This madness beats anything I've ever seen!
We had back-to-school bargains the first day of June.
In July we started the Labor Day tune.
There were goblins in August, and if I remember,
The Thanksgiving specials began in September.
Bikinis in winter and snowsuits in summer;
I tell you, these high-pressure sales are a bummer!"
The other ones snickered and laughed to themselves,
And kept piling Christmas wares high on their shelves.
"He'll learn like the rest of us," one of them said.

"If you want to make money and get 'way ahead,
You've got to have anti-freeze bargains in May,
And the week after New Year's start Valentine's Day."
So let's all bow down to the almighty dollar,
Let's worship and praise it and sing, wail and holler.
No holds will be barred in our race for the greed;
Let's crank up those seasons to jet airplane speed!
And since it is destined that Christmas is nigh —
Let me wish you and yours a great Fourth of July.

Mail-order trees

October 15, 1989

I know it's too early to be writing about Christmas. Nonetheless, this is something that must be done now if you want to avoid the rush.

You need to order your upscale Christmas tree.

The deadline isn't until December 1, but be not lulled into a false sense of security. There is much to do in the meantime. These days, you can't just say, "Tree-schmee, they're all the same," and expect Santa to include your name on his good-guy list.

You need to put on your L.L. Bean slippers, your L.L. Bean sweater and walk into your den. Step off a safe distance from the fireplace where your L.L. Bean logs are crackling beautifully and . . .

Oops, wait a minute. We're going too fast. We're preparing for the season of good cheer and we need to make the best of it. Go back to the kitchen and get down your L.L. Bean drinking glasses. Mix a bourbon and water, light up your L.L. Bean pipe and put some L.L. Bean mood music on the stereo. Then return to the den and take out your L.L. Bean tape measure and figure how much room you can spare between the L.L. Bean coffee table and the L.L. Bean magazine rack for your L.L. Bean Christmas tree.

I am not fibbing. Just when you thought the mail-order empire from Freeport, Maine, had exhausted all possibility of separating yuppies from their money, we have the L.L. Bean tree.

"The nicest Christmas trees we have seen," says the latest catalog. ("Latest" being somewhat vague in this regard, as L.L. Bean ships

2,876 catalogs per week to every home in North America.) "Exceptionally well proportioned balsam fir with thick, full, fragrant branches.

"Each tree individually hand-selected from Maine tree farms for symmetrical shape. Trees are tagged but not cut until order is received to ensure the highest degree of freshness upon delivery. Shipped in a durable, moisture-proof, waxed carton, all care instructions included."

To tell the truth, the L.L. Bean tree isn't all that expensive, given the hijack rates shoppers have come to expect for these things. The regular (64-72 inches) model runs $48. For a large (73-84 inches) tree, the tab is $55.

And it's not like we're still a nation of people who can sling an ax across our shoulders, gather the kids and Lassie and trudge through the snow to the Lower Forty to chop down the family's Christmas tree. For urban Americans, that myth died before Norman Rockwell picked up his first paintbrush.

Still, the idea of having a Christmas tree delivered by UPS leaves me colder than last year's fruitcake.

Maybe there's a solution.

L.L. Bean stands four-square behind the motto of customer satisfaction, right? If you don't like a product, feel free to return it for replacement or refund, no questions asked.

So what happens if L.L. Bean sells 150,000 Christmas trees through the mail — and then gets requests for 150,000 refunds on December 26?

Aaaah. Just thinking about it gives me that warm holiday glow.

Halloween

Buy soon — they're going fast!

October 30, 1987

If you've listened to the radio the last days or visited one of several Knoxville stores, you've probably heard about or seen one of those stupid jack-o'-lantern carving kits. What we have here is the finest example of UMGOMS (Useless as Mammary Glands on Male Swine) I've seen since the holiday season began.

The advertised price is $6, although this close to Halloween, I bet you could haggle and get a buck or two knocked off.

What do you get for your money? A special pumpkin-carving knife, for starters. Also instructions on how to create a jack-o'-lantern. Plus stencils to make sure you do it right and a small candle for the innards.

Please understand that I am a firm believer in capitalism, that I bow to the principle of supply and demand, that I have no qualm with those who would charge money to teach a special skill.

But a jack-o'-lantern carving kit?

Why not charge a fee to teach people how to eat a sandwich? Or enroll children in a special school where they can learn how to whine?

Knowing how to carve a jack-o'-lantern is instinctive in our culture. It's like knowing how to scratch an itch. If a skeeter nails you on the leg, you don't have to read a book or attend graduate school to know how to claw the welt with your fingernails.

What's worse is this business of stencils. Jack-o'-lanterns are supposed to be individuals. God did not intend for them to be mass-produced like vegetative Kens and Barbies. If so, he would have made sure they grew in the same size, shape and color.

On the outside chance there is someone who does not know how to carve a jack-o'-lantern, Uncle Venob is happy to assist.

The first thing to do is spread a newspaper on the kitchen table. (It IS a News-Sentinel, isn't it? If you intend to read instructions in The News-Sentinel and then do your carving on some infidel rag, I'm going to hush right now.)

Next, go find a knife. One with a long, slender, slightly serrated blade is best, but it really doesn't matter. As long as it will slice without excessive sawing and hacking, you're OK.

Cut a hole on top, up there around the stem. (Isn't it handy how the stem grew in just the right place to provide a handle?) Then use a spoon or your hands to remove the seeds and gunk inside.

Caution: This stuff is slimy and looks like orange hair. But it smells great.

Throw away the orange hair, but save the seeds. You can feed 'em to the birds, or else you can toast them in the oven and eat 'em yourself, like one of those health food nuts.

Now comes the fun part: carving the face. If you want a textbook-perfect job, sketch a rough outline of the eyes, nose and mouth on the outside of your pumpkin. Otherwise, just start cutting. Make two eyes (I prefer triangles), a nose (another triangle) and a mouth. (Be sure to include jagged teeth.)

Then go find an old candle, like the one you've been saving since the electricity went out last winter. You won't need it for a few months. Stick it into a small holder, put the holder inside the pumpkin and — *tah-dah!* — your very own, all-American jack-o'-lantern.

There is no charge for this information. Of course, if those six bucks are still burning a hole in your pocket, I suppose I could tell you we have just received a new shipment of that marvelously funny book, "A Handful of Thumbs and Two Left Feet," written by a bright man whose name escapes me at this moment. Six big ones gets you a copy; the autograph is free.

As we are fond of saying down at the Capitalism Club, "Uncle Venob didn't ride into town on the first load of punkins."

Elvira, real or otherwise

October 23, 1988

If there's anything I hate worse than a hunchback who stands straight, a ghoul who smiles, a witch with no warts and an angel without wings, it's an Elvira without bosoms.

That's why I am thankful we have people like Nellie Sue Acuff in our midst. Nellie Sue works at Big Don The Costumier on Central Street. With Halloween just over a week away, she's busier than the census taker on Noah's ark.

"It's crazy now, and it'll stay that way until Christmas," she was telling me. "Everybody wants a costume for some kind of party.

"We keep a photo album of all our costumes on hand. When people call, I ask them to come in and look at the pictures. We want to match their personality with the costume — whether they want to be a saloon dancer, an Arab sheik, a Dracula or whatever."

So what does all this have to do with an Elvira without bosoms? Plenty.

Elvira is the vamp who surfaces this time of year. She's the queen of Halloween, a raven-haired, black-dressed babe so identified with this season of the year that a beer company uses her image for its October advertising campaigns.

The dress Elvira wears — or is poured into, if you want to get technical — is low-cut. Veeeery low-cut.

Given the baggage she asks the dress to contain, keeping the garment up is a marvel of fashion, science or witchcraft. Maybe a little of each. Trust me when I say that any self-respecting Elvira needs to fit the part.

This makes for a real problem when a barely prospective Elvira comes into the store, an Elvira who matches in the personality department but not in physique.

"We also rent fake ones," Acuff said when I pressed for details.

"There was a gal in here the other day who had to use 'em to fill out her Elvira costume. A man was standing next to her, and he never seemed to notice."

That they were artificial, I think Nellie Sue meant to say.

I had called Big Don's and other stores to try to get a handle on the rage in Halloween costumes this year. After chatting with several sales clerks, there seemed to be no definite pattern.

However, it became readily apparent that the business of throwing on a worn-out T-shirt, ripped jeans, Dad's fedora and blackening your face with burnt cork is ancient history. These days, you gotta pay for your play.

At Kmart on Chapman Highway, Ellen Wright said Mickey Mouse and the Sesame Street gang were hot items among the kiddies. For the adults, gorillas were just the ticket. At $60 per.

Over at Hills on Broadway, Melanie Boles reported grown-up trick-or-treaters were choosing between Spiderman, Mr. and Mrs. Devil, clowns and vampires, plus a complete bunny-out-of-the-hat costume. Average price $30.

You can still roll your own, according to Jim Overcast at Target on Ray Mears Boulevard. He said $10 to $15 will buy enough fake hair, fake fingernails, fake teeth and glow-in-the-dark paint to transform any Plain Jane into a work of art.

And if you want to go to frightening extremes, Patricia Dilbeck at J.C. Penney's in East Town Mall can lay a Freddy Krueger mask ($35) and hand claw ($19) on you.

I just hope I'm not at a Halloween party when somebody with one of those Krueger Klaws tries to get fresh with an Elvira in falsies.

One wrong move and — BAAA-LOOOEY!

Election Day

Our sacred right and responsibility

November 6, 1988

I am tempted to say it's all over but the shouting. But since the shouting has been going on all year, perhaps it's best to simply say the end is nigh and leave it at that.

Seventy-two hours from now, the United States will have a new president- and vice president-elect. Then, mayhaps, we can enjoy the remainder of 1988 in relative calm.

Months of campaigning by the two major parties will cease. The need for millions of dollars to fuel these two giant machines will taper off — at least temporarily. Within a couple of years, however, the gears will start grinding again. And by 1992, they will be spinning like never before.

This presidential race has been the most interesting one of my life.

I have seen stronger candidates in the past. I have seen more pressing issues raised. I have seen more passion, more oratorical skill. But never have I watched more closely than when the beast known as Campaign '88 took on a shape and direction of its own.

No doubt part of the reason is regional prejudice. Tennessee had several sons who continued to surface as the months rolled on. We'll never see Howard Baker's name on a national ticket — oops, never say never in politics — but don't expect Lamar Alexander to retire at the University of Tennessee. And by all means, save your Albert Gore buttons; just scratch out '88 and insert '92. Or '96.

Even more so, being assigned to cover both parties' national conventions and watching this spectacle unfold was an experience I shall never forget.

I went to Atlanta and New Orleans as a newspaper columnist. I tried to interview and write as a newspaper columnist. But I freely admit that often, when seated in the crowded halls or weaving across the boisterous convention floors, I gawked like the hillbilly rube that I am.

You can't help it. This is everything you learned in sixth-grade civics. This is your high school American history class. This is World History 1100. And it is happening right in front of your eyes.

Fortunately, I am not alone. Late one afternoon at the Democratic convention, a bunch of us Scripps Howardites were racing the clock at our word processors when Pam Maples, a writer for The Rocky Mountains News, looked up and shouted, "I'm down on the floor, and all of a sudden it strikes me: This is the stuff I used to watch on television when I was a little girl. And now I'm here!"

Sam Donaldson and his big-time TV colleagues would probably laugh. But I suspect they felt the same way once upon a time.

We often hear that political campaigns aren't what they used to be, that today's pretty boy candidates lack the substance of old, that because of television and instant communication, politicians deliver cute jabs at each other instead of delving into the issues.

Indeed, packaging is a major consideration in any campaign. But what else is new?

Politicians are politicians are politicians. They bow, scrape, smile, make promises and try to look appealing in front of the electorate. And they do it whether the public eye happens to be served by an illustrator for Harper's Weekly, a baggy-pants flash photographer with "PRESS" in the brim of his hat or a neatly coiffed newscaster for a major network.

Yet even with all its plastic facades and behind-the-scenes trade-offs, despite its carefully planned media events and orchestrated "spontaneous demonstrations," regardless of the pollsters and analysts who claim to know our thoughts before we even think them, this system still relies on voters. You and me. I have always believed the right to vote is a sacred trust, and now I believe it more than ever.

It's like the air we breathe, easily taken for granted until it turns up missing. That's why I wrote the column a few weeks ago about Michael Lee Thomas, a convicted felon who has served his time and now is fighting to get his citizenship rights restored so he can vote. The next time you shrug off the opportunity to cast a ballot, think about being told, "Sorry, chum. You're not part of us anymore."

It's a weird system, all right. We endure shouting matches, misdirections, questionable choices, false starts, self-serving speeches and, occasionally, outright crooks. But amazingly, the crazy thing works.

That's why I'll be in line Tuesday morning.

Johnny Reb

November 11, 1988

It would be interesting to know what George Coleman might say about his predicament.

Perhaps now, more than a century after the fact, he would find a bit of humor in the situation.

Perhaps he would sigh, shrug his shoulders and tell us it really doesn't matter anymore.

Or perhaps he would be mad as hops. Old wounds can fester forever, you know. George might give us all a good cussing and a sound thrashing, then leap on his horse and ride toward friendlier territory.

Coleman was a captain in the Confederate Army during the Civil War. Company D, 9th Regiment, Kentucky Cavalry, to be exact. That's what his tombstone says. Other than that, there is no known record of his birth date, death date, place of death, his hometown, his peacetime occupation or his survivors.

But the one thing that sets him apart from other old soldiers who have faded away is the unique site of his final resting place.

George Coleman, the Confederate officer, is buried in a Union cemetery. On all sides, he is surrounded by his former adversaries.

"He's the only Confederate soldier I know of who is buried here," says Ramona Vaughn, director of the Knoxville National Cemetery on Tyson Street. "The others are at the Confederate cemetery on Bethel Avenue."

For the record, Capt. Coleman's grave is No. D-2538. It is positioned about 100 feet southeast of Vaughn's office. But at first glance, you'll have a tough time distinguishing it from the thousands of other military headstones.

Only when you look closely do you notice that it is not rounded on top like all the others. Instead, it comes to a point.

"According to tradition, the Confederates didn't want any 'damn Yankees' sitting on their tombstones," Vaughn said.

More than 8,100 bodies — 1,163 of them unidentified remains from the Civil War — are buried at National Cemetery. The known military veterans range from William Campy, who was killed March 2, 1862, to Anderson Sales, a World War II soldier who died last Sunday at age 70 and was interred Thursday. There's also Gen. Robert Neyland, the former University of Tennessee football coach who died in 1962, and Sgt. Troy McGill, a World War II Congressional Medal of Honor winner who was killed in action in the Philippines in 1944.

Not all the graves are filled with veterans, of course. Spouses and younger children of honorably discharged veterans also are eligible for burial at Knoxville and other national military cemeteries.

All of them will be honored today during Veterans Day ceremonies at the cemetery. The program begins with an Air Force flyover and includes the presentation of more than 50 medals to former prisoners of war.

If you happen to attend the ceremonies today, you might take an extra few minutes and wander around the 10-acre site, which is laid out like a wagon wheel. You'll pass by the markers of veterans from Vietnam, Korea, World War II, World War I, the Spanish-American War and the Civil War. These were proud men and scared boys, blacks and whites, officers and non-commissioned, some killed in combat, others who lived decades after hostilities ceased, all linked by the bond of military service to their country.

And while you're at it, take time to look up Rebel Capt. George Coleman. Give him a crisp salute and tell him not to worry, that things turned out pretty much OK after all.

Battle of the bulge

November 13, 1990

When the government of the United States issued military uniforms to Arnold Mullins and Troy Roe, it got the bargain of a lifetime.

Indeed, if Uncle Sam could squeeze the same longevity out of tanks, rifles, battleships, aircraft and other instruments of war, the Defense Department would be the most cost-efficient agency in the history of the republic.

Mullins and Roe were among hundreds of former soldiers who lined Gay Street for the Veterans Day parade. Unlike many in the crowd, however, they didn't have to suck in their guts when Old Glory came by. Both men were wearing their dress duds from long ago.

"It's the same one I've had since the early 1950s," said Mullins, a command sergeant major who served 27 years in the Army before retiring in 1979.

Mullins saw duty in Korea and Vietnam, then taught Junior ROTC in Kentucky after leaving the active military. He is founder and president of the Volunteer State Honor Guard and Hall of Fame.

Roe, 73, a retired milk salesman from Halls, looked spiffy in his World War II-era wool Navy blues.

"Actually, these aren't the ones I had in the service," he said. "I got them right after the war. I'm only 10 pounds heavier than I was in those days — except it's mostly in my stomach."

Roe's secret for keeping vast amounts of excess baggage in check as the years go by? "Walk a lot and watch what you eat."

Army Cpl. George Mathis, a Vietnam vet from Knoxville, had on the same size green camouflage outfit he wore in 1971. But this one wasn't Saigon vintage. Mathis gets new clothes on a regular basis, courtesy the same employer he had then. Mathis, 39, serves full time with the National Guard. He's with the 278th Air Cavalry and is on standby for duty in Saudi Arabia. If the order comes down, he'll switch to desert camo:

"We won't be wearing green. There aren't many trees over there."

Bruce Farr, a 61-year-old construction worker from Claxton, was in street clothes at Monday's parade. He's a trim 165. But as a Marine private in Korea, he was a lean, mean 135.

"I was ammunition carrier for a machine gunner," said Farr. "I hit Blue Beach No. 2 at Inchon carrying more than I weighed: four 20-pound boxes of ammo, a 50-pound pack, my carbine, a 9-pound helmet, plus a full cartridge belt with two quarts of water."

For some parade-watchers, the poundage process has worked in reverse.

Korea-era Marine Robert Blankenship, 63, ballooned to 200-plus at one time. Today, the retired pressman from Kingsport checks in at 135. A heart attack will do that to you.

So will the military regimen. See Lance Cpl. Tim Wade for proof. Wade, 20, entered the Marines two years ago at 155. He's 10 pounds lighter now.

But for the typical vet in downtown Knoxville Monday, Father Time has permitted an extra calorie or three to accumulate around the beltline.

"Sure, I've still got my military weight," laughed Knoxville businessman Ray Zuker, who piloted B-24s and B-17s on 27 success-ful missions over Europe. "It's somewhere inside of me, I just know it. And it's begging to get out!"

Capt. Jerry Taylor, 44, who served with the Air Force in Vietnam, still fits into dress blues. But, Taylor is quick to point out, the present uniform is not the same dimension as before — not even given the liberal truth-tampering former servicemen are allowed.

After all, a man of the cloth cannot lie.

"I weighed 138 in Vietnam," said Taylor, pastor of Ridgeview Baptist Church and chaplain for the honor guard. "I'm 211 today."

Chapter Four

MISTLETOE AND MASTERCARD: IT MUST BE WINTER

GEHRING

You're about to begin the largest chapter of this book. I made it big because there's so much to say about Thanksgiving, Christmas and the other special days of this joyous season.

It's impossible to speak of Christmas without thinking of Santa Claus. Crass commercialism notwithstanding, Santa embodies everything that is kind, caring and generous about this time of year. The innocent wonderment of Santa transcends the ages.

My mother tells of the time she and my father sat me down and tenderly tried to explain the facts of Christmas life. They spelled out who purchased the presents and who put them under the tree.

There was a long period of silence.

"Do you understand, son?" my mother finally asked.

"I think so. You and Daddy do part of the work. But then you all go to bed, and the REAL Santa comes and fills the stockings, right?"

Boy, my folks sure raised a gullible kid.

Thanksgiving

The people behind the scene

November 17, 1989

Since this is the time of year to be thankful, I propose a hearty hip-hip-hooray for the people behind the scenes. They always seem to get left out when the attaboys are dispensed.

Say you're at a fine restaurant, and the experience has been favorable. The prime rib was simply delicious, the best you've ever tasted. The service was beyond compare. Happily, you add a handsome tip to your check and make it a point to tell the waiter to please extend compliments to the chef.

That's all?

What about the dishwasher who scrubbed yesterday's cheesecake from your fork?

Or the laborer who harvested the lettuce and tomatoes for your salad?

Or the builder who took 2-by-4s, nails, drywall, carpet and wire and turned a drab, ordinary room into a beautiful dining hall?

Or the engineer who designed the machine that stamps your American Express card?

(On second thought, strike that last compliment. This time of year, I wish the people who invented credit card machines had sought a different line of work. By mid-January, my mild displeasure with them will have soured into downright bitterness. Nonetheless, I think you see what I mean.)

It's easy to gripe when things go wrong. Easy, nothing; it's the American way! And it doesn't matter if we have plunked down $4 for a screwdriver or $1,200 for a camcorder. If the product turns out to be a dud, we not only expect our money back, we also want a free sample of the item and a hank of hair from the person at the complaint desk.

But what happens when it works properly — which, if we're

honest, is most of the time? Do we ever stop to think about the human(s) whose genius and skill created an item so important to our lives? Usually not.

I got to pondering this a few weeks ago while hunting pheasants in southern Iowa.

If you're wondering how such a philosophical matter could penetrate my brain in the midst of 80 acres of picked corn, so am I. Maybe I'd been walking too long in the sun.

Anyhow, I was carrying a favorite shotgun, a lightweight little fowling piece I have owned for nearly 20 years. It fits me like a sock and is one of the few guns I can shoot with relative accuracy.

This is not an expensive firearm by any stretch of the imagination. Newspaper columnists cannot afford fancy toys unless they happen to be married to the publisher's daughter. Which I'm not.

But as I walked through the corn rows and briar patches and watched the bird dogs do their thing, the thought struck me that I would dearly like to meet the people who designed and constructed the very gun I was carrying.

For all I know, this montage of metal and wood represents nothing more than a 9-to-5 proposition for them. One more unit down the assembly line and don't let up till the whistle blows.

But I doubt it. Several craftsmen surely took pride in shaving a block of raw steel into a receiver and carving a blank of walnut into a stock. And for that I am thankful.

I would like to shake their hands and tell them how much pleasure I have received from their labors through the years. I'd like to sit down with them at the end of the day and take off my boots and sip a cold beer and swap hunting tales.

And I got to thinking that maybe we'd all have a brighter disposition if we took the time to thank — or at least think about — the nameless, faceless people who make such positive influences on our lives.

I missed the next pheasant I shot at with that little gun. Once at close range, twice going away.

Big deal. When it comes to gratitude, the people who sell ammunition must be brimming with thanks for folks like me.

Food for thought

November 28, 1985

"There are two spiritual dangers in not owning a farm. One is the danger of supposing that breakfast comes from the grocery, and the other that heat comes from the furnace." — Aldo Leopold

The late Aldo Leopold was a biologist by profession. More than half a century ago, he wrote the guidelines for a fledgling science known as "wildlife management."

Leopold's bold, new concepts were scorned initially; such is the fate of many a prophet. But time has proven him correct on most counts, especially his theories on the relationship between the quality of habitat and the amount of wildlife it will produce.

In layman's terms, that means if there is adequate food and cover, cottontail rabbits will sustain a healthy population despite the rigors of predation, disease, inclement weather and hunting. Remove the food and cover, however, and the rabbits will vanish, no matter how tightly the other factors are controlled.

So much for Wildlife Management 3100 and the good professor. But whether he was discussing the intricacies of ruffed grouse, whitetailed deer and ringnecked pheasants — or the people who hunted them — Aldo Leopold never strayed far from the subject of the land itself. He knew the quality of life for mankind was also directly related to the land. Particularly mankind's attitude toward the land.

As a nation, we grow further removed from the land with each generation, and that is unfortunate. No, it's worse. It's tragic.

It's tragic because as we shear this bond with mother earth, a bond mankind has known for countless generations, we literally bite the hand that feeds us.

Today is a day for feasting. All across America, millions of families will gather to gorge themselves on turkey and dressing, sweet potatoes and pumpkin pie. They will enjoy this bounty not because there's a supermarket two blocks away, but because a farmer, some-where, still plows the ground and prays for rain.

But how much longer will the farmer be around? How many more American farm families will find themselves skewered by the two-edged sword of rising costs and falling profits? How many more farms will be auctioned? What can be done to reverse the trend?

Obviously, there is no single, simple answer. But as politicians harrumph and haggle over various "rescue" measures, and country musicians sing to raise Farm Aid dollars, and bankers tack up notices of foreclosure, all I can see is the bond linking us to the land stretching tighter and tighter.

It is traditional for families to say a prayer over their Thanksgiving dinners. If you get called upon to do the honors today and can't think of anything to say, let me suggest a few lines I heisted from the Tennessee Farm Bureau News:

"Dear God, please give me the wisdom and patience to understand why a pound of T-bone steak at $2.50 is high, but a three-ounce cocktail at $1.75 is not. And a 50-cent soft drink at the ballgame is cheap, but a 15-cent glass of milk for breakfast is inflationary.

"And, Lord, help me to understand why $5 for a ticket to the local movie is a bargain, but $3.35 for a 60-pound bushel of wheat is unthinkable. Cotton is too high at 60 cents a pound, but a $20 cotton shirt is on sale for $18.50. And corn is too steep at 2 cents worth in a box of flakes, but the flakes are just right at 50 cents a serving."

Now belly up to the table, my friend. Laugh and eat heartily.

Just like it was your last meal.

A reason to be thankful

November 27, 1980

The preacher breathed heavily as he trudged up the woodland trail. Each puff sent a cloud of crystalized vapor into the sharp morning air.

No stranger to the mountains, he. A son of Appalachia, he had wandered all over these steep ridges and through the deep valleys, often with a shotgun cradled in the crook of his arm. For him it was a practical exercise, as well as recreational. Ruffed grouse and gray squirrels were a welcome addition to the table of a family man struggling through divinity school on a mountain minister's meager pay.

But this dawn, the load was less cumbersome. All he carried was a Bible and a book of Methodist rituals.

"Please come bless our house," the young couple had asked him the previous Sunday morning. "It would mean so much to us."

"Bless this house, indeed!" the preacher thought to himself as he walked. "What in this wasteland of worn-out strip mines and logged-over timber could possibly be worth blessing?"

Then he chased the thought out of his mind. There was a job to perform for the flock. If it was important to them, it was important to him. So he pressed on toward the top of the hill.

Their house, the stereotypic logging camp shack, was just as he expected. It was a leaning, two-room affair that clung to the face of the slope like a hairy nose on a witch's face. Two black and tan hounds announced the preacher's arrival briefly, then turned their attentions back to the vermin buried in their belly fur. Other than that, only a cluster of banty hens, pecking at barren ground, hinted of life.

The steps bowed and groaned as he climbed to the porch. But then the door burst open, revealing the freshly scrubbed, smiling faces of the young man and his wife.

He was dressed in his best pair of starched overalls, topped by a faded, but neatly ironed, flannel shirt. A thatch of coal-black hair was plastered to his scalp. His wife, barely into her 19th year, stood silently in her flower-print dress, a dress she had brought to life by recycling flour sacks.

The interior of the cabin was orderly, though sinfully plain. The scant pieces of furniture — a bed, four chairs, the semblance of a table and a cradle for the baby — had been hand-crafted from pallet slats and scrap lumber. Other old flour sacks, in the form of curtains this time, decorated the three windows. The soothing aroma of fresh coffee, warming on the wood stove in the far room, filled the tiny hut.

The wife spoke, breaking the preacher's trance. "Come join us. Have some coffee and a piece of pie."

The preacher had never eaten finer, nor enjoyed such pleasant company. This humble family, with fewer possessions than any he had ever encountered, filled his morning with excited talk about their baby and their plans for the future.

Thoughts of pity raced through the preacher's mind: How can this be? How can they go on this way? Surely they realize how very little they have!

But the hour was nigh. It was time for the man of the cloth to be about his religious business. He read from the book of sacraments. He quoted the proper Scripture. He offered the appropriate prayer. Then he stood to depart.

The mountain boy and his wife were still kneeling around the wood stove. Their hands were clutched tightly together. In the corner, from somewhere deep inside a bundle of homemade blankets, the baby cooed contentedly. The couple finally rose, tears in their eyes.

"Our home has been blessed!" the girl said to her husband. "How lucky we are. Now, honey, we have everything!"

(This column was based on a Thanksgiving sermon by the Rev. Jerry Anderson of Cokesbury United Methodist Church, the young preacher who trudged up that Polk County ridge more than 20 years ago.)

A tale of two turkeys

November 22, 1990

On this all-American day of giving thanks — when gentle feelings of tranquility pulse through our veins, when our hearts beat fondly for all the inhabitants of this orb, when we prayfully beseech higher powers for universal peace, when we celebrate with family and friends over mounds of rich food — let us consider the two turkeys sitting atop the Venable table.

(Three turkeys, maybe. Depends on whether I uncork a jug of distillates from Kentucky. But for the purposes of this essay, we shall limit discussion to the physical remains of birds, not corn.)

One was a wild turkey that formerly roamed the hardwood forests of southwest Virginia. The other was a domestic turkey restricted to the confines of an agri-business cage.

I acquired the wild bird early one morning last spring. I had hunted him off and on for three weeks. Twice, I got close. Close enough to goof something awful. Don't believe urban fairy tales about flightlessness; turkeys whose genes have not been mutated by generations behind screen mesh can shag like a Sidewinder missile.

But the beauty of mistakes is that they teach.

In the three weeks of failure, I learned this bird's habits. I knew his distinctive gobble. I could tell where he roosted. And, knowing just a little about avian biology, I was confident that one day, when the hens he had bred and re-bred all spring were sitting on nests full of eggs, he would do something foolish.

The moment arrived that morning in May.

Judging from the excited gobbles rolling out of the hills, the big tom was alone. And ready. Overdosed on testosterone, he bellowed his intentions at the top of his lungs.

I dropped off the ridge toward the west, crossed the valley and ascended the backside of his knoll. The gobbling continued, uninterrupted, as I sneaked across the crest.

I melted into the base of a white oak tree, disappearing through the help of clothes decorated with tree bark designs. I drew my legs into my chest. I pulled a camouflage mask across my face, rested the camo-painted shotgun across my left knee and stroked the lid of a cedar box call to issue the quiet *"yelp-yelp"* of a lovelorn hen.

Far down the mountain, from out of the pastel jungle of new spring growth, the gobbler thundered back.

I set the box outside arm's reach (the only prevention I know for over-calling) and snugged the shotgun's buttplate against my shoulder. Until ground zero, I could not so much as blink.

Less than 10 minutes later, the bird appeared out of the brush to my left.

He walked a few steps. Stopped. Searched for a source of the yelps. Walked again. He stepped behind a cherry tree, temporarily obstructing his view, and I took the opportunity to swing my barrel in his direction.

When the bird emerged seconds later, I put the bead on his wattles, pulled the trigger and launched two ounces of copper-plated, No. 5 lead pellets into his head and neck. Back home, after I finished cleaning his body, he went into the freezer.

There was no need for tree bark clothing when the second bird was acquired. You don't wear camouflage to the grocery store.

Nor was there a need to tiptoe quietly to the meat department. Or produce an imitative call. Or hold a shotgun motionless. Or pull the trigger. Someone had done it for me.

A lot of someones, actually.

Someone had watched over this turkey since he hatched in clinical surroundings. Someone had programmed the computer that activated his chemical-enhanced diet. Someone had loaded him, feet-first, onto a conveyer. Someone had slit his throat. Someone had run the machine that scalded his flopping, bloody body and yanked his feathers. Someone had inserted a pneumatic tube into his carcass and sucked out his entrails. Someone had weighed his remains, sealed them in a coffin of plastic and flash-frozen his flesh to the texture of granite. Someone had loaded him into a truck and shipped him hundreds of miles to a grocery store, where someone carried him to the meat department and someone checked him out at the cash register and someone toted him to my car.

Which bird enjoyed a better life? Which bird had a chance?

I do not know. Nor will I discuss the matter with hypocrites.

But the first time I encounter someone who eats no meat, wears no leather, lives in a cave, forsakes fossil fuels and slaps nary a mosquito, perhaps we can probe this age-old mystery through earnest dialogue.

In the meantime — a second helping, anyone?

By the numbers

November 25, 1990

U.S. Department of Meaningless, Erratic
    Dumb Details and Lunatic Excesses (MEDDLE)
MEMO FROM: J. Manfred Horsehinney, Director
    Red Tape Division
TO: Mr. Hiram Stringlouse, Obedient Citizen

Dear Mr. Stringlouse:

We at MEDDLE are reviewing your request for permits to send your true love a variety of Christmas gifts.

Although this unique selection of presents is a kind and generous expression of holiday cheer, I must point out a number of problem areas that must be corrected before any permits can be issued.

I will discuss each category in the order given on your application.

A partridge in a pear tree. Please list the genus and species of both the partridge and the pear tree, as well as the name of the nursery (or forest) from which the tree was obtained. Also, indicate the approximate location within the pear tree the partridge will be positioned.

Two turtle doves. Include serial numbers from your state hunting license and federal turtle dove stamp.

Three French hens. In accordance with Article 3, Paragraph 4, Line 6 of the NATO Agricultural Exchange Treaty, a poultry importation permit must be obtained before this transaction can progress. Forms are available from the French embassy in Washington.

Four calling birds. Will these birds be performing classical calls? Jazz? Country and western? Rock? Rap? Please include five (5) copies of lyrics for each scheduled performance. Use additional sheet if necessary.

Five golden rings. List the size of each ring and finger for which each is intended. No funny business about the finger, either.

Six geese a'laying. This gift, unfortunately, must be rejected outright. Because of the high incidence of salmonella poisoning, the Agriculture Department has banned all shipments relating to, or associated with, eggs. (Ova Order No. 6812-S.)

Seven swans a'swimming. Supply the name of stroke(s) each bird will be using. Also include certificates of lifesaving proficiency from the Red Cross or other accredited agency.

Eight maids a'milking. Using USDA Udder Form 38-D, describe breed, vaccination records, projected yield and butterfat content for each cow to be milked.

Nine ladies dancing. The Social Security number for Ladies 4, 7 and 9 were omitted on your original application.

Ten lords a'leaping. Height and weight of each leaping lord (as well as any stand-ins) must be recorded. Also, include notarized statement from certified engineer attesting that establishment in which lords will be a'leaping has sufficient underpinnings.

Eleven pipers piping. As with calling birds, the specific type of music to be played — or piped, as the case may be — must be submitted. Furthermore, include proof of royalty payments to American Society of Composers, Authors and Publishers.

Twelve drummers drumming. In order that equal employment opportunity was afforded each applicant for this job, please send all printed materials, including critique sheets, from the audition. OSHA requirements mandate the use of ear protection devices, to be supplied by the employer, for each drummer.

Due to the immense volume of permit requests reviewed each year at MEDDLE, please understand there may be a slight delay in processing this application. We appreciate your patience.

Say whaaaat?

December 5, 1989

I don't know whether you've noticed it, but everyone wants to change the music these days.

Go to church and see for yourself. You can't pick up a hymnal and find tunes like the choir used to sing when you were a child. That's because we are in the era of gender neuter.

I've never tried to neuter a gender before, but if it's anything like cutting hogs, I want no part.

Actually, I think it means you can't use words like "man" or "woman" or "brother" or "sister" or "mother" or "father" in a song anymore. So don't be surprised when the music director stands up some Sunday morning and asks everyone to join him in a rousing verse of "Faith of Our Persons."

The national anthem is under attack, too. There is a movement going on to change it from "The Star-Spangled Banner" to "America the Beautiful."

As far as I'm concerned, "America the Beautiful" paints a far prettier and more accurate picture of our nation. And it's dang-sure easier to sing.

On the other hand, if "The Star-Spangled Banner" gets the boot, what will George Bitzas do every Saturday afternoon during the UT football season? The poor lad will waste away from lack of work and I, for one, wouldn't want that on my conscience.

Proponents of song changes say it's important to keep up with the times. They say we need to take these steps because people don't talk the way they used to.

And they're right. People most certainly do not talk the way they used to. In fact, they don't talk at all. They interface.

Computers are largely responsible for this tragic situation. When computers were developed, we were told they would save us lots of time, money and work.

Suuuure.

Thanks to computers, Americans have been forced to work weekends just to stay abreast of latest (translation: expensive) software packages.

But that's not the worst of it. Because of the computer disease, our innocent children have had to learn an entirely new language. When I was in the first grade we read, "See Dick run." Kids today are taught, "Observe as Wellington creates delimiters for records in his data base."

It's bad enough that computer freaks and yuppies feel compelled to interface in such a manner at the office. But now they've gone too far. They're starting to mess with Christmas carols.

Someone passed along a list of modernized carols the other day, and I had to reach for my pistol. They might take away my four-wheel-drive pickup truck, but when they start messin' with time-honored songs of the season, it's time to call a halt to the madness.

The author(s) of this list — it was anonymous, with good reason — decided "O Come, All Ye Faithful" won't do. "Move Hitherward the Entire Assembly of Those Who Are Loyal in Their Belief" had a snappier ring.

"Nocturnal Hours when Stillness Is Unbroken" supplanted "Silent Night."

"Deck the Halls" became "Adorn the Edifices."

"The First Noel" was transformed into "The Christmas Preceding All Others."

"O, Little Town of Bethlehem" lost out to "Small Municipality in Judea Southwest of Jerusalem."

And through lyrical alchemy that should boggle musicians from here to Madison Square Garden, "While Shepherds Watched Their Flocks by Night" was wrung out and "During the Nocturnal Hours When Guardians of Ovine Quadrupeds Surveyed Their Charges" took its place.

It's enough to make our nation's forepersons agitate in their places of burial.

At a loss for words

December 16, 1986

It was a cold, snowy night, two weeks before Christmas. I was sitting around the house with nothing in particular to do.

"How odd," I thought to myself, as I stirred some chestnuts that had been roasting on an open fire.

"How can it be this close to Christmas and I'm not in a blind panic? The cards have been addressed, stamped and mailed. My shopping is done and gifts are wrapped. I've got four parties and three open houses to attend next week, but nothing tonight. How on earth can I spend this spare time?"

My first thought was to go walking in the snow. Yes, that's the ticket, I said to myself. Get out there and enjoy it!

You see, for the past few days, with virtually every Christmas card I had written, I had been dreaming of a white Christmas. You know the kind I'm talking about — where the treetops glisten and all that. So I put on my coat and headed out the door.

Jack Frost was nipping at my nose as I emerged from the house. But I didn't pay a bit of attention because my ears were instantly filled with Yuletide carols being sung by a choir. And the people looked hilarious — they were all dressed up like Eskimos!

Then for some reason, I remembered I had meant to buy a turkey and some mistletoe that day, but it had slipped my mind. Wish I had gotten them, for they sure do make the season bright. Ah, but it didn't really matter, because my heart was aglow. I thought back to when I was a tiny tot and how I couldn't have gone to sleep on a $10 bet.

Right off the bat, I noticed how many people there were on the city sidewalks. Boy, were they busy! And I cannot begin to tell you how pretty they were, all dressed up in holiday style. People were passing and children were laughing. It's hard to describe, but there was a real feeling of Christmas in the air.

I left the city, and soon I heard sleigh bells ringing. Sort of jing-jing-jingling, you might say. I glanced over into a lane and wouldn't you know it — the snow was glistening! It was a beautiful sight, and I was happy that night to be walking in a winter wonderland.

I hadn't gone 200 yards when I was gripped by the desire to leave

the lane and take a stroll into the meadow. I talked myself out of the
notion, though, 'cause sure as shooting, I'd want to build a snowman
and give him some silly name. Like Parson Brown. So I stayed in the
lane.

It's a good thing I did, for about that time I heard even more
jingling bells. I turned and spied something my tired old eyes hadn't
seen in a month of Sundays. Yes, sir; it was a one-horse open sleigh.
Hey! It really was.

And what's more, I thought I heard someone call the horse by
name. "Bobtail," if I'm not mistaken.

I thought to myself, "Oh what fun it would be to ride in that
sleigh tonight."

But they went on without noticing me. Shucks. So I kept wander-
ing. And, as is often the case for writers and other deep-thinkers, I
wondered as I wandered out under the sky.

It was a silent night. Almost a holy night. All was calm, and
because of the colorful decorations in people's front yards, everything
was bright. I felt very peaceful by now, almost like I could drift into
heavenly sleep.

I yawned and kept
walking and soon came
to a small stand of
trees. Hollies. They
had ivy growing in
them.

It's against the
law to molest holly
trees, but I could not
resist the urge to cut
off just a few limbs. I
wanted to hang them in
the front hall and also
put a few out on the deck. I didn't worry too much about the forest
ranger. It is the season to be jolly; besides, he's such a merry gentle-
man, he rarely gets dismayed.

It was nearly midnight by now. Clear as a bell. So clear you could have — why you could have even seen an angel if it had dipped near the earth!

But it was time to get home. Back to the busy city sidewalks and all that. I had a big schedule ahead of me the next morning. And, of course, soon it would be Christmas Day.

Later on, as I conspired by the fire and munched a few chestnuts, I was all but bursting with good tidings. So I decided to pour a big glass of cheer.

About that time, the doorbell rang. It was some neighborhood kids. They wanted me to go caroling. I thanked 'em for the invite, but said no.

"Why?" they asked.

"Because I never can remember the dadgum words."

O, Christmas tree! O, Christmas tree!

I-catching and festive

December 7, 1990

Anne Walker says decorating a Christmas tree is the perfect cure for holiday loneliness.

This is particularly true if hundreds of thousands of people — millions, perhaps? — turn out to see your handiwork. And when they leave a message about how much they enjoyed the experience — well, it simply makes the Christmas season come alive.

But I'm getting ahead of myself.

Anne and her husband, Fred, live on the shores of Watts Bar Lake in Kingston. They moved to East Tennessee in 1975, shortly after he retired from U.S. Steel in Indiana.

"We came here blind," she says. "We didn't know anybody. Fred liked to fish, so when we found Watts Bar, we built on the water.

"The first couple of years it was really lonesome. Our boys were grown up, so I came up with an idea to honor the Christ child and also make some motorists smile as they drove by."

What she did was turn your basic, seen-one-you've-seen-'em-all cedar tree on the side of the interstate into a sparkling Christmas tree. And she's been doing it every year since.

You can see for yourself by driving I-40 West toward Nashville. About two miles east of the Kingston Steam Plant, look to your right.

(OK. OK. So how are you supposed to magically know when you're approximately two miles east of the steam plant? That's your problem. Do this: If you cross the lake at the steam plant, you've gone too far. Turn around at the Midtown exit and try again. But trust me; if you're watching the right-hand side of the road as you travel west, you'll see this tree. If you *do* miss it, you're blind as a bat. Or else the grille of an 18-wheeler is welded to your rear bumper and your mind is occupied with matters of survival, or personal hygiene, instead of Christmas trees.)

"It's on state property," said Anne, "but nobody has ever given us any grief about it. In fact, one year we were decorating the tree and someone from the highway department stopped and said they'd been wondering when we would show up. The road crews even trim out the brush and undergrowth for us."

Fred's lost track of how long he and Anne have strung their decorations, but he thinks this is the seventh or eighth year.

"I do know this," Anne said with a chuckle. "I'm 5-1, and when we started, I was able to reach the top. Now, it takes three humongous ladders. I guess that tree is 25 feet tall.

"We've thought about finding another tree, but I hate to abandon this one. It's become an obsession with me. We usually put up the decorations around December 1 and take everything down right after New Year's."

Anne uses many of the same ornaments each year. Some are homemade; some came from stores. Others were left by motorists.

She also wraps a few empty boxes and places them under the tree. But these "gifts" rarely make it through the entire season. Thieves have no regard for the holidays.

"One of the best things about this is the notes people leave. I've got a boxful of them. Some are from local drivers, but we've gotten them from all over. I don't have a CB, but people tell me the truckers talk about it all the time, too."

One note was left by a woman who drove the route daily to take her father, critically ill with cancer, for treatment. The tree meant so much to him, they would stop each day and he would sit up in the back seat and gaze upon the scene.

"It's one of those notes that makes you cry every time you read it," Anne said.

There's no easy or economical way to string lights on this tree. But some day, Anne hopes to put a reflective sign that reads, "PEACE."

Given the international tensions of this precarious era, I hope she doesn't wait too long.

You shudda seen the one that got away

December 8, 1985

Nothing paints a quicker — and more pleasant — mental image of the Christmas season than a fresh, fragrant evergreen.

The tree can be a scraggy 2-footer for the coffee table or a double-wide that stretches to the top of a cathedral ceiling. No matter. Once the lights are strung and the ornaments hung, one is just as beautiful as another.

Like the people who celebrate the holidays, Christmas trees are individualists with histories all their own. Hence, some Christmas tree stories I have known:

• It was the perfect tree, Doug Jett was telling me. Just the right size. Just the right shape.

But there was this problem. Doug didn't have anything to reduce the tree to his possession.

"I had been duck-hunting all morning," he explained. "A few days earlier, my mother had asked me to keep an eye out for a tree. I was driving away from the lake that afternoon and saw it in some scrub growth near the launch ramp."

Doug pawed through the trunk of his car for something — an ax, a hand saw, even a tire tool — to chip away at the base of the small pine. Nothing.

Then he tried bending it over and wrestling it from the ground.

No way, and his temper was beginning to simmer.

So he did what any thinking hunter would do. He shot it.

"I just put the muzzle of my shotgun to the base of the tree and touched 'er off," he said. "Down it came, clean as a whistle."

Like they say, it's the spirit that counts.

• Lots of families make a Christmas ritual out of cutting their trees. But as I was growing up, the Venables' seasonal ritual revolved around the Y's Men's Club tree lots.

For years until his death in 1972, my father donated his time to direct the program for the YMCA. That meant the three Venable boys had plenty of work during the first three weeks of December.

But calling it "work" isn't wholly accurate. Imagine being: (a) 10 years old; (b) surrounded by Yuletide merriment which had not been tainted by the commercial cynicism of adulthood; (c) put in charge of opening dozens of bundles of balsams fresh from Canada; (d) paid the princely sum of 3 or 4 dollars a day.

If the truth be known, I would have traded my weekly allowance for the honor.

Gladly.

• Some years after I joined The News-Sentinel's sports staff, we began a Christmas tradition that continues to this day, despite the fact that our old gang has been splintered.

By "we," I mean yours truly, along with executive sports editor Steve Ahillen, sportswriter Thomas O'Toole (who jumped ship awhile back and now is assistant sports editor for Scripps Howard News Service) and other derelicts who enjoy a good time.

We conduct the Grand Hunt.

The Grand Hunt is the official gathering of Christmas trees for families within the newsroom. Here is how it works:

Staffers tell us what size tree they have in mind. Then Grand Hunters meet at my house. Then we launch my duck boat, the S.S. Venob, on a lake that shall remain nameless. (Grand Hunters are covetous of their Grand Hunting grounds.) Then we sally forth to some overgrown fields I happen to know that border the lake.

Then we cut the trees. Then we drag them back to the boat. Then we load them. Then we ferry them back to the mainland. Then we put them in my pickup truck. Then we deliver them to staffers' houses.

Oops, I just remembered one important part of the operation. Sandwiched between the gathering and the launching and sallying forth and the cutting and the ferrying, we drink large quantities of canned, foamy medicine. There are germs and snakes in those fields, even in December, and Grand Hunters have no desire to take chances.

I only participate in the Grand Hunt because of my love of fellow workers and the joy of holiday spirit(s). Strange as it may seem, a tree is not cut for the Venob home.

Amazing. After a lifetime immersed in Christmas trees, I decorate my own house with a put-together model that comes from a box.

Why?

Our son has asthma, and the real thing gives him sneezing, wheezing, coughing fits.

Jolly old Saint Nick

Santa Sam

December 24, 1980

They don't make Santas like they used to. Perhaps they never will again.

You can find imitations just about everywhere this time of year. Department stores and shopping malls particularly abound with bogus Kringles.

At first glance, they look the role. There's the red suit, the broad black belt, the flowing white beard. Children still sit on their laps and nervously babble the dreams of innocent youth. But that is where all similarities end.

The Santas I have seen lately are skinny — a by-product, perhaps, of the diet era in which we live. Those who do fill out the uniform show tell-tale bulges of pillows. And for a fee, one of Santa's helpers will photograph the tykes on his knee.

Humbug!

Someone forgot to tell the Santas of today about laughter and cheer and joy — freely offered, no price tag attached. That's the saddest part of all.

I have every right to make this callous critique. So do other members of the House of Venob. For we knew the real Santa Claus. He was a teacher, a giver, a specialist at helping others, a friend of youth, the most fair and impeccably honest man I have ever known.

Biased? Of course I am. Any son would be.

What separated Big Sam from other Santas was that he remained a jolly ol' elf all year long.

(Well, most of the time. I've seen him madder than seven hells at his first-born son. When it came to accounting for out-of-bounds behavior, this particular Santa knew all about keeping a list and checking it twice. Thrice, if required.)

But all sins were forgiven at Christmas, and that's when the round man's good will manifested itself in a red suit.

He was Knoxville's official Santa for the Christmas parade.

He entertained dozens of special groups — handicapped adults, Sunday school classes, underprivileged kids, senior citizens, servicemen's families — every winter.

He'd sit in a big sleigh in his front yard four or five nights in December and listen thoughtfully to the wishes of wide-eyed youngsters by the hundreds.

Yet Big Sam never "played" Santa Claus. That's what hirelings were for. He WAS Santa Claus — from the sole of his black boots to his 52-inch belt to his antique sleigh bells to the thunderous *"oooo-hoooo-hoooo-hoooo"* that boomed from beneath his beard.

My old man may have looked like he was acting. People probably thought he was acting. But he truly believed he could hitch a team of reindeer to that plywood sleigh and vanish into the starry sky.

And I'm still not convinced that he couldn't.

Some months before Christmas 1972, the sleigh bells were silenced forever. Not even a happy elf can pile 300 pounds on a 5'9" frame and beat the rap forever. The heart attack was massive. Fifty-seven years were snuffed in seconds.

As it always does, time healed the wounds. Most of them, anyway. No one in the Venob tribe can approach Christmas without fleeting thoughts of yesteryear. Happy memories, for sure, but laced with a lumpy throat, a moist eye.

Every now and then, I put on his old suit and cavort about. And if you'll pardon my bragging, I think I make a half-decent Santa.

Yes, I use artificial stuffing. My waist may be expanding, but I'm a stick in comparison to Big Sam. On the other hand, I can bellow a ho-ho that'll rattle the shingles. Why not? I had the best teacher.

My mother still keeps a file folder of Santa-era memories at her house. It's a ball to leaf through. My favorites are the letters penned years ago by shaky hands, the same hands that now write checks at the grocery store. There's also a mound of cracked photos — posed without charge, I point out — of exuberant youngsters who probably have kids of their own.

And there are pictures of the old man himself: laughing, cutting capers, giving candy canes, living out every holiday fantasy a mortal could possess. I'd give about anything to put my youngsters, Clay and Megan, on his lap for two minutes.

A lot of nice folks wrote a lot of nice things after Big Sam died that sunny morning in June. He was remembered for his contributions to education, to athletics, to environmental awareness, to racial equality, to peace and good will for all of humanity.

But I like to remember him as Santa, the real Santa. A ho-hoing, jelly-belly, eye-twinkling Santa who displayed the Christmas spirit every day of his life.

He left the kind of gifts they don't sell in stores.

You don't (gasp!) believe in Santa?

December 24, 1989

There are lots of reasons to feel sorry for Santa Claus this time of year.

For one thing, he has to spend six weeks in hot department stores — in full dress, no less — and entertain drooling, sneezing, crying, coughing, greedy children by the tens of millions.

If that's not bad enough, his shop is certain to be a madhouse of last-minute activity. Think about it. Overworked elves snarling at each other, reindeer poop on every boot, bicycle chains and doll arms scattered all over the joint, Mrs. Claus whining about the mess. I bet the poor guy drinks Maalox by the gallon.

And then there's The Journey itself. Arrrggh! What a killer.

I've been on some hectic whistle-stop tours in my life, but in my worst nightmare I can't imagine having to slither down every chimney in the land. Not to mention having to do it in the span of a single winter's night.

All that notwithstanding, surely the most frustrating experience for Santa Claus is trying to prove to grownups that he really exists.

Imagine being able to see other people and hear what they are saying, but they can't see or hear you.

Then imagine spending an entire year building Christmas gifts for your friends; but when you make the grand presentation, they shrug their shoulders and say, "Hmmmm. Wonder who did all this work?"

It's enough to turn your hair white.

Fortunately for the big guy, there is still a large contingent of adult followers. They believe in Santa Claus from the bottom of their hearts and souls, and all the logic this side of Socrates will not sway them.

My late uncle, Buck Spencer, was one of these people. After hearing his story, perhaps you'll know why.

It happened a few years before the United States entered World War II. Buck was 22 years old, not long out of school, and into his first full-time experience as a wage earner. Johnson Paint Co. had hired him to work in its Cincinnati office.

Funny thing about us humans. We're creatures of habit. We

always yearn to go home for Christmas, and Buck was no exception. He worked until closing time that Christmas Eve. Then he beat a path to the L&N depot, purchased a ticket and caught the southbound overnighter to Knoxville.

Sure, he wouldn't arrive until early Christmas morning, but what the heck. In matters of holiday homecomings with family and friends, late beats never, hands down.

But as he lay in his Pullman berth, nodding to sleep with the rhythmic clickety-clack below, Buck suddenly bolted upright.

Holy cow! This was Christmas Eve! The first Christmas Eve he'd ever been away from home! The first time he'd never hung up a stocking!

So Buck did what any rational person would do. He groped around at his feet until he found one of his socks. Then he dug into his ditty bag and produced a safety pin. And with peaceful knowledge that all was right with the world, he leaned from his berth and pinned the sock to the outside of the green curtain enclosing his quarters.

Buck has been dead for almost a decade. His children and grand-children are scattered from California to Georgia. But his stocking story is still a family favorite at Christmas. As far as I'm concerned, it's proof positive that Santa Claus is alive and well and prospering in the hearts of all who believe.

He simply has to be.

How else can you explain that when the train pulled into Knox-ville early Christmas morning and a homesick mountain boy arose from his bunk and eagerly prepared to greet his family, he retrieved his sock from outside the curtain — and found three pieces of chocolate candy nestled in its toe?

Santa hangs up his boots

December 25, 1990

NORTH POLE (Snow Job News Service) — Santa Claus, who turned a modest delivery service into the world's largest manufacturing and distribution center, is retiring.

Claus made the surprise announcement late last night after completing his 1990 rounds.

"This probably comes as a shock to many people," said Claus, dressed in his signature red and white suit, "but it's something I've been thinking about for the last five or six years.

"This job gets tougher every winter, and I've finally come to the conclusion it's more than I can manage. It's time to hand the reins, if you'll pardon the expression, to someone else.

"This business used to be simple. Some oranges, a few peppermint sticks, maybe a pocketknife or a cornshuck doll. But those carefree days are gone. Everything's so dadblamed high-tech. If I'd handed out Nintendo games in 1925, the kids would've had me swinging from the nearest oak tree. By the heels."

Trends in gifts notwithstanding, Claus said a near-accident was the deciding factor.

"We were coming over the Smoky Mountains, and I was already way behind schedule. I took a shortcut I hadn't used in, oh, a good 30 or 40 years. Maybe I misjudged the elevation, or maybe the load was heavier than I realized. It could have been that the reindeer were out of shape.

"In any event, we brushed the top of some spruce trees on Mount LeConte, and I don't mind telling you it scared the tee-totalin' eggnog out of me. I let out a Roseanne Barr squall, which caused Dasher to jump. Or maybe it was Blitzen; who cares? The sleigh swerved, and we nearly bought the farm right then. I managed to get it straightened up, but not before we dumped Billy Smith's train and Holly Wilson's bicycle. There wasn't even time to stop and search.

"I hated that for Holly's sake because she's a real sweet girl. It wasn't any great loss for Billy, though. He barely made the nice list in the first place. If he hadn't studied his math last week, and then helped his grandmother bake cookies, it would have been curtains for him anyway.

"So I said to myself, 'Claus, this is it. When you park this buggy tonight, it's over. Better to go out now as a winner than hang on till you drool.' "

Claus also cited acute health reasons for his historic decision.

"I'm not the most physically fit guy on earth," he said, patting his ample belly. "The doc's always on my case. Quit smoking that pipe, he says. Lose weight, he says. Stop lifting those heavy bags, he says. The guy's worse than a broken record.

"I don't have much trouble staying on a diet during the summer, but this time of year it's impossible. I only take one or two bites from each cookie the kids leave for me, but by the end of the night my calorie count's into six figures.

"Oh, and the milk — blech! They pour it into a glass around 8 o'clock, set it by the fire and head off to sugarplum land. You can well imagine how that stuff tastes when I show up five hours later. These kids never heard of brandy?"

Claus' retirement announcement sparked waves of panic and despair throughout this quaint village, as thousands of helpers pondered their futures.

"I hope he realizes what an impact this is going to have on the economy of our community," said Olaf Johannsen, master herdsman of reindeer. "Everybody around here works for Santa. He pulls out and we're history. There must be 750 Barbie doll makers alone. Start adding the GI Joe makers and the Teenage Mutant Ninja Turtle makers, and you've got a financial holocaust."

Some workers reacted angrily.

"Why'd he spring this on us at Christmas, for Pete's sake?" said Sven Shortbread, president of the International Brotherhood of Elves, Local No. 15. "We all busted our buns for him this year, and what thanks do we get? A layoff notice. Not even a 60-day warning. It ain't fair."

Only one person in the town seemed unaffected by the news.

"Is he spreading that old retirement baloney again?" asked his wife, Mrs. Claus. "You'd think people would see through it by now. He's been saying the same thing since Rudolph was a fawn.

"Every Christmas morning, he drags in here and moans about his aching back and swears he's calling the whole show off. He limps around like a whipped dog and begs for sympathy.

"Nonsense. By the middle of January, he'll be back in the toy shop from dawn until dark and all the elves will be complaining about overwork. It never fails.

"Face it. Santa knows he's onto a good thing, and he isn't about to let it slip away. He's got the most famous face in the world, knocks out a couple of million a year from commercial endorsements and gets to travel free.

"Retire? Him? Hah! He's been on a pension his entire life!"

'He looked like Santa Claus'

December 21, 1990

In a busy, bureaucratic world, where names and circumstances of the downtrodden can be conveniently dismissed with the stroke of a computer key, does anyone really care?

Yes. Elaine McGavin does, for one. And I am pleased to tell you how this former Knoxvillian walked the extra mile for a family of total strangers and helped them unravel a 25-year-old mystery.

McGavin — you might remember her as Elaine Jackson, Bearden High class of '72, University of Tennessee class of '77 — has a pretty good handle on the complexities of governmental operations. She is a former FBI agent, is married to a current FBI agent, and works as a medical social worker for Virginia's Potomac Hospital on the outskirts of Washington, D.C.

Recently, a 71-year-old man was wheeled into the emergency room. We'll call him Bill.

Bill had collapsed near his home. He was dead on arrival. He was indigent. He had no family.

In big city hospitals, Bill's kind are a dime a dozen. Just another name. Another statistic. Another body for the county to cremate.

"I had seen this man before," McGavin told me via telephone

from her hospital office. "He had a chronic respiratory problem. He'd been admitted several times.

"He was a kind man. He led a very simple life. He stayed in a rundown trailer and made a little money picking up scrap metal. He had no telephone, no car."

You know what else attracted Elaine to Bill?

He looked like Santa Claus.

"He really did," McGavin said. "He had long white hair and a white beard. He was about 5-10 and heavyset."

Whatever the case, Bill was about to be treated like any other ward of the state. McGavin couldn't bear the thought of it, particularly at this time of year.

"A funeral is something a family takes for granted," she said. "I mean, there's always *somebody* to take care of the details."

Since Bill didn't have anyone, McGavin appointed herself a committee of one. After getting clearance from her supervisors, she threw herself into the task.

"I remember he once told me about serving in the Army," she explained. "My husband is also a veteran. He said if Bill had been in the military, he would be eligible for burial benefits. I started checking with Veterans Affairs and the Social Security office, and the snooping finally paid off."

Among Bill's meager records, she located an old Florida address, plus a wife's name from long ago. McGavin placed a call to the number, certain it would prove to be fruitless.

Not so.

"His wife answered the phone. She hadn't heard from this man since 1965, but she'd never gotten a divorce. He also had a daughter and a son, who are now adults."

As McGavin talked with these strangers, she learned that Bill's wife was a war bride from Italy. She and Bill operated a successful restaurant in Florida for more than a decade.

But in 1965, a member of the wife's family became ill. She traveled back to Italy. When she returned to Florida, Bill had vanished without a trace.

McGavin doesn't know what made Bill leave home. It could have been a flashback from the war, financial woes, domestic troubles. His family never figured it out, either. They had spent years trying to locate Bill but were unsuccessful.

"I can only imagine the demons that must have been running around in his head. My guess is he wanted to go back, but after a while it became harder and harder to do. So he just stayed up here."

Bill's wife and children traveled to Virginia to claim the body and attend a funeral. Through the efforts of McGavin and veterans' officials, Bill's body was laid to rest at Quantico National Cemetery. The presidential color guard from the Tomb of the Unknown Soldier participated in the ceremony.

"It was sad, of course, but at the same time the family was glad to know what had finally happened to Bill," she said. "This closed a chapter in their lives."

Has the experience made an impact on her celebration of the holidays?

"It certainly has," McGavin answered. "I've experienced hardships in my own life, but they seem so trivial now."

Peace on Earth

The impossible dream

December 26, 1983

This peace on Earth business never ceases to amaze me. It's just like the weather. Everybody talks about it, especially this time of year, but nobody seems to find the answer.

Politicians tell us how they have endlessly labored so this miracle can become reality. Military leaders are quick to point out that might makes everything right, that soldiers are the true ambassadors of peace. Clergymen repeat the same story of hope and love and try to make us believe all nations will someday beat their swords into plowshares.

Maybe. Maybe not.

For thousands of years, we have been killing our brothers and sisters. We have killed for food, for living space, to oppress and to banish oppression. The paradox is that in every conflict, all parties involved truly believe their missions are inspired by God. He's always on "our" side, never on "theirs."

Now we stand on the threshold of 1984, the ominous year of Big Brother that George Orwell predicted 35 years ago. Will we be around 12 months later to ponder what '85 will bring? Will tensions be eased in the Middle East and Central America? Will they erupt elsewhere? Will the shouts, threats and boasts between Washington and Moscow ever subside?

I would like to think so. But in truth, I know they never will.

As long as there are haves and have-nots, there will be strife. As long as there is terrorism, people will live in fear. As long as I insist on testing the strength of my right hand with someone else, there will be war, war that could tie a mushroomed ribbon on this speck of galactic dust until the end of time.

We talk of megatons and B-1 bombers, of tanks, Pershing missiles, infrared scopes and all the other play pretties of death. Yet all we really know about them is that they cost billions of dollars and often are produced just in time to be rendered obsolete.

But do we ever stop to think what these things really do?

Their purpose is to tear human bodies apart. They crush bones and rip tendons. They burn flesh. They destroy life.

And what is so frustrating is the knowledge that you and I and 99/100ths of humanity are powerless in the decision-making process.

You will never convince me that the average Ivan-on-the-Street in Russia wants war or that he is a three-headed ogre determined to rule the world. No, he's just an ordinary guy like me, with a wife and kids and more belly and less hair than he prefers.

His form of government is different from mine. So are his economy and his speech. But he merely asks of life what we all do. He wants to hear his babies laugh and be able to stick around to see his grandchildren and die in peace.

So tell me why his chiefs and my chiefs, who surely hold those same hopes and dreams for their own families, keep putting chips on their shoulders and daring each other to knock 'em off?

Perhaps it doesn't have to be this way.

In 1968, the Tasaday tribe was discovered in a remote, mountainous section of the Philippines. Amazingly, these people are still living in the Stone Age. They eat roots and grubs. They cook and warm their bodies over fires ignited with a friction drill. By our standards, they are almost apart from the human race.

But consider this interesting fact about the Tasaday: In their language, there is no word for fighting. Or for enemy. Or weapon. Or bad. Or ugly.

Here are the most primitive of people on the face of this earth, yet they live in an atmosphere of peace and understanding that transcends the ages.

It all came crashing home to me one day last summer, when we stopped in Chattanooga on the way back from vacation.

The kids had never been to Lookout Mountain, so we took a cable car up the slope. On top, National Park Service employees told us about the Civil War battles fought along these steep ridges. We looked at the war memorials and statues. I had seen these, and others just like them, many times before.

Then I walked to an overlook and peered down to the Tennessee River and the city along its shores. The world was green, bristling with life.

But just over a century ago, this was a burned-over, battle-scarred, hellhole of a place. There were moans and screams, the roar of cannons, the acrid bite of black-powder smoke in the air. Not the stuff that goes away when a director yells "cut!"

I left the overlook and went downhill to the Ochs Museum and looked at photos made during the fierce battles of Chattanooga and Chickamauga. I didn't see any proud soldiers or hear the spirited refrain of "When Johnny Comes Marching Home."

Instead, what I saw were the gaunt, scared faces of boys. These were someone's sons. They were fathers, nephews, brothers, uncles. Each face reflected that same hollow, terrified stare we have become all-too-familiar with — whether from Shiloh or Normandy, Bataan or Hue, St. George's or Beirut.

Whenever hostilities break out, government bookkeepers tell us how many people are killed. But all the military experts and physicians on this globe will never know how many Einsteins die in these encounters. Or how many Henry Fords and Jonas Salks are destroyed before they can touch the world with their genius. Or how many great thinkers and peacemakers return to dust before their time.

The thoughts and images from Lookout Mountain burned in my mind throughout the day and into the night. Even at breakfast the next morning, I could not shake them.

That's when I opened a copy of The Chattanooga Times and read where President Reagan was rattling swords with Khadafy and double-dog daring him to make another move. El Salvador and Nicaragua were about to burst at the seams. At the same time, 10-year-old Clay was pulling on my sleeve, reminding me I had promised to stop at the next store so he could spend his vacation money for a model of GI Joe.

And I just got to wondering if we ever learn a damn thing.

A message from the past

December 23, 1990

In May 1864, Union and Confederate forces clashed near the North Anna River in Virginia. It was not one of the major turning points of the Civil War.

The federals abandoned their effort after four days and moved on to other campaigns. One source lists 642 killed and wounded; another simply says the number of casualties was equal on both sides.

But whether they are sketchy or detailed, there is an inherent problem with cold battlefield statistics. They cannot describe the pain and the loneliness of those involved, the longing to be with their loved ones so very far away.

Soldiers know these emotions all too well, for they have seen the horror firsthand. They have heard the screams and felt the wounds and tasted the blood of their comrades.

One of those injured at North Anna was Pvt. George Cramer, a member of the 11th Pennsylvania Volunteers. His left arm was shattered by enemy fire, and he spent months in recuperation.

In some respects, Cramer was lucky. The standard treatment for limb injuries in the Civil War was amputation. But some surgeons had begun to tinker with the notion of salvaging body parts, and Cramer was among the guinea pigs.

The ultimate effectiveness of his treatment is debatable. All his descendants know is that George Cramer, a tailor by trade, died several years after the war of complications from the old injury.

But one thing remains. Cramer's letters to his wife, Mary, have been handed down, generation to generation. They are now owned by his great-great-grandson, Martin Gehring, the talented News-Sentinel cartoonist who works his magic four times a week beside my columns.

Martin has spent the last few months transcribing these letters to a word processor. He hopes to compile them into a series for his family.

But I've asked him to share Pvt. Cramer's 1864 Christmas letter with all of you. Perhaps it may help shed some insight on the Mideast nightmare that could be triggered within a month:

Mount Pleasant Hospital
Ward 2
Washington, Dec. 22, 1864

Dear wife,

Next Sunday we will again be called upon to keep in memory the coming of the Prince of Peace. But alas, it is not so with us. Men still stand in Hostil Array, ready to strike destruction to men who they are commanded by him who preached mercy and gives Salvation to love as thyself.

Again is our National Counsel in Session, but there is no sign of their delibaration of conciliation, but strife to the bitter end, heedless of devastation, deaf to the Cry of the Stricken, blind to the Suffering of broken up Familys, not heeding the widowed mothers surrounded by wanting little ones. Still the cry is three hundred thousand more. More war is the watchword, both North & South.

This, I suppose, you rather think is discomforting congratulation of Christmas. So it would be if we only look at the action of man.

But there is a higher Power, a more kind & more merciful Ruler than man for whose protection and care we can & should be thankfull, allthough we have felt the Evils of War to some extent.

But when I look around, look over the past, I must acknowledge that we have been favored above what we could command. I do not deny that when I think how I will return to my Family, it makes me feel sad sometimes, but then again, knowing it might be worse, it is encouraging to trust in God's Care for the Future.

Having said this much, and being assured you respond to what I expressed, I will say a happy Christmas to you all, wishing you will kiss my little ones for me. I for my part will try to feel as happy as possible under the hope that I may return ere very long to stay for good with those who are near & dear to me. In the meantime, I will say God bless you all & will close with my Love.

Your affectionate Husband,
George Cramer

As we approach Christmas 1990 and the United Nations' January 15 deadline for withdrawal of Iraqi troops from Kuwait, I cannot help but wonder how many American service personnel are writing Christmas letters to their own families.

And I pray no newspaper columnist 126 years from now will be using those letters to describe the pain, despair and suffering our fighting forces experienced in the last decade of the 20th century.

Mysteries and miseries

December 13, 1990

CALHOUN, Tenn. — The haunting refrain from Glen Campbell's "There's No Place Like Home, Especially Christmas Eve" had barely faded from the radio yesterday morning when I rolled to a stop at the site of the worst traffic accident in Tennessee history.

It was a stinging, sobering moment. Perhaps the most cruel twist of coincidence I have encountered in 23 years of writing.

For the families of more than a dozen motorists who died on Interstate 75 in a fog-shrouded, 80-vehicle, chain-reaction inferno, Christmas will forever be linked to sorrow. Despite the healing effect of time, it will be impossible for them to separate the holidays from the horror.

Be that as it may, the future will have to take care of itself. The pressing task right now is identifying the victims and contacting their loved ones. It is a grisly mystery, compounded by the scarcity of clues.

"Thirteen bodies came here," said Dr. Iris Snider, McMinn County's acting medical examiner, as she stood near the makeshift morgue at Jerry Smith Funeral Home in Athens. "Four had enough physical features for positive identification. It's going to take more time for the others."

Teams of specialists from the FBI and the Tennessee Funeral Directors Association were literally piecing through the remains yesterday afternoon.

"The most frustrating part is we don't have an exact victim list to work from," said Knoxville mortician Jerry Griffey, a member of the funeral directors' disaster response team. "If this was an airplane crash, for example, you would have a pretty good idea of who was on board. But these people could have come from anywhere."

Indeed. By noon yesterday, an estimated 600 frightened, anxious callers had contacted the funeral home. Many more were expected to telephone overnight, as worried people around the nation checked to see if their relatives are among the victims.

"They're calling from everywhere," said Snider. "Knoxville and Chattanooga, of course, but also all over the East — from Ontario to St. Petersburg, Fla.

"We're encouraging people to get hold of us, but we also want to know if the person they're calling about eventually shows up. Until then, we have no way of knowing if they're still a potential victim."

Because many of the bodies were burned beyond recognition, Snider is asking families to provide as much background information as possible: "We need any clue — jewelry they might have been wearing, dental records, any type of surgery that would have left a metal pin or plate inside the body."

Back on the interstate, orange-vested crews from the Department of Transportation were alternately shoveling and sweeping the last bits of smoldering debris from what used to be asphalt on I-75. A grader rattled along the battered pavement, leaving a line of rubber, glass, wire and other auto parts in its wake. As soon as the path was cleared, dump trucks began spreading sand to absorb motor oil, gasoline and diesel fuel. The air reeked of burned cargo.

"As soon as the rest of the cars and trucks are removed, we can start repaving," said Tom Collins of Cleveland, area superintendent for the state agency.

Removing these vehicles? That's one thing. Identifying them is another.

I walked around the mounds of charred, twisted rubble for more than an hour yesterday morning, and I'm still not positive I could tell you if some pieces belonged to cars, trucks or buses. Many were simply burned-out hulks of metal.

One, however, was distinctly a pickup truck. It bore North Carolina plates. Nothing burnable remained; no tires, no dashboard, no seats. The entire chassis was warped, perhaps as much from heat as impact.

Rounding the rear, however, I did spy one fragment of organic material. And the rush of emotion it brought forced me to turn away.

All that remained in the pickup's burned-out bed was the blackened trunk of a Christmas tree.

Christmas in Vietnam

December 25, 1988

Lonnie Daugherty will not be having ham and lima beans on saltines today, thank you just the same. Nor will he be eating his meal while crouched on the hood of a flatbed truck loaded with hundreds of thousands of rounds of small arms ammunition. Other than that, he's not too picky.

"You had to sit on the hood," Daugherty recalls of that December day in 1968 near Ninh Hoa, South Vietnam.

"You didn't dare step out onto the road or into the ditch. Not even to use the bathroom. You never knew where a land mine might be."

So he squatted atop the truck and wiped the sweat and red dust from his face and opened his C-rations. Then his convoy continued its journey to resupply infantry units.

Somehow, it didn't seem much like Christmas Day.

Oh, officially a cease-fire was in effect. A full 72 hours' worth of cease-fire. That's what the Army was saying. That's what the TV commentators were telling the folks back home, too.

Now tell it to the grunts.

"Cease-fire?" they chuckle with a quizzed expression. "What cease-fire? Christmas was just another day."

Ask Dale McCoy about the Christmas cease-fire of 1969. He'll tell you how several of his buddies were wounded in an enemy grenade attack near Pleiku.

Or talk to Jim Obenschain, who spent his 1967 Christmas cease-fire filling sand bags for bunkers near Da Nang while snipers spat terror from afar.

Or Dan Weirich, who worked late into the night of Christmas Eve 1969 setting up a listening post near Xuan Loc.

Or Kent Rowland, whose platoon was socked in by fog and rain in Quang Tri province during the Christmas cease-fire of 1969 and was forced to wait nine days for resupply.

"You never trusted the Christmas truce," Rowland says. "It was a very unpleasant time. That may be one of the reasons I still get real depressed this time of year."

"You were always lonely and homesick in Vietnam," says Mark Baldwin, who found himself in the jungles north of Saigon during the cease-fire of 1966. "But Christmas was the worst. I was desperately homesick. I never wanted to be home so much in my life.

"I had two months of duty before I returned to the States. My mother left the tree up at her home. On March 1, we finally celebrated Christmas."

A lot of crazy things happened in that crazy war, Christmas Day notwithstanding. And I don't mean to mess up your holiday by starting things off in such a downer mood.

But amid the festivities today, along with the singing and dancing and feasting and toasting and worshiping and praying and greeting old friends and exchanging gifts and all the other trappings of this most wonderful and joyous moment, I wish we would all pause long enough to remember the men and women who once suffered through the mockery of a "cease-fire" in a hellhole halfway around the globe.

Merry Christmas, my friends. God bless you every one.

A Handful of Helpful Holiday Hints

November 25, 1988

Today is the official start of the Christmas shopping season So let's flex those billfolds and whip out those credit cards and go out there and act like Americans!

I have been a full-time Christmas shopper since, oh, about 1955 or 1956. That's more than 30 years of pushing and shoving, hassling and waiting, stomped feet and sore backs and other delightful pleasantries of the season.

With such vast experience under my belt, I'd like to give you an early present by outlining a few rules of the road.

A Handful of Helpful Holiday Hints, as it were.

RULE NUMBER ONE: No store will have the size and color of merchandise you want. This is an iron-clad truth of Yule shopping, and the sooner you accept it the better.

If you wish to buy a brown coat for Cousin Roy, the midget, all you will find are XXLs in green and orange.

Disgusted, you go back to the same store the following day and try to buy a coat for Uncle Jim, the giant, who is partial to green.

Sorry. Sold out.

RULE NUMBER TWO: If *(chuckle-chuckle)* you do find an item to buy, you will wind up in the longest line at the checkout.

It matters not that there are only three people in front of you, and the other lines stretch past the pantyhose display and spill into kitchen appliances.

The first person will spend 22 minutes, 37 seconds fumbling for an ID.

The second will forget something and beg the clerk to hang on "just a minute."

The third will be carrying a sick child who screams, between spit-ups, like a tortured prisoner.

And when you finally advance to the cash register, five new checkout lines will open.

RULE NUMBER THREE: Even though a store continues to run advertisements about a particular product throughout the Christmas season, it will be out of stock until March 23.

At the earliest.

RULE NUMBER FOUR: So you're going to skip the mall madness and shop by catalog?

Ha!

Your gift will wind up being back-ordered for six months or, if

readily available, mailed to a similar address two states away.

What's more, the $15.75 purchase you made will be listed on your credit card account as $15,750. When you call long distance to complain, you will be put on hold till the telephone receiver melts in your hot little hand.

RULE NUMBER FIVE: If, through some fluke of fate, you actually purchase a suitable gift and make it home without being trampled, you will never — repeat, never — be able to wrap it as pretty as they do in the store.

In less than 60 seconds, a professional paper paster can reduce an eight-dimensional object to a gold-gilded, fancy-ribboned work of art.

An amateur can spend two hours trying to wrap a book, a box of candy or a deck of playing cards and it will still end up looking like it fell off a garbage truck and was run over by a tractor.

Trust me.

Tacky gifts for tacky people

December 11, 1990

An outbreak of sexual inequality erupts across this country each December, and I say it's time Gloria Steinem, Democrats and the ACLU launched an investigation.

You'd think we would know better by now. You'd think the consciousness of America had risen to a higher plane. You'd think we had moved beyond stereotypes based on gender.

Apparently not.

I make this accusation after learning that electric razors are stronger than ever on the Christmas gift market.

According to a recent article in "Advertising Age" magazine, the four leading shaver companies — Norelco, Remington, Panasonic and Braun — will spend an estimated $70 million on commercials during the 1990 Yule season. That's a 30 percent jump from last year. And it translates into a giant batch of ink and air time just to convince the Missus that Mister Big needs a new razor to hone the wire edge off his chops.

Oh, sure. I know what the shaver companies say. They say their products are designed for women, too. And, in truth, some ads do casually mention that the Shaverooski 007 is gentle enough for a lady.

But tell me this: How many commercials show Mrs. Claus scraping her legs or armpits with the Shaverooski 007? I rest my case.

You know and I know who they're *really* after. They're after us men. To those mega-billion corporations, men are nothing more than fleshy faces festooned with fuzz. They couldn't care less about our minds.

But that's not the worst of it. A razor is a tacky present for a man OR a woman. It's a subtle way of saying, "Shew! Do you ever need fixing up! That skin of yours is like 100-grit sandpaper. Take this thing and go into the bathroom and don't come out till you there's been a vast improvement!"

If personal products like razors continue to be socially accepted as Christmas presents, I shudder to think what's next. Mouthwash, mayhaps? Underarm deodorant? Toilet tissue? Nose hair clippers? Air freshener? Wart removers? Dental floss? Hemorrhoid ointments?

Yuck. Gag me quickly with an extra-large spoon.

Give us a break, Madison Avenue. Please promise us our worst holiday nightmare won't turn out like this:

"Merry Christmas, darling. I hope you like my present."

(Rattle-rattle. Unwrap-unwrap.)

"Oh, John! A two-gallon bottle of Scope! How utterly kind of you. It's what I've always wanted. But you shouldn't have; I mean, this stuff costs so much . . ."

"Cost is never a consideration with your Christmas present, my angel. I know how much you need this Scope. Why, my eyes are watering already. So skip on over to the sink and lavish yourself in all its glory."

"I will in just a minute, sweetness. But first, you must open my gift to you."

(Rattle-rattle. Unwrap-unwrap.)

"Yeeee-ooooo! A two-month supply of Charmin!"

"Do you like it?"

"LIKE it? Whadaya mean LIKE it? Honey, I LOVE it! I can't think of anything I'd rather have from my true love on Christmas morning. Why, I've been dropping hints about this since Thanksgiving."

"I know, you sneaky devil. It was that wonderful night when we were in Kroger. We were walking hand-in-hand through the household paper supplies and you started whistling 'Here Comes Santa Claus.' I knew exactly what you were thinking."

"Gosh, I'm so lucky to have a thoughtful wife like you."

"And I'm lucky to have a caring, sensitive '90s guy like you."

(Smooch-smooch-smooch.)

Aaaargh! The thought of such madness makes my stomach absolutely boil with acid.

But relief is on the way. All I gotta do is find the holiday decanter of Maalox that Mary Ann gave me last Christmas, and I'll be back in the pink before you can say "Jacob Marley."

Mice? How nice!

December 26, 1989

Even without the benefit of pre-season peeking, Lillian Waggoner knew what to expect for Christmas this year.

So?

Lillian knows what she'll find under her tree next Christmas, too. And the next and the next. And the one after that.

Oh, there might be a surprise box of candy somewhere along the line. Or hand lotion, a sweater, a book, scarves, perfume or any of dozens of other traditional gifts. But there is one thing she can always count on.

Mice.

You heard me, cheesebreath. M-i-c-e.

Well, not real, live, twitchy-nosed mice. These are mice replicas. Dozens of them. Mice on the Christmas tree. Mice on the knicknack shelf. Mice on top of the dresser.

"I've got so many, I've never stopped to count," Waggoner says. "It's mostly my daughters who give them to me, but the sons do, too."

Should one of the kids forget, no problem. There's always some-body else in the tribe of Waggoner to take up the slack. We're talking about a woman with seven children, seventeen grandchildren and eight great-grandchildren. They can account for a lot of mice.

This bizarre holiday tradition began many years ago. It was one of those things Lillian would just as soon forget.

"There's only two things on this earth I'm afraid of — snakes and mice," she said. "I was sittin' in my living room one night and saw this little mouse go running into the bedroom. It scooted under the bed.

"Well, sir, I went in there and put on my gown and sat down on the side of the bed, thinking that little booger would come runnin' out. But he didn't.

"Oooooh, it worried me a lot! I could just imagine him jumping into the bed when I was sleeping. So I yelled to my youngest son, Steve. He hollered back to take a broom to him."

What followed were three nights of mayhem, the likes of which could prompt a visit from the ASPCA.

"Normally, I'm soft-hearted," Waggoner said. "I wouldn't hurt a flea on a dog's back. But I meant to get rid of that mouse. I chased him all over the house with a broom. I even tried pouring hot water on him. I slowed him down some but never did kill him."

Finally, the pesky rodent was seen no more. Waggoner assumed she had won.

"I'd either scared him out of the house or else he was dead."

Nope. When one of Waggoner's daughters was visiting a couple of weeks later, the varmint showed up again.

"Linda saw him and went to hollering at me. I came into the room, and there he sat between the coffee table and the oil heater. I touched him with the toe of my slipper, and he took off again. Larry, my son-in-law, grabbed a wastebasket and smashed it down on him. At last, he was dead."

Normally, this would be end-of-mouse, end-of-story. But Waggoner's kids kept teasing her about the mighty quest. And when Christmas rolled around that year, a mouse ornament showed among her presents.

That started it.

"They've given me so many over the years, I've started naming some," Waggoner said. "There's the mouse with an apron who sits by the sink. I call her Rosie. Sandy (another daughter) crocheted one. Its name is Luella. Then there's the mouse with great big ears: Smiley."

Lots of the Waggoner clan will be visiting over the holidays, so there's no telling what additions will be made to the mousery. But one thing's for sure: the Real McCoys are still not welcome.

"Ever since this thing began, I've kept a baited mouse trap by the stove," Waggoner said. "Never have caught anything in it, but I always keep it handy."

Dollars and scents

January 7, 1988

We have just finished the smelliest season of the entire year.

No, I'm not talking about evergreen and peppermint. Those have been throw out or eaten, respectively, and shan't surface again for another 11 months.

The scents I refer to are the ones that come packaged in bottles.

Little fancy bottles stamped with high price tags. You know — the perfumes, aftershaves and colognes given and received for Christmas.

I don't know if anyone has ever taken the time to do the calculations, but I'll bet Americans buy thousands of gallons of smell-good each year. Fortunately, most of it is shipped to Aunt Bertha and Uncle Horatio who live in Boise. It's safe for them to remove the cork and splash on freely because the only living things within 10 miles are elk. And the elk love it.

But no matter how offensive or delightful the solutions may smell, I am amazed people buy any of the stuff after glancing at the name on the label. This is especially true of men's cologne.

The purpose of a fragrance is to attract/please/excite the opposite sex, right? So why would a guy want to shoot himself in the foot by wearing an after-shave lotion named along the lines of Fish Factory, Diesel Dump Delight or Armpit?

Don't take my word for it. Go to the fragrance counter of any department store and see for yourself. You might be gripped by the same thoughts I had when I gazed upon such honest-to-gosh products as:

Chaps — This stuff is supposed to smell like a cowboy's pants, for Pete's sake? I'd just as soon use Trigger Sweat, thank you.

Adidas — Aaaak! A tennis shoe? C'mon, please tell me this is someone's idea of a sick joke. On the other hand, perhaps it's just the ticket for people with a foot fetish.

Brut — This is what every woman wants? A goon with 5 o'clock shadow, a ketchup-stained undershirt and a 10-cent cigar clenched between his teeth? Suuuuure.

Stetson — Look, I wanted something to splash on my face after I shaved, not put on my head to keep out the sun and rain.

Canoe — One time I left a rainbow trout, a pair of wet socks, a dozen nightcrawlers and part of a sardine and mayonnaise sandwich in the bottom of my canoe. I found them three days after they started to bake in the August sun. Now some fool wants me to pay $12 for a tiny bottle of solution so I can be reminded of that wonderful occasion every morning?

Royal Copenhagen — I refuse to believe this is cologne. It sounds more like some fancy brand of snuff dipped by kings, princes, lords, dukes and bishops.

Polo — Back to the horses again. Thanks but no thanks. Not only does Trigger Sweat smell better, it's not nearly so expensive.

Musk — Apparently nobody who manufactures, sells or uses a musk-based fragrance has ever skinned a skunk, muskrat, mink or any other beast possessed of a musk gland.

If it takes the aroma — I use the term loosely — of musk to excite the little lady, I'll settle for a vow of celibacy.

Out-thinking the other guy

December 14, 1986

Cheeseburger & Chips, the woman sitting next to me at the cafe, had a problem.

"I asked my brother what he wanted for Christmas," she was saying to her companion, Chef Salad/Thousand Island. "He said a warm-up suit. Black. It had to be black. And it had to be a certain brand."

Cheeseburger & Chips named the brand, but it's not important to this discussion. So we'll just keep it generic.

"I went to the mall and started shopping," she continued. "You know how much they were?"

"No," Chef Salad/Thousand Island answered.

"Ninety-nine dollars! For a warm-up suit! I was figuring they'd be $40, maybe $50 at the outside."

"So what did you do?" Chef Salad/Thousand Island asked.

"Two things," replied Cheeseburger & Chips. "First, I kept shopping till I found the lowest price. Eighty-nine bucks. I hated to spend that much, but that's what he said he wanted, so I bought it.

"Then, I called my mother and told her how much I had spent. I told her the next time she saw my brother to casually mention how much money his present cost. I want to make sure he spends the same amount on me."

"Reckon it'll work?" Chef Salad/Thousand Island said.

"It better," said Cheeseburger & Chips. "I'm not about to fork over $89 for his present and then have him give me a set of el-cheapo earrings, the kind that turn green in three weeks."

I was tempted to leap to my feet and give Cheeseburger & Chips the Chamber of Commerce Giver of the Year Award. But then I noticed how deftly she handled a knife when carving her cheeseburger and elected to remain silent. It didn't matter anyway, for she and Chef Salad/Thousand Island began conversing about their work, and I heard no more talk of Christmas giving and getting.

But the discussion did start me thinking about how the exchange of gifts has been honed, fortunately or otherwise, into a fine art.

Even if your heart fairly glows with the spirit of the Magi, even if you live by the theory of it's-the-spirit-that-counts, even if you would never measure friendships with a monetary rule, it still is possible to find yourself in an embarrassing situation at Christmas.

You know what I'm talking about. In fact, you've probably been there before: You've just handed a friend a gift pack of Life Savers (including exotic flavors like wild cherry, butter rum and Pep-O-Mint), and your friend returns the honor with a sweater.

A wool sweater.

An imported wool sweater, no less.

Complete with your monogram.

This is not the time to panic, my friend. Instead, you've got to save all your energies for quick thinking. You need to chuckle confidently and say something like, "The fruit flavors in these Life Savers are only a table of con-tents. Your real Christ-

mas present will arrive all year long. You see, I signed you up for Fruit of the Month."

Or you might try this: "Drat the luck! UPS still hasn't shipped your present, so I got these Life Savers as a symbol. I've ordered a set of custom-made life jackets for you and the kids. You know, lifesavers — get it?"

Of course, this means you must then dash out and sink a small fortune into a Fruit of the Month membership or a set of custom-made life jackets. One-upmanship is not cheap, particularly at the 11th hour.

But just remember. Never let 'em see you sweat.

Out with the old, in with the new

Extending the fun

December 26, 1986

Welcome to the saddest day of the year.

All those pretty papers and ribbons have been stuffed into the garbage can. The shiny new toys are neither shiny nor new, and their batteries have long since run out of steam. The tree, which only a few days ago stood tall and majestic in the living room, now looks as forlorn as a wet dog.

Sound familiar? Of course, it does. What we have here are the raw materials for a super-duper dose of the post-Christmas blues.

It's typical of The American Way, I guess. We are experts at working ourselves into a holiday frenzy and then changing directions — blam! — just like that. Since Thanksgiving Day, people from New York to Los Angeles have been overdosing on Christmas. They have gone shopping and baked cookies and sung carols and attended parties and listened to concerts.

And for what?

So they can whack the festivities with a meat cleaver the very second midnight strikes and Christmas Day is officially declared over.

It doesn't have to be that way. Really. I know this smacks of heresy, but I submit it is possible to stretch the fun and excitement of Christmas a little longer.

Don't take my word for it, though. Listen to Naome Beaman,

wife of Knoxville Realtor Clarence Beaman. She spent much of her childhood in Stockholm, Sweden, where people have had a few more centuries to refine their celebrations. Perhaps they have a lesson to teach us.

"The Swedes make an occasion of everything," she said. "They have to, because the days are so short and dark in winter."

To begin with, they taper Yuletide at the start and finish. There's no quantum leap into Christmas, a massive escalation, and then a brick wall stop on December 26. The season doesn't start perking until the observance of Lucia Day on December 13.

The way Beaman explained it to me, the festivities of Lucia Day are somewhat akin to homecoming on a college campus. A queen is selected by popular vote. Girls in homes and offices dress up and serve coffee and cookies to their families and co-workers. That night, there is a big Christmas parade.

The general excitement builds to Christmas Eve when Santa makes his visit. But in Sweden, he comes before folks go to bed. Even before they eat supper. And he doesn't come down the chimney.

"Our presents always were in a bag by the front door," Beaman said. "Then we would sit down to a big dinner where my father read the Scripture. The house would always smell like spruce. Swedes don't use anything artificial, even if it's nothing more than a twig out of the forest."

After the meal, it's package-opening time. Then it's off to bed because "Julotan" is observed early the next morning.

"This is like an Easter sunrise service in America," she explained. "We would get to the church about 5 or 6 a.m. It would be beautifully decorated, and the choir would be singing. It was a wonderful experience."

OK. So far, so good, eh? Not a great deal of difference from some customs in the United States, wouldn't you say?

But here's where the Swedes start to really enjoy themselves and slowly let the holidays wind down.

"We extend the season until well after Epiphany (January 6, observed as the time of the Wise Men's visit), sometimes as long as the end of January. It is a time to relax and visit friends. It's a fun time.

You don't get depressed during those cold, dark days of midwinter."

There's even a special celebration for taking down the tree.

"It's called 'Christmas tree plundering'," Beaman said. "All the breakable objects are removed, and the tree is taken to the center of the room. It is redecorated with candy and apples, and the children dance around it, like a May Day celebration. Then, after everyone has enjoyed a treat off the tree, it is thrown with great fanfare out of the house."

Hmmm. I don't know how keen I am on seeing the flicker of Christmas tree lights on Valentine's Day. But the thought of restructuring the holidays and spreading out the fun sounds marvelous.

Too bad it won't work in America. It's just not the nature of the beast.

Sure as the idea would catch on here, people would invent new ways to rush about madly, shop till 10 p.m., burn their holiday spirit until it is charred, and tell themselves they're having a great time.

New Year's (un)resolutions

January 1, 1987

Today is the day you start paying for your play.

You're going to shed 20 pounds and crush out those smokes for the last time and jog two miles every afternoon, right?

Yeah, you and 40,000 others.

I hate to begin the year on such a pessimistic note, but let's be honest with each other. Not many will make the goal. The rest will become despondent in a few days, plop down in front of the TV and take out their frustrations with food, booze and cigarettes.

That's why I always like to pause on New Year's Day and offer an alternative.

I've said this before, and I'll say it again: The secret to keeping New Year's resolutions is by promising NOT to do something. Especially if it's something you hate doing in the first place.

I have followed this procedure for the better part of a decade, and I am happy to report a 100 percent success rate.

Here's a resolution hint: Always hedge your bets, especially the iffy ones. If the U.S. tax code can have six exceptions to every rule, why shouldn't you?

Enough of background, however. Let's get down to business.

In the Year of Our Lord 1987 I, Sam Venable, being of relatively sound mind and ample body, do solemnly swear NOT to:

Talk with a nasal twang like Sen. Jim Sasser.

Buy a pair of gray, pointed-toe shoes that have those itty-bitty low heels, a suit with a double-breasted coat or a hat without a bill in the front.

Play bridge.

Enjoy 95-degree weather.

Put mousse on my hair, although a mouse is permitted to nest there during my annual overnight stay at Mount Le Conte.

Go bowling.

Attempt to perform mechanical or electrical tasks, especially those involving VCRs, automobiles, outboard motors or heat pumps. (Exception: Insertion of flashlight batteries, but only if I have clear directions and 20 minutes advance time to study them.)

Wear gold. (Exceptions: my wedding ring and crowns on my choppers.)

Eat cooked cauliflower, cabbage or lentils.

See how easy New Year's resolutions can be? Go on and get a pencil and write a few for yourself.

Oh, and while you're up, would you mind passing me that platter of fried chicken?

Snow daze

February 14, 1985

At the present rate of snowfall around Knoxville, my kids will be 21 before they enter high school. Assuming they attend classes 'round the clock — summers, Easter breaks and Saturdays — for the next 10 years, of course.

And even though I burn wood to supplement electric heat, I'll probably need to remortgage the house just to pay my January and February utility bills.

One snowfall is OK, especially if it comes on or around Christmas. I can even abide two snows per winter — sometimes as many as three — if they are of short duration. But 24-belows and six or seven inches piled up every time you part the curtains is getting ridiculous. What is this, Bangor or Knoxville?

Granted, snow is pretty to look at. I love to walk in it. Matter of fact, if you have never eased through deep woods on a silent, snowy day, you have no concept of contentment.

But enough, by Celsius, is enough!

The TV weather people really get off when they talk about snow. They pull out all those charts and maps and radar pictures that are colored like something you see in a nightmare. They start speaking in tongues and batting their eyelashes. They would have you believe snow comes from highs meeting lows and cold fronts from Canada riding moist northers and stuff like that.

What sort of fools do they take us for?

You and I both know where snow comes from. It comes from grocery store owners.

Mister Big, who is vacationing in the Bahamas, calls the home office and asks for a stock boy. He discovers there is an oversupply of rutabagas, guava paste, anchovies and water chestnuts.

"This is terrible!" he sputters around a $2 cigar. "Put out the word!"

So the kid starts whispering, ''Did you hear what's coming

tonight? Three inches of snow and 20 degrees."

The guy he tells it to bumps into a friend on the street. "Five inches of snow and 12 degrees," he says. "I just got the word."

Then it goes to 12 inches and -4 and, well, you get the picture. Chicken Little herself couldn't do as good a job.

People leave work. Schools turn out. Everybody speeds to the store in a nervous panic. A primeval spirit, the will to survive, awakens throughout society.

"Give us bread, milk, eggs and cereal," they say to the store manager.

"Sorry," he replies, "we're sold out of those. How 'bout some rutabagas, guava paste, anchovies and water chestnuts?"

Of course they buy. At twice the price.

The TV weather people hear what's going on and take a spin to the store. They see checkout lines stretching to the meat counter. They stay just long enough to buy a six-month supply of rutabagas, guava paste, anchovies and water chestnuts; then they boogie back to the station to spread the news that 15 inches and -18 are on the way.

Can 150,000 Knoxvillians be wrong?

The truth about snow skiing

December 3, 1989

If God had meant for humans to ski, he'd have given us boards instead of feet. Bigger buns, too — so we would bounce like tennis balls after crashing to the ground.

Also lots of broken bones. If skiing were part of the master plan, we'd come into this world with fractured fibulas, shattered skulls and ankles mangled like rusty bed springs. What's the use being born with a perfectly good skeleton when you're going to trash it later on some stupid slope?

Ski people, however, refuse to accept the obvious. They put on their designer bib overalls and come swooshing down the mountain like they had good sense.

You'll start seeing ski people any day now. They're easy to spot. They wear colorful sweaters. They have ski racks on their cars. They drink wine and eat cheese — which is convenient, as many of them have no front teeth.

Nonetheless, this is the time of year skiers are happy. Winter is nigh and that means snow.

Not real snow, of course. That's another aberration of the natural order skiers have wrought upon us. They don't rely on clouds to bring snow. They push a button and a giant ice cream machine does the work.

Against my better judgment, I once attempted to learn to ski. I spent four weeks one afternoon under the guidance of a veteran instructor. We finally shook hands and agreed it would be safer for all concerned if I concentrated my efforts on tending the fire at the lodge.

If you could simply walk onto a slope and ski — like going to a gym with friends and shooting basketball — perhaps this sport would make more sense. But nobody ever said skiing was simple. Or sensible.

First, you have to suit up. This takes between six and eight hours, depending on your ability to use buttons, zippers and straps while in bondage. Imagine the Michelin man in a suit of armor trying to scratch the back of his neck. The ski people have a name for this routine. They call it "layering."

You put on one layer of thin material to absorb sweat. Then a layer of heavier insulation. Then another. And another until you have gone through longjohns, sweaters, goose down, bibs, gloves and wool hat.

Now that I think about it, the term "layering" is quite appropriate. You are stacked like a layer cake, and the guy who sold you all that junk is laying away big bucks for retirement.

But that ain't the worst of it. Before you get to the skis, you must put on boots. Big, thick, heavy boots. Boots with all the comfort and flexibility of a seasoned oak log.

Don't worry if you have no boots. Most ski resorts have plenty of pairs for rent. You give them a fistful of dollars and they direct you to the woodpile to find two logs roughly the size of your feet.

Then — *clunk, clunk* — you're ready for action, assuming you aren't white-eyed from heat stroke or crippled by a permanent foot disorder.

Skiing itself is impossible.

It is a figment of the imagination fostered by resort moguls who strive to give the impression that balancing on a pair of barrel staves and going 50 miles per hour down a 65-degree slope is child's play. This is an incredible lie, and I keep hoping a crusading newspaper like ours will expose it.

The fact of the matter is this: People do not ski.

Not real people, anyway. Those things you see at ski resorts, or on TV during the winter Olympics, are high-tech robots. Real people, the ones who fall and scream and break legs, are hidden in remote valleys well away from the main event.

How can robots be so lifelike? I don't know exactly. Machinery has forever been a puzzlement to me.

But I do know this: After you have mounded up truckloads of dirt and built a fake mountain and then covered it with 10 feet of fake snow, anything is possible.

Fireside meditation

March 2, 1989

Decadence. One-hundred proof decadence. Inexcusable, immoral, incorrigible decadence. The sort of turpitude Sunday school teachers warn you to avoid at all costs.

We each have our own unique brand. Could be chocolate. Or liquor. Or gluttony. Flashy clothes. Fast cars. Faster women. To each his own.

My personal poison is sleeping away a cold, gray winter day. On the sofa. In front of a fire.

When I set out to sin in this manner, I want it to be mean outside. Really tearing up jack with wind, rain, snow or sleet; a regular dose of environmental madness. Because on the inside, I'm going to be snoring like a bear in the depths of hibernation.

The other morning, I did it. I did it with full malice aforethought and hang the consequences.

It was the day Knoxville arose to a couple inches of snow on the ground and an avalanche of wet flakes still floating down. The same day for which weather forecasters 12 hours earlier had pledged nothing but rain.

You remember it, don't you? You cussed and pulled on old shoes and slopped to the car and slipped — sideways, backwards, anywhere the laws of motion and gravity dictated — until you finally reached your place of employment. Right?

Not I. Confession being good for the soul, I am going to tell you precisely how I sinned.

Yet the trouble with confession is that it also includes a provision for repentance. And I shall not repent. Indeed, if I get a similar chance to sin in the coming days, I shall sin with devout conviction.

You see, I had come to the office the previous weekend and gotten a bunch of work out of the way. Rare is the time I'm even caught up. But for once, I was actually ahead. The only truly pressing matter facing me was an after-dinner speech in the evening.

So I climbed out of bed — Mary Ann, due at her computer instruction classes in one hour, was long-since up and glaring at me — and walked down to the living room. The only pause I made was to plug in the coffee pot.

I gathered scraps from an old newspaper and wadded them upon the grate. Next, I arranged seven or eight sticks of kindling. Maple.

Maple does not good kindling make. I much prefer pine. In fact, I usually cut me a fencepost-sized pine each spring and spend the better part of one week filleting the long, skinny trunk into box after box of fragrant starter wood. Preferences notwithstanding, however, I had fallen into a treasure trove of short, slender maple some time back. Reasoning that poor kindling beats no kindling, I had committed countless hours of hatchet labor, rendering it into an acceptable pine substitute.

With the base of the fire laid, I criss-crossed three or four sea-soned oak logs, opened the flue and touched the paper with a wooden match.

Then I curled up on the sofa for 3 1/2 hours, a full 210 blissful minutes, rising only to add more logs and swallow a few gulps of coffee. After each arousal, it was gently back to Snoozeburg, drifting off to the music of crackles and hisses from the fireplace.

Then — and only then — did I take a shower and put on decent clothes and drive to the office.

There are two reasons why I took the time to tell this tale. Aside from bragging about my personal brand of decadence, I mean.

First, I wanted to see if I could eat up an entire column on some-thing as worthless as idle slumber in front of the fire.

Second, I wanted to know if my boss — the boss who was at his desk shortly after the crack of dawn on that same snowy day — truly reads my stuff.

If I'm still employed this time tomorrow, he probably doesn't.

Mum's the word!

February 1, 1990

If nobody speaks to you today, don't suspect bad breath or faulty deodorant. It's nothing personal. Honest. It's just that they are observ-ing National No Talk Day, a full 24 hours dedicated to the principle of peace and quiet.

No Talk Day is the brainchild of Marilyn Bachelor. She's a third-grade teacher at Garner Elementary School in Clio, Mich.

Fourteen years ago, Bachelor declared February 1 as a day of complete silence in her classroom. She handed down this decree with no regard whatever for mayoral proclamations, congressional resolu-tions or anything else of a legal nature. Teachers can do stuff like that and get away with it.

Then a funny thing happened. Someone at Chases's Annual Events, the official book of holidays, got wind of it. No Talk Day was canonized and has been observed all across America ever since.

I called Garner Elementary School earlier this week and tried to interview Miz Bachelor. Unfortunately, I'm not the first journalist with this clever idea. Soon as I identified myself, I heard someone in the background ask, "Is it another reporter?"

"It happens this way every year," said the school secretary, Delores Gradowski. "Reporters call from everywhere. They especially call on No Talk Day and try to goad Mrs. Bachelor into saying something."

The poor woman gets so many requests for interviews, she simply leaves a prepared statement in the principal's office. Here's part of what it said:

"I created No Talk Day to bring excitement to a long winter school day. The first one was so successful, I decided to repeat it.

"It promotes an awareness of our dependence on oral communication. Scratch paper is left on each child's desk. I tie a pencil and paper around my neck. We can write notes to each other, use the chalkboard, the overhead projector, demonstrations or pantomime. But there's no talking at all, except during lunch and recess.

"At first, the newness is exciting. But after a while, it becomes frustrating when we can't understand what each other is trying to say."

How well I know. This feeling of utter helplessness sweeps over me whenever I play charades. After 15 minutes of acting out song lyrics and book titles, I want to grab my teammates in a chokehold and scream, "It's 'Swing Low, Sweet Chariot,' you blithering idiots!"

Still, the idea of No Talk Day has merit. If it could be applied to select groups, the rest of us would rejoice in quiet celebration.

I propose No Talk Day be enforced upon: Politicians and bureaucrats at all levels of government. Rap singers. Hard rock bands. TV preachers.

Also any professional tennis player whose initials are John McEnroe. And car salesmen who SHOUT THAT NOBODY BEATS THEIR RED-HOT DEALS, SO COME ON DOWN FOR A FREE COKE AND GET IN ON THE SAVINGS OF A LIFETIME! Plus Sally Jessy, Donahue, Oprah, Geraldo and others of their ilk. As well as telephone solicitors, humanoid and computerized.

Aaaah! Things are starting to sound a lot better already, don't you think?

Actually, we could do everyone a favor by declaring No Talk Year for these loud-mouthed people. All in favor say, "Aye!"

Oops. I mean raise your right hand.

Who cares about the game?

January 28, 1990

Across America today, there are approximately 575 people who won't be watching the Super Bowl.

Everyone knows that the Super Bowl is the most over-hyped, over-analyzed, over-commercialized non-event in the history of television. Entire civilizations have lived and perished with less fanfare.

Here is what will happen after weeks of pre-game fluff are boiled away: Twenty-two young, athletic millionaires will spend 60 minutes running with a football, passing a football, knocking each other down, licking their fingers and scratching their groins. Despite the final score, the sun will rise tomorrow morning.

Still, we watch it.

We watch because the Super Bowl has evolved into a national happening. We know it will leave us empty, void of any hint of lasting importance. We feel compelled to watch nonetheless. We're afraid of missing something.

Most of us, anyway. The 575 Super Bowl refuseniks are not affected by this pox. They will spend the entire afternoon in non-football pursuits.

They will not gather with friends for a Super Bowl party. They will not stuff their bellies with cheese curls and onion dip. They will not hover around The Tube for over three hours, intently following the progress of every play, replay and replay commentary.

If you'd like to swell their ranks to an even 600, here are a few fun-filled activities to occupy your time:

• Read an unabridged dictionary from cover to cover — including the copyright, contents, preface, explanatory chart, explanatory notes, history of the English language, pronunciation guide, abbreviations, pronunciation symbols, foreign words and phrases, biographical names, geographical names and index.

This exercise will improve your mind immensely.

When everyone in your office gathers 'round the coffee pot tomorrow morning to rehash San Francisco's runaway victory, you can impress them with the likes of: "pennoncel, noun, a small triangular or swallow-tailed streamer borne at the head of a lance in late medieval or Renaissance times."

And boy, will they be sore they wasted all afternoon watching some stupid football game.

• Count the amount of cereal in your cupboard.

Not the number of boxes. The number of individual flakes.

Then make a detailed chart showing how wheat flakes stacked up against corn flakes, sugar-coated compared with plain, high fiber vs. low fiber, that sort of thing.

Large biscuits of shredded wheat don't qualify. They're too easy. Then again, you needn't count each grain of oat bran, unless you seek extraordinary challenges.

You ought to fling your oat bran into the garbage, come to think of it. As anyone who keeps up with medical news knows, this stuff has recently fallen from dietary grace.

If you don't get rid of surplus oat bran immediately, you run the risk of turning into a gigantic ball of axle grease.

• Disassemble your wristwatch.

If you own an all-America watch with hands and springs, gently clean each part, oil lightly and snap everything back in place.

Your timepiece will reward this effort with years of faithful service.

If you own a communist digital watch, arrange all the parts on a firm surface and beat them soundly with a brick.

Not only will you be shed of an irksome device that blinks, your blood pressure will settle into a healthy pattern, and you will have a vibrant, optimistic outlook on life.

Which is a lot more than Denver fans can hope for tomorrow morning, no matter how frantically they waved their pennoncels during the game.

Martin Luther King Jr. Day

The quest continues

January 19, 1989

When you sit down to order lunch these days, does it ever cross your mind that more than a quarter of a century has passed since Martin Luther King Jr. and 75 college students were arrested for daring to eat at a whites-only diner in Atlanta?

Or that 33 years have gone by since Rosa Parks refused to give up her bus seat to a white passenger in Montgomery, Ala.?

Or that an entire generation of Americans has graduated from college since James Meredith challenged tradition, state law, an army of deputy sheriffs and Gov. Ross Barnett to become the first black student enrolled at the University of Mississippi?

Or that it's been over three decades since towns like Clinton, Tenn., and Little Rock, Ark., were rocked by violence in the wake of court-ordered school desegregation?

A lot of social customs have changed since those bloody, bitter times. A lot of laws have changed, too. It is not that difficult, relatively speaking, to change social customs and laws.

But changing hearts is another matter. As per:

NEWS ITEM: "He lived a hero's life," said President-elect George Bush, speaking earlier this week at a ceremony to honor King on the national holiday that commemorates his birth.

"He dreamed a hero's dream. And he left a hero's indelible mark on the mind and imagination of a great nation.

"So, today, we remember the man; we pay tribute to his achievements; and we pledge once more our nation's sacred honor in continuing the pursuit of his dream."

NEWSROOM HAPPENING: "You keep spelling my son's name wrong," the angry father announced when a staff member in our sports department answered the telephone. "We don't spell our family's name like that nigger boy spells his. I'm tired of it, and I want it stopped.

"By the way, how come you people can't ever get the white players' names right? You always seem to know how to spell those nigger names over at Austin-East."

NEWS ITEM: The Metropolitan Planning Commission and City Council voted unanimously to change the names of East Vine and McCalla avenues to Martin Luther King Jr. Avenue.

After a six-month transition period, the change becomes permanent on November 1.

The action was taken after nearly 400 persons living and working along the thoroughfare petitioned MPC for the renaming. Officials say this was the most organized and ambitious campaign of its type ever brought before the planning commission.

NEWSROOM HAPPENING: "Well, I see they're gonna change the name of Vine Avenue," the visitor to our office was saying. "Good. The next time I have a letter to send to someone over there, I'll just address it 'Nigger Avenue'."

NEWS ITEM: In honor of King's birthday, residential mail service was suspended and government offices and banks were closed last Monday.

NEWSROOM HAPPENING: "Has anything really changed in the last 25 or 30 years?" the man was asking me.

"Everywhere I've been this week, I've heard, 'If it wasn't for that nigger, the bank would be open. If it wasn't for that nigger, we'd get our mail. We ought to be celebrating James Earl Ray Day instead of National Nigger Day'.

"So much for one man's dream," the man lamented. "So much for the changes he brought to our country."

Brotherhood?

Sometimes I wonder if we have the foggiest notion what the word means.